I0678263

# Imagining You

## Cloudberry Inn Series #1

Karice Bolton

Copyright © 2020 Karice Bolton

ISBN: 979-8-9851947-4-6


All rights reserved. No part of this book may be reproduced in any printed or electronic form, or stored in an unauthorized retrieval system, or transmitted in any form without permission from the author.

This is a work of fiction. Names, places, incidents, and events either are the author's imagination or are used fictitiously. Any resemblance to actual persons, living or dead, events, or locales is entirely coincidental.

Edited by V. Clifton

Cover Design: Didi
Adobe Stock: ©2mmedia

Interior: B&B Formatting
Adobe Stock: ©volff

# DEDICATION

To My Family. You are everything.

# CHAPTER ONE

*Samantha*

We live in a day and age where texts, emails, and quick cell calls are the norm. Yet, my sisters chose to write a cryptic letter to me asking me to come home to Cloudberry Inn. I tried calling and messaging them in return, but they ignored every single attempt.

I let out a sigh and stared up at the beautiful old inn. The place that I'd called home growing up sat in the midst of tulip fields as far as the eye could see. It felt good to be back in Washington again.

Tulip season was over and the inn was surrounded with goldflame honeysuckle climbing up the porch and stretching along the white-shingle siding. The brilliant yellow door drew guests right in.

I saw that my sisters had kept up the perennial flower beds just like our mother had through the decades, and a smile touched my lips. Maybe that had softened Vera. Or could it be Lana who fell into the gardening trap? None of us really had a green thumb, but I was sure it was something that could be learned. I wouldn't know since I lived in an apartment in Manhattan and managed to kill most of my houseplants.

My heart skipped a beat before diving into a tangled web of nerves as I stared at the inn. I should just charge up the steps and announce my arrival. That's what I would have done when I was eighteen, but a lot had changed between eighteen and thirty-three.

For starters, I hadn't seen my sisters for seven years.

Not by my choice.

My mother's funeral—seven years ago this July—was the last time I saw Vera or Lana. Not that I hadn't tried, but I lived in New York, and they always had some excuse as to why I shouldn't visit. The inn was too full, repairs were being done, it was the wrong season...the list was endless.

I let out a sigh as I gripped my bag and swallowed down the twinge of worry. I'd only brought two bags, and one exploded in the backseat of the car on the way here. I'd deal with it later. Now, I needed to focus my energy on what was about to greet me on the other side of the door.

This was my home as much as theirs.

They reached out to me.

Everything would be fine.

I brought in a quick, sharp breath as if that were the final boost of energy I needed and trudged toward the inn. The sweet smell of honeysuckle drifted over as I got closer to the house, and I closed my eyes for a brief second as memories from my childhood wrapped around me like a warm embrace.

"Maybe spending a few days out here will do me some good," I whispered to myself just as the large door opened slowly, revealing my sister, Vera.

She looked just like she did seven years ago, shiny brown hair cut into a perfect bob, sparkling blue eyes that seemed to dull when they focused on me, and a thin frame that I'd gladly trade any day for the lumps, bumps, and curving protrusions I'd seemed to inherit from my mom. Lana and Vera took after my dad when it came to physique. I was the lucky one who could be mistaken for a sack of potatoes at first glance.

"You made it," Vera sad flatly.

I'd partly expected a phony smile or arms up for a hug or something, but I got nothing.

"I figured I'd better head out since you wouldn't return my calls, texts, or emails."

"Those messages told us you got the letter." She folded her arms across her chest and didn't budge from the doorway.

I wasn't sure if she were standing guard and I was the enemy or what. It certainly felt that way, which made no sense to me.

It never had.

I cleared my throat. "I called Dad right away to make sure he was okay."

"Why wouldn't he be okay?" Vera frowned at me. "He's happily plopped down in Arizona, pretending the inn never existed."

I shrugged. "I don't know, but you sent a letter asking me to come out here when you haven't reached out for years. I got worried. Once we lost Mom..." My voice trailed off when I saw Vera frown. "Anyway, I'm here, and I'm really happy to see you."

Vera drew in a deep breath and let her arms down to dangle by her sides, but she still didn't offer any affection. She was the oldest of my sisters. Lana was the middle sister, and I was the youngest. We grew up loving one another.

I think.

I didn't know what had happened since.

"The inn is fully booked, so we're putting you up in the attic." She stepped to the side of the entry with barely enough room for me to slither through, and the space wasn't a small one. "We added a bathroom up there a couple of years ago, so you should be fine."

"Thanks." I glanced around the foyer of the old inn, and my heart ached for my mother. The space was so large that it actually acted as the lobby for the inn. A large stone fireplace anchored the space and offered a place for guests to congregate if it ever got packed when checking in.

From the appearance of things, the home hadn't changed much in the seven years since my mom's death. A large vase filled with flowers from Cloudberry's own perennial beds had been placed on the oval table that was polished daily to a high shine to show off the cherrywood, just like my mom always did. Paintings of the tulip fields dotted the walls, and family heirlooms were tucked into the corners of the inn. The enormous red wool rug had been rebound along the edges to hide any hint of wear.

I drew in a breath and looked at Vera as I placed my bag on the floor. "The flowers look nice."

"The gardener does a great job." Vera gave a quick nod without connecting her gaze with mine.

Surprise hit me upside the head. "Oh, you guys don't do them?" I blurted the words without realizing the ramifications.

Vera's hands flew to her hips as fast as her gaze locked on mine. "We barely have time to take care of the guests, let alone garden all day. You have absolutely no idea what it's like to keep this place going."

She dropped her hands to her side and clenched her fists.

There was no point in mentioning that Mom had managed all those years. It was stamped across the inn.

"I'm sorry. That's not what I meant. I know running Cloudberry is a full-time job."

"How would you *know* anything?" Vera rolled her eyes. "You're busy pretending this place doesn't exist while you're clear across the country. Just like Dad."

"Vera, I don't know why you asked me to come." I glanced toward the door. "But maybe it's best if I leave."

"Oh, no, you don't." Lana's chipper voice echoed down the hall as she wandered toward me.

Her lean figure hadn't changed since last I saw her. She looked fabulous in a pair of cropped jeans, a white tee, and her brown hair pulled into a high ponytail. Brown hair was what we all had in common, but each of us had different colored eyes. Vera's were blue. Lana's were green. Mine were brown. I was pale. They were tan. I stayed indoors most of the time, and they obviously got sun. Getting some rays here would probably do me some good. Maybe that would be the silver lining to this trip.

A tan.

My sister walked toward me, and the room immediately thawed. Lana raised her arms and beckoned me for a hug. I glanced at Vera, who looked completely annoyed, but I complied and wrapped my arms around Lana. I drew in a breath and clenched my eyes shut when I realized she smelled just like Mom, same perfume.

"It's so good to have you here." Lana let go and took a step back. "You haven't changed one iota."

"I put on about ten more pounds, but I like to think with the other thirty, no one will really notice." I smiled, and Lana chuckled.

"You know it's all muscle, Remember? That's what Mom always told us. She was all muscle and you took after her." Lana winked, and my chest slowly unclenched.

I grinned and nodded, finally letting out some of the air I'd been holding.

"So, I take it you, not Vera, wrote the letter?" I asked Lana since the letter had arrived signed with nothing more than *Your Sisters.*

Lana nodded and reached for my hands. "I did, and I'm so happy you came."

I smiled and pointed at Vera. "I'm not sure she is."

Lana waved her hands at Vera. "She'll get over it. She's just upset because the North brothers showed up for some engagement party."

I gasped, and my eyes widened. "Drew North was here?"

Lana shook her head. "No, he was the one missing, which is what put her in a sour mood."

Vera rolled her eyes at Lana. "Whatever. I couldn't care less. You're just as bad as Samantha, spending your time making up stories."

Lana chuckled. "The difference is that Sammi gets

paid for hers."

Vera gritted her teeth and shrugged. "I told her she's in the attic."

I nodded and Lana reached for my bag. "It's a lot different from when you were here last. I promise. We even had an elevator put in to get to the second floor."

Shocked registered on my face. "Really?"

"Yup. We're big time now." Lana winked and chuckled.

"Cloudberry has always been big time in my book." I smiled and glanced at Vera.

"You don't mind sleeping in the attic?" Lana asked.

"Not at all."

"What do you know? The princess hasn't stomped off yet." Vera's snide comment stabbed me in the heart as she marched toward the kitchen.

I never thought I was a princess.

I never thought much of anything.

I just... existed.

"What's that all about?" I whispered to Lana before she started to the stairs.

"She's not thrilled that you're here." Lana bounded up the stairs.

"Yeah, I already got that message loud and clear. But princess?" I shook my head. "I don't get it."

Lana didn't answer me as we made our way around to the other set of stairs that went up to the attic. They were behind a door at the end of the hallway. My sisters and I always made up stories of ghosts living on the third floor. Actually, our mom helped us in that department as well.

She had all kinds of tales about Cloudberry Inn, and rarely did we ever venture to the top floor unless we had no choice, but I was older now and certainly wouldn't let a few ghosts ruin my trip. I had sisters for that.

I spotted where the elevator had been placed at the end of the hall between two bedrooms where the laundry room and linen closet had been. It looked functional and tiny but exactly where I wouldn't want to get stuck.

My sister reached for the door to the attic, and my hands got clammy. Amazing what old childhood stories could do to a person as an adult. I rubbed my palms on my jeans as Lana flipped the light switch on.

I laughed. "That's new."

"Yeah. We thought a little dangling string and a lightbulb weren't really inviting to guests."

"So, guests sleep up here?" I asked in surprise.

A lot had changed.

As a family, we'd always kept this space off-limits to guests, packing it with old photo albums, Christmas decorations, and dusty boxes that hadn't been opened in far too long.

She turned around on the staircase and looked down at me before wiggling her brows. "It's our honeymoon suite. Not that I'd know what happens on a honeymoon."

I laughed and shook my head. "If I remember correctly, you've gotten plenty of practice without one."

"Ouch. Burn." Lana chuckled as we made our way up the stairs.

It felt nice to be able to joke around with my sister. It had been a long time.

"Hey, at least you've had plenty of men to know which ones to stay away from. The only men I've had in the last ten years are between the pages I write."

Lana chuckled. "Might be better that way."

When I made it to the top of the stairs, I was blown away. The attic had been completely transformed to a beautiful airy space. The window at the far end was wide open, and sheer white curtains blew from the gentle breeze, sneaking secrets inside. An oversized bed with an ornately carved wooden headboard sat to my right, piled high with bright white pillows and an embroidered white comforter.

"This is beyond inviting." I smiled, taking in the beautiful artwork adorning the walls. "I think most brides would just want to wrap themselves up in the blankets and sleep away their honeymoon."

Lana let out a wry laugh. "Then honey...you've never been with the right man."

I let out a wistful sigh and nodded. "You're probably right."

"Through here is the bathroom we added, complete with a clawfoot tub."

I followed Lana into the addition and was in awe. "I might never go back to New York."

Lana winked and put her finger to her lips. "Don't say that too loud or Vera will cause World War III."

I crinkled my nose and shook my head. "Why is that? I seriously don't get what I've done."

Lana cocked her head slightly and narrowed her eyes on me. "You don't have any idea?"

# CHAPTER TWO

*Garrett*

"The two Roberts sisters are maddening." I looked at my stepbrother, Wyatt Elliott. He was visiting from the islands.

"Over at Cloudberry?" Wyatt asked, scratching his beard.

He'd been to the jobsite while it was being completed, but he'd met both women on and off through the years at various community events around town.

"You got it." I shoved the Roberts' overdue invoice to the side and stared out the window.

I felt for the two women. I really did. I wasn't sure they'd ever wanted to be in charge of the old inn, but once Sarah Roberts passed away, the cards were dealt.

"I've had this overdue invoice for months. I don't think it's an issue about money, but I wouldn't know because they don't return my calls."

Wyatt laughed and shook his head. "I don't think it has anything to do with the money you're owed, and everything to do with the fact that two beautiful women have the nerve not to return the one and only Garrett Mason's phone call."

I grunted and shook my head. Wyatt could always make me laugh. "Are you calling me a man whore?"

"I would never use that language. No." Wyatt laughed even harder and glanced at the invoice. "Why don't you take it upon yourself to stop by the inn and see what's going on? Maybe you can charm the truth right out of them."

"I doubt they'd answer the doorbell." I winked at my stepbrother. "Besides, there's no charming those two. I'm pretty sure they hate men."

"You're just saying that because neither of them is interested in you." Wyatt clapped his hands and turned his baseball cap around. "You can't fool me."

Even though we were both in our thirties, Wyatt managed to look like he'd stepped right off some college campus somewhere.

"Got me all figured out, huh?" I grabbed the overdue invoice off my desk and stood. "Why don't you make your way over to the inn with me, and I'll show you that I'm a professional? I don't mix business and pleasure."

Wyatt shook his head. "Now you're just flat-out lying."

I laughed and nodded in agreement. The truth was that I'd met plenty of women on the job, and some of those encounters even spawned into my version of a relationship.

Three months, tops.

"Fine." Wyatt grabbed the can of soda he'd left on the desk and followed me out the door.

It wasn't that I was hurting for money. I'd inherited a pretty decent business from my dad the moment he'd turned sixty and retired, and I'd managed to spin it in several directions.

My dad had built up the largest general contracting firm in the area. When I took over, I expanded from residential to commercial and had finally finished my first development project. It didn't come without risk, blood, sweat, and tears, but it paid off.

I pulled off the first apartment complex in our town of twelve hundred. Of course, the old-timers in the town were in up arms the moment my application went into town hall, but after enough charming, explanations, and promises, my permit was granted, and the thirty-four-unit apartment complex became a reality.

I'd still managed to keep the other portions of our business up and running smoothly, which was how we did work for the Roberts sisters over at Cloudberry Inn. They wanted a sunroom built off the back of the inn, and I happily obliged. A few years back, they'd had us add an elevator to the old mansion, so I wasn't worried about taking on this job.

Everything went fine this last job too. They made all the payments on time... right up until the final lump sum that was due upon completion.

"So, why haven't you stopped by the inn before today?" Wyatt asked as we climbed into my 4X4 pickup.

"Honestly, I didn't have time to go chase down the money because it was precisely when the apartment project ended. We were skating into a barely completable deadline to pass final inspection and get the occupancy permits handed over before the big end-of-school-year crunch began and ended." I started the truck, and Wyatt shrugged.

"Ah. Now that you're big time, you can't be bothered with such small—"

I rolled my eyes. "I never said that."

"Tell me why the bookkeeper isn't handling this?"

I glanced at Wyatt as I pulled onto the main road out of town. "She's tried. Libby's the one who's already left all the messages, sent all the invoices, and finally had it. She handed me the folder and told me to solve it." I shrugged. "I've left a couple of messages myself."

"It's a good thing I rolled into town or you'd never get this taken care of," Wyatt teased.

"Keep talking and you won't have a bed to sleep on tonight." I smiled at my stepbrother and let out a happy sigh.

So much had gone right in the last year that it was harder to remember what all had gone wrong so many years before.

I suppose they called that progress.

Or at least my therapist two towns over did.

"Tell me this." Wyatt adjusted the air conditioning to point at his seat.

It wasn't that warm for this time of year, but it felt muggy, especially to a guy who was probably used to the constant island breeze over on Fireweed Island. I rather liked the weather now.

"What now?" I grumbled, giving him a sideways glance.

He wiggled his brows. "Which Roberts sister would you... you know?" He cracked another smile out of me as I let out a deep breath.

"Neither."

"Please. They're both beautiful."

I nodded. "They are, but I don't feel a connection with either of them."

"Maybe you haven't gotten to know them well enough."

I shrugged, holding onto the steering wheel tighter than usual. Truthfully, I didn't always feel connections with the women I slept with, so I didn't know why this hypothetical question stumped me. I was rarely a man at a loss for words.

"Come on. You can't tell me you never thought about asking one of them out."

Wyatt didn't know when to stop.

Never did.

I nodded. "It's the truth."

"What if one of those two women is meant to be your future wife?"

"You need to go back to Fireweed and find your own woman." I laughed. "You're starting to sound like Mom."

"Your mom, not mine. My mom is completely against my getting married," Wyatt confided.

I shook my head. "Funny that hasn't rubbed off on you. Just promise me one thing if the sisters open the door."

"Can't be too tough of a request," he chided.

I smiled at Wyatt. "Just don't say anything that I'll wind up regretting."

Wyatt whistled and let out a low chuckle. "I'll try not to embarrass you, *honey*."

I spotted the sign for Cloudberry Inn and pulled down the one-lane road. There were a few cars in the parking lot, and the gardener was tending to the millions of flowers that made this place famous. I found a spot under a large maple and turned off the truck before reaching for the past due invoice.

"This sucks." I glanced at Wyatt. "I hate tracking down money."

And it really did. If the women couldn't afford to pay, I'd work with them. I didn't want to bring this up, but I needed it settled one way or another—payment plans, credit cards, whatever.

"Better you than me." He climbed out of the truck, but had we not been in public, I would have slugged him for old time's sake.

Brotherly love and all that.

We walked across the parking lot, and I nearly barreled into a woman whose rear end was sticking out of the back of her car with an armload of clothes. It looked like she was moving into the place for an extended period.

When she spun around after sensing us, her eyes smiled before she said a word.

"Oh, sorry," she mumbled from under the pile of clothes she clung to as she straightened up.

Her gaze met mine, and every thought I'd had escaped me.

If Wyatt had asked me why we were at Cloudberry Inn, I wouldn't even know. All I knew was that the most beautiful set of chocolate-brown eyes locked onto mine.

"My apologies." I stepped aside when Wyatt jabbed me in the side, reminding me of my manners. "Did you need help carrying anything? It looks a little crazy."

She laughed nervously but pulled the bundle tighter to her chest. "No, I'm fine."

I reached out. "You sure?"

Her fingers wiggled around a piece of loose fabric that managed to float away, but she didn't seem to notice.

When Wyatt and I looked down on the ground, we saw a bright white pair of granny panties. The woman turned on her heels and started toward the inn without a clue of what she'd left behind.

I scratched the stubble on my chin and let out a deep breath. "Do we leave 'em here? Take 'em? Turn around and go back to the office? Call it a day?"

Wyatt kneeled down and laughed. "There's no way the woman standing in front of us two seconds ago wears these. They'd fall right off."

The thought amused me. And other than her gorgeous brown eyes, I had no idea what she looked like behind the pile of clothes she clutched.

Although, I did get a pretty good glimpse of her from behind as she stomped her way to the entrance of the inn.

And her body was amazing.

Curvy in all the right places.

And yeah. Hard to believe the granny panties were hers.

Which was the exact opposite of the Roberts sisters.

Not that I imagined either of them in their underwear, but if I had let my mind wander there, it wouldn't have been the granny variety either. Vera and Lana were tall, skinny, and perfect for some runway in Europe or something.

Totally not my type.

I knew a ton of men who salivated over that look, but I liked some meat on the bones. I wanted to feel a woman's curves as I had her on top of me or beneath me. I wouldn't mind if the woman actually filled out the underwear that were carelessly lying on the ground.

"What's that wicked grin all about?" Wyatt asked.

His gaze landed on mine, and he laughed. "Never mind. I don't want to know."

I nodded and bent over to pick up the rogue underwear. "Good call."

As we made our way to the front of the inn, I knew Wyatt was having a hard time keeping his mouth shut.

He understood my type.

He saw her drop her knickers right in front of me.

He knew she was a guest at the inn, which meant no strings attached.

And I had managed to stuff the woman's underwear into my front pocket.

Before I knocked on the door, I spun around to face Wyatt. "No, I will not be hooking up with her or any of the guests or employees staying at the inn."

A woman's laugh echoed through the air, and I let out a sigh as I turned to see Vera staring right at me.

"Well, that's a relief, Garrett. I guess I can let you inside then." Her eyes fell to the paper I was holding as Wyatt and I walked into the lobby.

Lana came to greet me from down the hall as Vera crossed her elbows over her chest.

Typical.

These two always played the good cop, bad cop scenario.

"Nice to see you, Garrett." Lana's friendly smile worked on Wyatt, but I wasn't falling for it.

I was being avoided, and no amount of sugar and spice would make that better.

I smiled and glanced around the foyer before bringing my eyes back to Lana's. "Do you enjoy the sunroom?"

Lana and Vera traded glances. "We do. It's a beautiful addition."

"So, no issues with it, then?"

Lana shook her head.

I nodded. "Good. I'm glad you like it. I was starting to worry you felt there was a problem with it or something."

Lana drew a deep breath. "I know why you're here."

"Really?" I grinned. "So, does that mean you *have* been getting my messages?"

A woman's laughter from up the stairs caught my attention, and I turned to see the same woman from the parking lot coming down the stairs.

Only this time, I could actually see just how perfect she was all over.

"Interestingly enough, they don't return my calls either." The woman smiled and stuck out her hand. "We met briefly in the parking lot."

I stared at the gorgeous woman in front of me, and it

felt like the rest of the world had slipped away for the second time in one afternoon.

She smiled wider. "I'm Samantha Roberts."

"Roberts? Did you say Roberts?" I asked, surprised.

"Yeah. We're sisters."

I turned to Vera and Lana. "Oh, I thought there were only two of you."

Samantha chuckled. "I think they'd like to think that too."

"Ouch," Wyatt whispered under his breath.

Samantha turned to face us and laughed. "True story."

I noticed the sisters didn't correct her and wondered what kind of dynamic they had. Wyatt might not have been my brother by blood, but he was definitely my brother by heart.

"Well, I'm Wyatt, and this right here is my brother, Garrett." Wyatt pointed at me as if he'd suddenly become the matchmaker of the century.

"You two don't really look alike," Samantha pointed out.

"Stepbrother," Wyatt corrected, and I laughed.

Samantha nodded. "Gotcha. I'm just relieved I'm not the only one being ignored by these two." She pointed her thumb behind her and chuckled.

"So, if you don't return my calls and you don't return your sister's calls, why on earth do you have a phone?" I asked, and I saw Samantha smile wider, which made my day perfect.

It didn't matter if I got paid or not.

Samantha Roberts had snark and fire like Vera, but she did it with a smile and a twinkle in her eye. I could really learn to like this woman.

Vera just scared me.

Lana let out a deep breath and glanced at Samantha before motioning for me to follow her.

"Do you mind coming with me to the office?" Lana asked. "It sounds like we have some items to discuss."

"Just one item." I shook my head, following Lana down the hall. "And no, I don't mind."

I glanced behind me to get one more look at Samantha Roberts, but she was gone.

# CHAPTER THREE

*Samantha*

"Great. I know I brought that pair of underwear. I had exactly three comfy pair and now I only have two." I stood next to my rental and bent over to look under the car in case I kicked it under the wheels or something. I groaned and stood back up.

Nothing.

Nowhere to be found.

Both hands whipped to my hips, and I shook my head in annoyance.

It wasn't the end of the world, but I had three pair that I absolutely loved. They were roomy, they didn't cut into any part of me, and they always worked well under sweats. It wasn't that I didn't have other underwear. I packed another five pairs, but they were all...

Confining.

And I hated to be confined.

Especially on vacation.

"Ugh." I bent back down and looked under the car.

"Looking for something?"

I recognized *his* voice immediately.

The man from inside.

*Garrett, I think his name was.* I spun around and smiled.

I waved my hand to dismiss his curiosity. "Just must have dropped something earlier. Doesn't seem to be here."

Garrett's striking green eyes connected with mine, and electricity immediately zipped through my veins. His blond hair had some wave to it as he ran his fingers through the strands, and my stomach tightened as I imagined his fingers elsewhere.

I looked away quickly to compose myself and wondered what had gotten into me.

I'd always loved writing those scenes in my books.

The first encounters.

The quick glance.

The soft, mistaken touches that lead to those incredible first kisses.

The thought of writing about first encounters got me excited all over.

But I *rarely* lived it.

Okay, fine. I *never* lived it.

I let out a sigh and noticed that Wyatt had already climbed into the truck, so I slowly brought my gaze back to Garrett's and swallowed hard.

And sure enough...

The moment our eyes met, I felt a tingling sensation rush through my body as if I'd just jumped off a cliff.

Maybe not jumping off a cliff but zip-lining.

Garrett smiled and it about did me in. I would definitely be writing this man into my next book.

I guess it was good to set foot outside of my Manhattan apartment every now and again. Washington was already turning into an awe-inspiring trip.

Which was good because my editor expected something from me by the end of summer.

Garrett's deep voice nearly hummed as he spoke, but I didn't actually hear what he said.

"Pardon me?" I asked, and his smile grew.

"I think I might know what you're looking for."

I let out a gasp, and my eyes fell to a huge lump near his crotch.

The man was huge.

Garrett was huge and hard, and I shouldn't be looking.

My cheeks flamed red, but I couldn't look away.

For the life of me, I couldn't pull my eyes away.

A perfect roll pointed away and over just to the left of his pocket, outlined in a dark pair of jeans that fit him a little too well.

"I doubt it." I shook my head, finally ripping my gaze away and up.

And up. And up. Had to keep the gaze up.

Since when did I start looking at men's crotches?

Garrett laughed. "No, I'm pretty sure I found what

you're missing."

I smiled and shook my head. "And I'm pretty sure you didn't."

"Oh, I'd be willing to bet I found what you were looking for."

I wiggled my index finger in front of him and rolled my eyes. "I'm a hundred percent sure you didn't, so whatever you might have found, you should turn it in to my sisters. Another guest probably lost some precious valuable."

"No. We saw it fall."

My eyes widened, and my stomach roiled like I was out to sea. "Saw... what... fall?"

Garrett reached into his pocket, his fingers sliding next to the lump.

My heart started hammering as so many dirty thoughts raced through my mind.

I had absolutely no idea what came over me.

I wrote for a living.

I purposefully stayed indoors and avoided people.

Interactions.

Encounters.

Just about anything, really.

That involved people.

I liked writing *about* people.

Not dealing with people.

I loved making up my own best and worst versions using my own personal encounters.

My fear, however, was that I'd soon run out of experiences to pull from.

Yet, this thirty-second encounter was filling me up with so many wonderful thoughts and feelings I thought I'd explode.

Until his hand slipped free from his pocket, the large roll in his pants disappeared, and my bright white tighty-whities hung between his fingertips.

Just dangling in the air for all to see.

I gasped and snatched the underwear right out of his hand.

"Told ya." Garrett smiled, and the tingles happened all over yet again.

"So, that's what filled your jeans up." I smiled, and he cocked his head slightly in confusion.

"I'm not following."

I pointed at his crotch and nodded. "You looked like you were saluting a second ago, but it was just..." I clenched my underwear between my fingers.

"You noticed my—" He couldn't finish because his smile was so big.

"Don't turn this around." I shook my head. "Why would you keep these?"

I bundled them in my fist and scowled at Garrett.

"I didn't *keep* them, but I also didn't think you'd appreciate me pulling them out of my pocket in front of your sisters." He smiled, and my eyes drifted down to his less bulky pocket. "It seems you have enough trouble with those two already."

I hid a chuckle and grinned, noticing that things still

weren't completely flat and back to normal.

"You gathered that, did you?"

I drew a deep breath and it finally felt like I'd actually gotten enough oxygen since I arrived at the inn.

Garrett scratched his chin and his smile warmed me right up. His green eyes sparkled in a way that stirred my thoughts in all kinds of crazy ways. I didn't know if he looked at everyone like this, but it certainly made me feel good.

Really good.

Definitely going in my next book.

"Did you show up unannounced or what?" His lip curled in a way that kept his mouth slightly parted as I imagined what it would be like to be kissed by those beautiful lips.

I shook myself out of writing mode and grinned.

Not every part of life had to be captured for some story. It was okay to live in the moment.

But I did wonder what it would be like to be kissed by this sexy stranger.

Garrett narrowed his eyes on me as if he could read my mind, and I quickly straightened up and dropped the dopey expression from my face.

"Actually, they invited me out here." I rocked back on my heels and looked toward the Inn. "But I don't think they expected me to show." I swallowed back the embarrassment. "And I'm not even sure why they invited me."

His expression fell slightly, and it looked like he wanted to tell me something.

Instead, he just nodded and glanced at my clenched fist. "If that were a turnip, you'd have a quart of blood by now."

"Huh?"

"Your undies. You're squeezing them as hard as—"

"Oh, right. Squeezing blood out of a turnip." I grinned.

"It's not every day I have an attractive man track me down to hand me a pair of my own underwear."

He winked. "I don't believe that for a second."

I giggled unexpectedly, and his green eyes brightened. "I don't know if that's a compliment or not."

Garrett laughed. "Yeah, I suppose it could go either way." He glanced back toward his truck. "Hey, are you going to be in town long?"

My stomach felt like a hive of bumblebees was about to take flight. Apparently, that feeling really *did* exist in the real world.

I sucked on my bottom lip and kept my gaze on Garrett. "I was only going to be here for the weekend, leaving on Monday afternoon."

He let out a hiss and shook his head. "Too bad. I'd love to take you out for a drink. Think you can squeeze me in?"

Was he asking me out on a date?

Wait.

No.

This wouldn't qualify as a date since he knows I'm leaving.

"Umm." I pressed my lips together. "I don't really sleep with men on the first date."

Who was I kidding?

I didn't sleep with men even on a tenth date because I never got to the tenth date.

Garrett laughed and shook his head as his eyes stayed locked on mine. "That's really admirable."

"Thank you." My cheeks warmed.

At least I set the record straight.

"But I wasn't asking you to sleep with me. Just have a drink."

I laughed nervously, feeling completely flustered. "No, I know, but if I'm leaving in a few days, then having a drink isn't really so we can get to know one another on some deep level." My brows furrowed. "So, I assumed you'd want to skip over all that getting-to-know-you stuff and go for the hook, line, and sinker. I just didn't want to waste your time."

He looked utterly amused, and I had no idea why. "Do you always jump right to the conclusion?"

"What do you mean?"

"Well, you completely took the wind out of my sails. I kind of think there's a lot of fun stuff that can happen between two people who meet. The middle of the story is where all the good stuff happens." His brow arched and he scratched his chin. "And it sounds to me like you just jumped us right to the conclusion."

I shrugged. "It's a quirk."

That served me well when writing. I always enjoyed knowing the end of the story I was writing. I needed to know where I was headed. Sure, there were those times when where I thought the story was headed and where the story actually went were two different things, but I'd say for the most part, I rarely started a relationship with my keyboard unless I knew the ending.

And I knew the ending with Garrett. I'd get on an airplane headed back to New York, feeling cheap and wishing I hadn't slept with him.

Then I'd wonder if everyone in town knew.

If my sisters found out.

It would be a whole mess that I wasn't willing to deal with.

I froze and glanced at the inn. I had the distinct feeling I was being watched.

Garrett let out a heavy sigh.

"You know what? I changed my mind." I smiled, watching the complete look of surprise wash over his face. "Pick me up tomorrow at seven."

"Okay, then." Garrett nodded as his gaze drifted to my clenched fist. "I'm glad you changed your mind."

"Well, don't get any ideas. This is the only time you'll be seeing these."

"Wouldn't dream of it." Garrett smiled and shook his head. "I'll pick you up at seven."

"Great."

He turned toward his truck before I made my way back to the inn, and my legs felt like two wet noodles.

What had I gotten myself into?

I moved my underwear to my other hand and trudged up the steps to the inn and stepped inside.

The old mansion was as quiet as a high school library, which was completely unusual.

I didn't hear any noise from the kitchen, no creaking from the upstairs, and no voices on the phone. It was eerily quiet.

I decided to make my way down the hall to the study.

As I approached, I heard my sisters talking in hushed voices and put my ear up to the door to listen, except the door wasn't completely closed and I tumbled forward into the room.

My sisters both looked up at me, completely surprised, as I straightened and cleared my throat.

"I didn't know it was open." I looked at Vera, who flashed me a fresh scowl, and over at Lana, who was sitting at the desk my mom sat at for decades.

All sorts of memories drifted into my mind as I thought about the days that I'd crawl onto her lap as she tried to use the ten-key or the days I'd slump in the chair across from the desk and complaining about school. The familiar ache washed over me as I stared at my sisters.

I missed my mom.

It had been seven years, and I missed her as much today as the one she'd left this world.

"Anything I can help with?" I asked, not having any clue what I could actually do.

Vera shook her head. "A bride-to-be is having her bachelorette party here, so the second floor is booked, but they aren't getting here until tonight. Just going over details."

That was the longest sentence from Vera since I'd arrived. Maybe things were turning around.

Lana nodded. "We're pretty much set. Linens have been changed, chocolates laid out, new flowers in all the rooms. Why don't you go to town and just relax a bit?"

My brows furrowed and I looked around the study. It, too, was like a time capsule with secrets tucked onto the bookshelves along with figurines. The floral couch under the bay window hadn't been moved an inch, and the mini-refrigerator by the desk hummed as it always did.

But what stuck out to me most in the room were my two sisters acting as if everything were normal.

"Are we just dancing around the elephant in the room here or..." My arms lifted high into the air when I realized I was still holding a balled-up pair of underwear. I quickly dropped my arms and stared at Vera and Lana. "I fly across the country because you asked me to come and then you want to send me off to town?"

"You didn't have to come," Vera muttered under her breath.

I pointed at her with my free hand. "You're absolutely right, which is why I'd like to know why you invited me out here when you haven't wanted me to visit for years, and I'm not sure you actually want me here now."

Lana stood and let out a slow breath. It had always been her way of trying to defuse a situation, buying seconds of time to produce calmness.

It rarely worked because we had Vera as a sister.

"Don't act all high and mighty because you took a flight out here." Vera glared at me, and I threw my head back in frustration.

"If you'd like me to leave, I have no problem packing up and going back. I just thought you needed me." I swallowed down the emotion that went with those words.

Why would I think my sisters ever needed me? They

made it clear that they never did.

"No, Sammi." Lana walked over and reached for me. "Don't go."

My stomach knotted, and I wanted nothing more than to be back in New York. It wasn't like I had a huge circle of friends waiting for me back there, but I had a life.

My life.

The one I created so many years ago.

The one my mom helped me create.

Vera brought her gaze to mine and she cleared her throat. "I'm sorry."

When the words tumbled out, nothing else mattered.

Maybe we were making progress.

# CHAPTER FOUR

*Garrett*

I certainly didn't want to get in the middle of three quarreling sisters, but I had a bad feeling that one of them was getting the short end of the stick.

When Lana had called me back into the office, I expected to leave with a check.

Instead, I left with a lengthy explanation and a promise.

Of sorts.

I tapped my finger on the table as Wyatt stared at me. We'd stopped off at my favorite diner and were waiting for our food.

Wyatt waved his hand in front of my face. "Are you going to tell me what's going on or what?"

"There's really not much to say." I shook my head. "I can't tell whether they have the money and just don't want to pay me, or they actually don't have the money but would pay me if they could."

"Even after you talked to Lana?"

I scrubbed my face with my hands and groaned. "Yeah. I'm more confused than before I went."

"Did she give you any timelines?"

"Soon." I did air quotes and shook my head. "I wouldn't put up with that from anyone, so why I'm suddenly walking away feeling like I'm lucky to be in their presence, I do not know."

Wyatt laughed. "Great. So, you've got the hots for one sister and the other two sisters have cast some sort of spell on you."

I laughed and shook my head as I stared at Wyatt. "You've spent a little bit too much time alone on that island of yours."

"Nah." Wyatt shifted in the booth. "I'm just calling it like I see it. And I don't spend much time alone."

I rolled my eyes and grinned.

"I don't have the hots for anyone, first of all," I corrected. "And I don't believe in magic."

"Then, why are you taking out the mystery sister for a drink?" Wyatt looked amused.

"I want to help her."

Wyatt's carefree expression turned serious. "Help her?"

I nodded. "I think her sisters are up to something, and I'm not sure she knows about it."

"Okay." Wyatt frowned. "And this pertains to you how?"

"Well, I kind of feel bad for the girl."

"She's no girl." Wyatt wiggled his brows. "She's fully a woman."

"Dude, would you get your head out of the gutter for one second?" I laughed, shaking my head.

"Do you think she always wears that type of underwear?" Wyatt asked.

"Really? That's where your head is?"

"I don't know where else it would be." Wyatt shrugged and smiled. "In all seriousness, though, what makes you think she's in the dark?"

I thought back to Samantha and how sweet she was. It was hard to believe she was related to Vera and Lana.

"When you were at the inn, didn't you feel the tension as soon as Samantha came downstairs?" I asked.

"I don't think her jokes helped, to be honest." Wyatt grinned.

"But her sisters didn't dispel them, either," I pointed out. "I think she just uses humor to make herself feel better."

Wyatt nodded. "Could be."

I thought back to Lana in the study. She was pacing in front of her desk and apologized for the delay in payment but promised that I'd be seeing a check for the balance soon. She was just waiting on something.

I let out a sigh. "It's not my business."

But I wondered what that *something* was.

"It kind of is your business since you're not getting paid," Wyatt pointed out.

The server brought over the two cheeseburgers and

fries we'd ordered.

"Listen, the last thing I want to do is start trouble in someone's family." I stopped talking and popped a fry in my mouth.

Wyatt nodded. "Right. But I think the trouble is already there."

"I wonder if Samantha was invited out here for a reason that benefits the other two sisters."

My sudden interest in Samantha Roberts was no doubt going to lead me into trouble. I could just feel it, but for some reason, the thought almost excited me.

Or maybe it was just her that excited me. I smiled to myself when I thought back to the disappointment that covered her face when I pulled out the rolled-up underwear.

"Could be." Wyatt took a bite of the cheeseburger as I thought about Samantha. "Just be careful. Family drama can get really messy."

I laughed and ate another fry. "You don't say."

Wyatt grinned and nodded.

We'd both had experience with drama growing up, and most of it stemmed from his biological father. My dad married his mother, and Wyatt lived with us full-time right away. There was no shared custody between his parents, but his father certainly wanted to make his mom's life a living hell, which he managed to do for quite a few years until he found someone else to torment.

His new wife.

"The Roberts sisters have always been really nice over the years, but the last few encounters have been off." I took a sip of Coke. "I mean, Vera's always been ornery, but I could pull a smile from those lips now and again."

"Not today, you couldn't." Wyatt pretended to shudder. "She's as cold as the glaciers up north."

"But not Samantha," I pointed out. "She's genuinely nice, and she seems curious about life."

She was all light and warmth, and I didn't ever remember a time when I thought back to a woman and felt actual emotion and feelings and...

I was merely taking her out for a drink.

And then she'd be flying back to wherever she lived, as she so aptly pointed out.

"You need a chaperone for your date?" Wyatt teased.

"I think I'll be just fine. She let me know that we wouldn't be sleeping together."

Wyatt's brows shot up. "She what?"

I nodded, smiling as I thought back to her explanation. "She puts a lot of work into..." I stopped and laughed before continuing. "Thinking about outcomes."

Wyatt shrugged. "Sounds like a lot of work."

"Probably so, but she's already outlined how things are going to be, so I don't have to worry about spinning my wheels. She's explained that there's not enough time to get to know one another and that she wouldn't sleep with someone until she did, so..."

Wyatt clasped his hands together. "Then why on earth did she agree to go out with you?"

I smiled and shook my head. "I have absolutely no idea, but I'm glad she did."

"Do you know what she does for a living?"

I shook my head. "Something analytical. Maybe an attorney."

"She doesn't strike me as one." Wyatt pushed his lips into a frown. "Don't see it."

I agreed. "She's too sweet and gets ruffled too quickly for that profession, but she's definitely intuitive."

And she has a mind that goes places that could be fun. Catching her staring at my overly stuffed jeans was a kick and something I never expected.

"Well, she's gorgeous." I sat back in the booth after taking another bite of the burger. "And at least I might get to the bottom of what's going on at Cloudberry."

Wyatt nodded. "Just keep telling yourself that's the reason for your date."

"It's not really a date." I shrugged.

"You know what I mean." Wyatt flashed a coy smile. "You can turn anything into a date."

"Not with this one," I assured him. "I have a feeling she's a woman who sticks to what she says."

"We'll see." Wyatt seemed amused.

"Enough about the Roberts women." I wiped my mouth with the napkin and had a sip of Coke. "How's Dad doing? When I talked to him, he seemed happy as a clam with the monster of an RV they just bought."

Even though there was plenty of drama with Wyatt's biological father, my dad was the one true figure of stability in Wyatt's life, and I know he appreciated it.

"That thing cost more than most people's homes." Wyatt grabbed his phone. "Have you seen pics?"

I shook my head. "Dad sent over one, but it was in the

middle of the RV lot, so I didn't really get the feel."

Wyatt tapped on his screen and slid the phone to me. "There it is. He named it. I think he's in love with it."

"Seriously?" I asked. "And your mom is okay with it?"

Even though Wyatt could refer to my dad as his dad, and he rightly should, I never felt comfortable calling his mom by mom. I knew it wasn't a betrayal if I did, but I just couldn't bring myself to do it. I knew my mom could never be replaced, and my father wasn't trying to do that. But my mom was and still is a constant figure in my life and Wyatt's father was not. So, I never called Wyatt's mother *Mom*. I called her by her name, Twila.

"Well, he named the RV 'Twilight', so it's kind of an ode to my mom."

I laughed. "Oh, to be that age."

Wyatt snorted and took a sip of his pop. "Oh, it's creeping up on you sooner than you think."

"Same goes to you, buddy."

Wyatt nodded in silence and brought his gaze to mine. "Did you think you'd still be single at this age?"

I drew in a deep breath and let it out slowly. It wasn't something I thought of often.

"No," I confessed.

"Do you think we do it to ourselves on purpose?" Wyatt seemed fully intent on having a deep relationship conversation after we'd both stuffed ourselves with cheeseburgers and were basically comatose.

"Do what?" I propped my elbows on the table.

"Zero in on women who don't want to settle down."

I furrowed my brows. "Who says I do that?"

Wyatt laughed and nodded. "So, you're still in denial."

"I'm not denying anything." I shook my head. "It might be worse than that. I might just be an idiot."

Wyatt tapped the table with his hand. "That could be it."

"I knew you'd like that answer."

Wyatt shrugged. "I don't know. Sometimes, I get a little jealous when I see some of my buddies going back to their home, a wife there waiting for them..." His voice trailed off, and I realized he was serious.

This really was a serious conversation.

I straightened in the booth and nodded. "No, I know what you mean. There are nights I wonder why I can't get my shit together and just focus on finding a healthy relationship that lasts longer than a trimester."

"And that's if you're lucky," Wyatt was quick to point out.

I smiled. We both had the same problem. We loved women, but we hated to commit.

I had committed once, but it left me a ruined man.

Wyatt twisted his lips into a wry grin. "I just wonder if I'm going to be collecting my social security and wandering the assisted-living halls looking for my very first bride."

I gave him a thumbs-up sign. "Nothing wrong with that. Don't knock it until you try it."

"Seriously, man. Don't you worry that you'll never find that one?" He held up his index finger.

"I don't stay up at night worrying about it, but I do hope that someday, she'll just bump into me."

"What about Samantha?"

I looked at my brother like he had three heads. "I don't even know her. Why would you bring her up as if she's the one? Sure, she's hot as hell and has curves in all the right places..."

"Go on." Wyatt motioned with his hand to keep going.

"But I don't know the first thing about her. She could have ten husbands buried in her back yard somewhere, and that's why her sisters out here want her money."

Wyatt whistled. "You think that's why they invited her out here? To borrow money?"

The moment the words left my mouth, I wished I could pull them right back in. The thought had crossed my mind. But I didn't have a clue why Samantha might have money and they wouldn't. It was probably not even the case. Her sisters probably just wanted to visit with her.

I pushed down the thought and cleared my throat. "I don't know. It's not my business."

But the timing was hard to ignore.

"Remember what I said earlier? It kind of is your business until you get paid."

I let out a deep breath. If the sisters had money issues, I certainly wasn't going to come down on them. I'd take payments, even if it took twenty years. But I couldn't even get that out in the conversation when I was talking to Lana. It was weird. She just had this way of steering the conversation and controlling the outcome without my even blinking an eye. I just wondered what all they kept from one another, what secrets drove them apart.

"I don't know. I'm just going to take Samantha out for a drink and see where it leads. But if she's being used by her sisters, I don't think I'll be able to keep my mouth shut."

Wyatt nodded. "You never can."

# CHAPTER FIVE

*Samantha*

I'd woken up early. I was still on East Coast time. Even though it was five o'clock in the morning in Washington, I couldn't make myself sleep any longer. Last night with my sisters wasn't any more revealing than the day with them had been. I was wide awake, yet exhausted.

It didn't help that there were footsteps pitter-pattering up and down the stairs to the attic room all night long. I tried to catch the culprits, but every time I opened the door to the stairwell, whoever it was had vanished.

Probably the drunk bridal party.

I also spent the night wondering about my sisters. Once the apology was uttered into the air, I guess I thought that was about to be the start of mending our relationships. I was ready to apologize too. But I just hadn't figured out what for yet.

When I thought we might actually get into some sort of deep conversation, the guests arrived early, and the entire evening was dedicated to taking care of the soon-to-be bride and her wedding party.

So, I sat here in bed wondering why my sisters called me out here. I only had a couple more days here, so hopefully, they'd spit it out before I headed back to the airport. There had to be a reason.

If we'd been friendly over the years and visits were the norm, I wouldn't think twice, but this was completely out of the ordinary, and neither of them expected that I would show.

I texted my dad that I'd arrived, and he'd wished me a happy time with my sisters, but he didn't reveal anything either.

I'd always made it a point not to bring my dad into my drama with my sisters.

Or the lack thereof, really.

Once Mom passed away, all I wanted to do was make his life easy, and I think I did.

I hope I did.

The inn carried too many memories for him, and he wanted to be far away. I made that possible.

I stared at the rafters in the ceiling, admiring the discolorations from age that made them even more beautiful. My sisters had done an amazing job with this attic space. And the sunroom out back they'd added on this year was brilliant too.

My sisters belonged here. They did an amazing job running the inn. My only hope was that I could tell them how proud of them I was, but I wasn't sure it mattered to them.

I felt my stomach tense, and I let out a slow and steady breath.

I hated this.

I hated walking on eggshells with my sisters.

Feeling like I'd done something to wrong them in some unknown way.

When I'd first gotten the letter from Lana, I worried that one of them was ill or had an accident. Why they wouldn't call over something like that, I didn't know, but I was panicked.

Once my dad assured me that everything was fine with them, I relaxed a little.

But once I realized they had no intention of following up after the letter, I just booked a trip.

And now I was fully immersed in the Lana and Vera show. I'd do whatever they'd tell me to do and I'd try to constantly apologize for the life I'd made away from Cloudberry Inn.

I pulled the crisp white sheet over my head and groaned.

Why did I bother to come?

Vera hated me and Lana was just sugarcoating life. I just wasn't sure whose.

I shoved the sheet off my head and decided to get up. I'd be as quiet as possible to not wake up the guests below. The last thing I needed to do was upset my sisters and make angry guests.

Although, I was surprised that I wasn't hearing the floor creak with each step I took toward the bathroom. My sisters must have made sure the contractor took care of all those sounds too, which made me wonder about the noises last night.

After brushing my teeth and pulling my hair into a ponytail, I pulled on a bathrobe and tied the sash before heading downstairs. Hopefully, I could avoid bumping into any guests.

The closer I got to the kitchen, the more I could smell a fresh pot of coffee. Pastries were laid out on a platter next to frilly dishes and a stack of linen napkins.

*Just like Mom used to do*, I thought to myself. The familiar ache touched my chest, and I swallowed down the pesky tears.

I knew the pastries were off-limits, but I grabbed a mug from the cabinet and poured a cup of coffee before wandering into the newly built sunroom where I found my sister, Lana, curled up on the couch with a shawl pulled over her.

Her eyes were closed, and the soft heaves of her chest told me she'd just fallen back to sleep. I didn't want to wake her, so I quietly turned around and went back into the kitchen and out the door to the patio.

Late spring in Washington state still made for crisp mornings no matter the time of year, but it felt good. There wasn't the constant thick dampness that lingered like a wet blanket as with New York, which was ironic considering Washington's reputation for constant rain.

I found a chair with a cushion and shook off the glistening morning dew before taking a seat.

I leaned my head back against the chair and took a sip of hot coffee as I scanned the gardens in front of me. Everything was meticulously planted, groomed, and in full bloom for the season. The fields behind the gardens had only the fading greenery the tulips had left behind.

Cloudberry was peaceful.

No doubt about it.

As I let my head loll back and forth, I closed my eyes and Garrett popped into my head. He certainly was good-looking and good-natured, considering what I'd managed to lose and he'd managed to find in the driveway.

I'd pretty much gotten over that I'd dropped the ugliest pair of underwear known to mankind. But it made my life easier. He wouldn't be getting any kind of crazy thoughts about me.

Nope. Not a one.

That pair of underwear was like the warden of all other underwear. They'd keep watch over the thongs that stay tucked away in the back of the drawer, the lace tongas that leave little to the imagination, and even the low-rise boy briefs. Those all offered fun and flirty alternatives, but not the granny panties. They saluted and stood guard.

Those sent a clear message.

I was off-limits and didn't need to be bothered with something sending the wrong message.

I smiled thinking back to Garrett dangling them in front of me. He had such a great look in his eyes, like he held some secret that only the two of us shared.

Except I knew no secrets, and I highly doubted he did either.

I let out a happy sigh and blinked my eyes open to see my sister standing next to me.

I smiled and looked up at Lana, blocking the sun with my arm over my eyes. "Boy, you know how to sneak up on people a little too well."

"You're up early." Lana smiled.

I nodded and squinted as I put my arm down, and she took a seat next to me. "Still on New York time."

Lana stretched and eyed my coffee cup. "I always love mornings."

I chuckled. "You've always been a morning person."

"And you've always been a night owl, which is why I was surprised to see you out here."

I took a sip of coffee and let out a deep breath as I wondered if we'd ever get past superficial chitchat.

There used to be a time when we shared secrets, stayed up until late at night laughing and crying, and played up one another's dreams. The sad part was that the last time any of us did that was when we were teenagers.

"What happened to all of us?" I asked, staring at my sister.

She'd already gotten dressed for the day and had on a pair of pink leggings and a white linen peasant blouse, looking absolutely stunning.

I tugged on my bathrobe as she bit her lip and shrugged. "We grew up."

"It's that simple?" I asked, feeling the heavy weight of guilt spreading through me.

"Why wouldn't it be?" She watched me carefully for my reaction.

"I just feel like there's a lot of unresolved stuff between us all. I mean, Vera looks like she'd toss me off a cliff if she had the chance, and you just keep the same smile plastered on your lips with me that you use on strangers."

"We grew up and we grew apart." She kept the smile on her lips. "Don't overthink everything. Not every sibling relationship has to be as perfect as the ones you write about in your books."

A stab to the heart.

"I don't write perfect relationships. My characters are flawed, emotions high, and stories layered, which is why I don't believe that we just grew apart."

Lana crossed her legs, but she didn't say another word.

"So, that's it? We aren't going to get anywhere?" I asked, feeling completely hollow inside.

Pretending like this was absolutely exhausting, and it made me feel like a shell of a person.

"There's nowhere to get. We're all fine." Her lips pursed into a fleeting smile as she folded her hands on her lap, but I wouldn't stop staring at her. "I don't know what you want me to say."

"Let's start with why you suddenly wanted to see me after seven years?" I swallowed down the humiliation. "I didn't think I was that bad of a person, but it's like you two want nothing to do with me."

"That's not true. We're just busy running things here."

"I've always offered to help." I felt my hands fisting into little balls of anxiety.

"You can't be pulled away from what you do. Mom made that clear eons ago." Lana rolled her eyes, and I finally caught a glimpse of something.

Something that looked like pure disgust.

"What do you mean?"

Lana's brow arched. "You can't be serious."

"Completely serious." I thought back to my mom and her unrelenting belief in my ability to write.

It started with the first story I wrote in kindergarten and continued all the way through grade school and right on up until the first year in high school when I finished my first novel. She pushed it out to dozens of agents, catalogued all my rejection letters, and helped me come up with the next story in the series.

All while I was in high school.

Lana stared at me blankly before saying the words that dug deep into my soul. "You were always Mom's favorite."

I parted my lips to say something and then slammed them shut. Mom never had favorites. She loved us all the same. I swallowed down a lump in the back of my throat and looked over at the hot pink geraniums lining the nearest flower bed.

Mom loved Lana's determination and commitment to perfection in all things she did.

Mom loved Vera's feistiness and her inability to ever let her feathers get ruffled.

Mom loved my ability to be sensitive to others and follow my intuition.

Yet, I felt like I had absolutely none of that when it came to my sisters. I could never tell what they were thinking. I had no gut feelings with them at all, and I rarely had the opportunity to be sensitive to their needs.

"So, you and Vera decided to boycott me because you think Mom liked me more?" I shook my head. "That's ridiculous."

"It's not ridiculous, Samantha. It's how it was, and we always accepted it."

I drew in a shaky breath. "Mom didn't play favorites.

She loved you both more than any of us will ever know. You're disgracing Mom's legacy by even suggesting that. The woman ran herself ragged making sure we were all taken care of, along with the inn, the guests, and Dad." My eyes narrowed on my sister. "And *she* didn't hire out gardeners."

The moment I said it, I regretted it.

Lana sucked in a sharp breath and stood quickly. "Maybe it was a mistake asking you out here."

I stood, glancing toward the inn as I tightened the sash on my robe. "Why did you invite me here, Lana? There had to be a reason."

# CHAPTER SIX

*Garrett*

Samantha was standing outside Cloudberry Inn wearing a pink floral dress while glancing at her phone.

As I pulled up, I couldn't take my eyes off her. She was the most beautiful woman I'd ever laid eyes on. Her hair was back in a ponytail, and she had a pink purse over her shoulder. Even her shoes were pink, and I wasn't usually one to pay attention to stuff like that. But there was something about her that made me want to memorize every single detail.

I hid a smile as I slowed the truck and rolled the passenger window down.

"Hey, stranger." I smiled. "Wanna go make some trouble in our tiny town?"

Samantha laughed, and her eyes connected with mine.

It felt like the entire world tipped off its orbit when her chocolate eyes rested on mine. Her cute little lips curled slightly, and she drew a deep breath as if she were reconsidering the date, but then she giggled.

And I thought I'd finally heard angels sing. This girl was going to drive me crazy.

"Damn." I sighed and shook my head as she climbed in.

"What?" she asked, slamming the door of my truck.

"You're going to make this date that's going nowhere hard on me."

Samantha buckled and slowly crossed her right leg over her left and stretched it in front of her.

I knew better than to let my gaze wander up her legs, but damn, she was sexy.

She blinked her eyes innocently at me. "What do you mean?"

I let out a low growl of laughter. "You're damn sexy, and all I got you to commit to was a drink before you leave town."

She turned and faced me. "And what more would you like, Mr. Mason?"

I spun the truck around in the gravel and smiled, shaking my head. "Don't ask me that."

Samantha giggled. "You're such a man."

The attraction to her was undeniable.

I glanced at her and grinned. "What's that supposed to mean?"

"Men only have one thing on their minds. It's a fact."

"Interesting."

"What's so interesting?" She licked her bottom lip,

and I immediately thought about those lips elsewhere.

Maybe she was right.

"You were the one who'd thought what I had in my pocket was my—"

She whipped her head back in the seat and laughed, cutting me off. "Don't even turn that whole thing around on me. What was I supposed to think? It didn't even look normal. Not to mention, what man rolls up a lady's underwear?"

"What lady can't keep track of her underwear? And not that you'll ever find out, but I'm no average Joe in that department."

Her cheeks flushed with color, and I smiled.

"And what is average, anyway?" she asked, staring out the window.

I smiled. "I think I've heard six inches."

She brought her gaze back to me, and I snuck a quick look in her direction. "You're certainly giving me plenty, and then some, to write about."

"What? Are you a reporter?" My insides tensed.

The last thing I needed was to be fodder for the town's paper.

She laughed and brushed a stray piece of hair from her face. "Why? You have something to hide?"

I turned into the parking lot of the café and parked before answering.

"No. I'm just a man with very few tricks, and if they're all exposed, my dating life will turn even more dismal than it already it is."

"Ah." She nodded her head. "I see. Do you expect me to believe that you have any difficulty in the dating area?"

The way she looked at me made my pulse race. This was ridiculous. Women didn't do this to me merely from conversation.

"Well, when you live in a town this size, I don't know how active a person can be." I watched her expression turn from intrigue to something else. Something I couldn't put my finger on. Remorse? Regret? I didn't know.

"Duly noted." She hopped out of the truck, never answering my question, and gasped.

"Is that Violet?" She squealed. "Oh, my gosh. I haven't seen her since..." Samantha's voice trailed off and she glanced over at me. "Sorry. I shouldn't—"

I laughed. "Go for it. Far be it from me to hold you back on some long, lost reunion."

She jumped a little and clapped her hands together before calling for Violet Smith across the parking lot.

Violet was a lifer. When my father had moved us and the business here, we'd learned who all had been in town for generations, not because of any real investigating but because they made it known—loud and clear.

Violet turned around, looking somewhat startled as she heard her name being called until she caught Samantha running at her.

"Samantha? Samantha Roberts? As in *New York Times Bestselling Author* a million times over?"

I frowned.

Famous author?

How did I miss that?

I thought back to what Samantha's sister promised me, and I drew a breath. I really hoped I was wrong.

As I slowly made my way to the two women catching up in front of the restaurant, I saw happiness spread across Samantha's features. Worry from the day before had all but slipped away, and she seemed genuinely thrilled to have run across Violet.

Violet's eyes narrowed on me as her voice flattened. "Oh, Garrett."

I probably failed to mention that I'd gone out with Violet a few times over the years.

"You two know each other?" Samantha asked, smiling.

"You could say that." Violet rolled her eyes but quickly turned her attention to Samantha. Violet touched Samantha's arm and smiled. "Why don't you have dinner with us?"

My chest tightened. There was no promise of anything with Samantha. I knew she was leaving town in a few days, but I had one shot.

Tonight.

Samantha turned to me and smiled, shaking her head. "Another night, maybe? Tomorrow? I'm here with Garrett and..."

Violet got the look in her eyes that always worried me while dating and she smirked.

We'd never slept together, oddly. But I was the one who'd turned her down each time, which didn't exactly leave her with warm and fuzzy feelings toward me.

"Your call." Violet scowled at me before plastering a smile across her narrow features. "Let me give you my number, and maybe we can catch up while you're in town.

I know everyone would love to see you."

Samantha looked a little embarrassed as she traded numbers with Violet, and we all walked into the restaurant. Violet joined her family in the far corner while the hostess sat us at a window overlooking an empty pasture with a barn that had been begging to fall over in every single windstorm we've had, yet it just wasn't its time.

"You were popular back in school." It turned into more of a statement than a question.

Samantha blushed and took the menu from the hostess while specials were being rattled off.

Since she didn't answer my question, I drew a breath and tried a new tactic. "Have you kept in touch with many people from here?"

She shook her head and didn't bother opening the menu. "I already know what I'm having."

"You do?"

"It's one of my favorite places. We've been coming here since I was a little girl."

I sat back in the booth and nodded. "That's right. You and your sisters were born and raised here." I laughed, wondering why I felt like I had to show her the town when she already knew the town. "What are you having?"

"Chicken-fried steak with mashed potatoes and gravy." She cleared her throat. "With a side salad."

"That's quite a drink." I laughed.

She giggled, which made me wish this date could be more. "Hunger took over."

"A woman after my own heart."

"Which part?"

"The side salad." I smiled and watched her fuss with the tattered corner of the menu. "Do you miss this place?"

She tilted her head and let out a heavy sigh. "I don't know if I do. I think I miss what I used to have here but not necessarily what's here now."

I nodded, completely understanding what she meant. It's exactly why I was so eager to take over my dad's business here rather than where I'd done most of my growing up south of here. We'd moved here when I was twelve.

"Since my mom passed away and my dad moved to Arizona, nothing really feels the same. My sisters hate me, and I'd rather just not deal with it, to be honest. New York is a bubble."

"I can understand that." I pressed my lips together and thought about my stepbrother. We'd dodged that kind of family drama, but I knew it existed. I saw it within his family and it could destroy people. "But I doubt your sisters hate you." A few seconds passed as I watched Samantha scan the restaurant. "I can't imagine *anyone* hating you."

Samantha brought her gaze back to mine, and I suddenly felt like the luckiest man in the world as her eyes warmed and her dazzling smile wiped away her pout.

She laughed softly and drew a breath. "I'd like to say that's the case, but I'm afraid they don't like me very much."

The server came and took our order and trundled off as I watched Samantha glance at her phone.

"Sorry. I've been waiting for an email from my editor

all day." She looked embarrassed, shoving her phone back into her purse.

I shook my head. "No apologies needed. I know how work never stops. Back to your sisters."

I had no intention of telling her my suspicions, not until I knew more, understood the dynamics, and could prove that my hunch was right.

"Do we have to go back to them?" Samantha teased.

I shook my head. "Nah."

"Well, maybe you would be a good sounding board since you're completely objective, and we've already established that nothing much will come from this dinner."

I touched my heart and laughed. "Ouch."

She laughed. "You know what I mean."

"I'm getting to understand pretty quickly," I agreed, still feeling a pull to the woman sitting across from me.

Maybe the pull was purely because I knew I couldn't have her.

"Basically, I haven't been in my sisters' lives much. In the beginning, I blamed it on living clear across the country, but after my mom's death, I realized it was more than that."

"How long have you lived away from Cloudberry?" I asked, genuinely curious.

Even though we'd moved here when I was twelve, and then I took over the business, I'd been in and out of town helping out enough to come to know the Roberts family, but I never ran into Samantha, which was odd. I suppose it could be blamed on the age difference.

But shoot. I'd never even heard of her.

Samantha sucked in a breath. "Boy. A really long time. Before I even finished high school, actually."

I couldn't hide my surprise. "Really?"

She nodded, and I wondered how to bring up what I'd heard.

"Does your distance have to do with your job?"

Samantha smiled "It does."

"Which is?" I knew what I thought I'd heard outside, but I needed confirmation from Samantha's lips.

"I told you. I write."

"But what?" I prodded.

"Does it matter?" Her brow arched, and she looked extra sexy.

Damn this woman.

"Like I said, if you plan on doing an exposé about my lack of dating skills, then it matters."

A wicked look spread across Samantha's delicate features as she took her phone out of her purse and slid it to me.

"Doesn't sound like Violet thinks you have a lack of experience in the dating department. She sent a text when we sat down."

I looked at the screen and had to laugh.

*Watch out. He's a man tramp.*

I laughed and shook my head. "If only."

"You dated Violet, I'm assuming?"

I nodded. "We dated. Never slept together."

"I didn't ask."

My brows shot up. "I knew you'd wonder."

"I'm headed back to New York, so it's none of my business." A wry grin spread across her features.

I could see a bit of mischief behind her gaze and couldn't help but shake my head.

"You must keep men guessing back in Manhattan."

"Hah," she blurted, throwing her head back in a fit of giggles.

I hadn't had a woman giggle like she did in...

Well, never.

She brought her gaze back to mine. "I don't have time to date. There are no men."

"You write."

"I spend my days locked in my apartment coming up with characters and stories and loving every second. I rarely go out." She tapped her finger on the table. "Which is why I thought tonight would be good for me. I don't want to dry up on ideas."

"Are you like an advice columnist or... ?"

She beamed. "You really have no idea."

I shrugged. "Why would I?"

She let out a wistful sigh as our dinner arrived, and she thanked the server before bringing her gaze to mine.

"It's refreshing."

I glanced down at the plate of food and nodded, really having no idea what she was talking about other than the food. "I guess it is."

She laughed. "No. The fact that you could care less about me."

I frowned. "I wouldn't say I cared less. I'm actually trying to get to know you."

She pointed her fork at me and leaned in. "Exactly. You have no idea about me. No preconceived notions. No ideas on how I should act. Who I should know. What I should be thinking."

I cocked my head slightly, confused. "Why would I?"

She nodded. "Precisely."

I laughed and scratched my chin. "I usually consider myself somewhat sharp, but I'm really not following you."

"Living in Manhattan is all about who you know, and in order to know anyone, you have to know everyone."

I shook my head, laughing. "It seems that would be nearly impossible in a city that size."

"You would, wouldn't you? Yet, every time I've tried to get to know someone, they know more about me than I do." She shrugged. "So, long ago, I decided to stay indoors and do what I do best."

"Which is to write."

She nodded and took a bite, closing her eyes as she chewed. It was almost a mesmerizing act. When she blinked her eyes open, she smiled and blushed. "It's been too long. This is so good."

"It's too bad you're flying out of here in a couple of days."

She took another bite and her head lolled. "I will miss this gravy."

I smiled and shook my head. "About your sisters..."

She laughed. "Them again? They want nothing to do with me. That's been established since I arrived."

"When was the last time you've had a girls' night with them?"

Her big brown eyes widened, and it just made me wish even more that I was wrong about her sisters' intentions.

"Well, I'd say... never."

I was surprised. Every woman I'd dated always made an excuse for a girls' night. I assumed it was the norm. "Never?"

She shook her head. "Like I said, I left home before I'd even finished high school and haven't been back there pretty much since then." She shrugged. "We've just never had that kind of relationship since I left. It's one of the many reasons I wonder what on earth made them invite me out."

"Maybe tonight's the night?"

She scowled, and even that expression on her pouty lips and doe eyes turned sexual. "What do you mean?"

"Why not stop by the store on the way home and get some bottles of wine and try to get them to loosen up a bit? Maybe they'll finally talk if you give them some liquid courage."

She laughed, shaking her head. "The one thing those two don't need is courage."

"Vera is a firecracker," I agreed. "She's usually very

upfront."

Samantha smiled. "And ornery."

"You said it. I didn't."

"I just think there was something that made them want me out here, and they decided for whatever reason to change their mind, but I'd already booked the ticket so they're stuck with me."

I nodded, swallowing a piece of steak as I thought about Lana's promise to pay me *soon*.

"I couldn't help but catch that Violet said you were a New York Times Bestselling Author." I watched her squirm across from me. Her shoulders dipped slightly, and I watched her cheeks redden as she brought her gaze to mine.

"I am."

I smiled, wishing I could take her hand in mine. "You said earlier about locking yourself away, imagining characters and stories."

She nodded, her eyes staying on mine.

"So, you write fiction, I'm guessing?"

Samantha sucked on her bottom lip for a brief second as if she were contemplating what all to say. "I do."

"And you obviously do it well."

"I don't know about that. I've just been lucky."

"It's not just luck to hit the bestseller lists."

Her eyes fastened on mine and electricity shot through me. "No. You're right. It takes a huge publisher who knows what stores to send your books to that get them counted. A huge marketing spend and—"

I interrupted. "A good story. Give yourself some credit."

Her lips curled slightly. "Fine. And a decent story."

I looked at the woman sitting across from me who'd accomplished more than most people could ever dream of achieving, and yet, you'd never know it by looking.

"It's okay to know you're good at something," I pointed out.

"I suppose there's nothing wrong with it."

"And hitting a list isn't shabby." I grinned. "Especially that one."

She grinned wider, and I saw a coy look flash across her expression. "Fifteen times."

"You've hit the list fifteen times?" I was shocked. "How many books have you written?"

"Fifteen." Her eyes sparkled.

"And have you celebrated fifteen times?"

She laughed and shook her head. "I don't even think I've celebrated once."

My eyes narrowed on the gorgeous woman sitting across from me, and I smiled.

"Well, that's going to change starting tonight."

# CHAPTER SEVEN

*Samantha*

I stumbled into Cloudberry Inn a little before nine o'clock at night, holding a carton full of wine bottles and great expectations of mending fences. After Garrett ordered me two drinks and made me chant that I was worthy of my bestseller status, I agreed to let him swing by the store so I could pick up some alcohol for my sisters. The grocer assured me that buying six bottles of wine was the better deal, so here I was.

Armed and ready to liquor up my sisters and force them to like me.

The bridal party was still enjoying their weekend at the inn and a few other guests had checked in during the day, so I did my best to keep quiet as I made my way down the hall, through the kitchen, and into the family room where my sisters usually spent their evenings, just as my mom and dad had before them.

Sure enough, Vera and Lana were sitting in the room with a couple of dim lamps turned on and the overhead light turned off. The gas fireplace was on in the corner, but

Lana still had a pink afghan draped over her shoulders.

Vera was reading a massive hardcover, and Lana was cross-stitching a pillow that I'd seen earlier in the day.

Only Lana looked up when I came into the room holding my bright idea.

"Wine, anyone?" Lana glanced at Vera, who slowly looked up from her book.

"I'm good. Thanks." Vera flashed a fake smile in my direction, but I traipsed forward with the carton of wine.

"What about you, Lana?" I smiled. "It's a Friday night. Let's live a little."

Vera let out an exaggerated sigh. "Just because you're busy back in New York partying all the time doesn't mean we want that out here."

My brows shot up in surprise as I set the carton of wine on the coffee table.

"Partying?" My hands flew to my hips. "You think I'm out partying?"

"I've seen the photos," Vera mumbled as she put her nose back in her book.

I looked at Lana, who seemed far too amused with this interaction, and I scowled at her.

"What do you think I'm doing back there?" I asked anyone in the room who would answer.

Vera, annoyed by the very fact that I wouldn't just go away, slowly shut her book and brought her attention to me.

"Well, I imagine you're busy attending functions, hobnobbing with people you don't know, and pretending we don't exist."

My jaw dropped open, but I quickly brought it back up and pressed my lips together as I looked at Lana, wondering if she thought the same thing.

"You know what?" I asked. "Hold that thought."

Garrett was right.

These women needed to loosen up. Instead of the quick edge of anger that roared to life so I could defend myself, I decided to try a different angle.

I spun on my heels and went into the kitchen where I grabbed three cups from the cabinet.

Who needed wine glasses in a moment like this?

I pulled open a drawer, found the wine opener, and marched back into the family room where my sisters hadn't moved a muscle.

"What do you want? Merlot? Cab? I'd offer white, but it hasn't been chilled."

"I'm fine," Vera repeated, and I spun around.

"Clearly, you're not." I handed her a cup and picked up the nearest bottle of wine, opened it right up, and poured the deep crimson into the cup Vera was still holding.

I did the same for Lana and myself and took a seat in the recliner nearest the fireplace.

The recliner was actually Dad's favorite place to sit, and I was surprised he didn't take it to Arizona with him.

I glanced at Vera, who was happily sipping the wine, and I nodded.

I smiled. "Good. I'm glad to see you having a sip, after all."

Lana chuckled as she drank, and I took a deep breath,

wondering if Garrett was on to something.

"I've had enough of this," I declared. "I need answers. Why did you invite me out here when it's painfully obvious that Vera could care less whether I lived or died, and Lana, you do your best to flash your plastic smile in my direction every time I make a sound, but you can't even talk to me?"

"Why do you care?" Vera asked over her cup as she took another sip.

"I care because I received what I thought was an emergency summons, and then I got the cold shoulder once I arrived. I want to know what prompted the invite. It obviously wasn't out of sisterly love."

Vera snorted and took another sip.

Garrett's plan really was working.

I hadn't heard Vera snort for years.

I just hoped I'd be strong enough to hear what they had to say.

"I don't think it's anything we should discuss while we're all drinking," Lana answered.

"Then let's tackle another subject." I took a giant swallow of the merlot and wished I hadn't mixed the wine flavor from tonight's drinks with Garrett, but I probably needed the liquid courage as much as anyone.

"What subject?" Lana asked, setting her cup down.

"Why do you two hate me so very much?"

"Isn't that the same topic?" Vera asked.

A chill settled over the room as Vera and Lana traded glances. It didn't take long before they both picked up their cups and took another swallow. We'd be breaking into the second bottle of wine in no time.

Lana began." We don't hate you."

"But?" I prompted. "You don't seem to like me very much."

Vera tucked her feet under her and looked over at me. "We don't really know you."

"That's not my fault. I wanted to be close," I started and stopped as soon as Vera rolled her eyes, untucked her legs, and got up to pour herself more wine.

*At least they aren't stomping off yet*, I thought to myself.

"I highly doubt that." Vera plopped back down on the couch.

"It's true."

"You've got so many friends, I doubt you think twice about us most days." Vera chortled as she quickly took another sip. "Especially with that redheaded dude you're always pictured with."

"That redhead is my closest friend and editor." I let out a slow breath as the drinks from earlier and the wine sloshed around in my stomach. "He's about all I have back in New York."

"Please. Let me get the violin out while you complain about your fancy life back in the city with no cares in the world." Vera popped up from the couch suddenly and looked a little tipsy. "I don't have anything to say. Our lives don't intersect, and they don't have to." Vera glanced at Lana. "You deal with her."

Vera stomped out of the room, leaving me to wonder if I should go after her or give her space.

"She's still pretty crabby since Drew North avoided this place like the plague," Lana explained.

"I doubt that's the whole reason." I let out a deep sigh. "Is there ever going to be a way for me to make things right?" I shook my head and groaned. "I honestly don't know why there's so much animosity toward me."

"It's complex." Lana poured herself the last of the wine from the bottle.

"Well, I'm here and ready to listen."

Lana's expression hardened. "The problem is that I don't think Vera cares to explain."

"Then why won't you?" I watched Lana's gaze drift toward the fire.

"It's not my story to tell."

I sighed as my head lolled to the side. "How noble."

"Let's change the subject," Lana suggested.

I straightened in the chair and looked at her. "To what?"

"How was your date?" she asked, plastering her perfect smile onto her face.

"It wasn't a date," I corrected. "He just offered to take me for drinks, and it led to dinner."

"Whatever." She shrugged. "You don't have to tell me."

I thought back to Garrett and my insides instantly warmed. I didn't know if it was the genuine soul he had beneath the rough exterior or the fact that he was just plain sexy that made me very confused about my time around him, limited as it might be.

"He's refreshing."

Lana leaned forward. "How so?"

"For starters, he had no idea who I was and—"

"Do most people?"

A callous laugh left my lips. "Surprisingly, yes. Back in the city, they seem to make it a point to know things like that."

My sister stared at me. "Do you subscribe to that thought?"

I laughed. "Not at all. I can barely remember my own name, let alone anyone else's. Contrary to what Vera thinks, I don't go out much."

"It's hard to believe." Lana bit her bottom lip as her gaze fell to the floor. "You don't have a care in the world. You spend your days making up stories. You don't have to worry about money or business problems. You're out of touch, and I think that bothers Vera."

I sat in stunned silence. That was the exact opposite of the world I lived in.

I spent my days wishing I could fall into the stories rattling in my head. Instead, I was left with a blank screen most days. My biggest fear each day was that I'd have to come up with some crazy reason at the last moment as to why I didn't want to go out for some social event my publisher thought would be good for me. And all I thought about was money because if I didn't make enough of it now, I might be under a bridge when I hit ninety.

Not to mention, it was more than difficult to get publishers to get behind authors nowadays. I even spent a significant amount of my royalties advertising just to stay ahead of the curve and pray that they keep offering deals. But it would be foolish to not recognize how fortunate I'd been and continue to be. I was grateful every single day.

As I stared at my sister, I realized I couldn't tell her any of this. Not because she wouldn't understand but because she wouldn't care. She already had the narrative made up about me and my life back in New York, and anything I said to the contrary would be considered whining.

I knew how my sisters thought.

I drew a deep breath and let it out slowly. "It sounds like you think that too."

She shrugged. "Partially. You left home before you could even vote, and prior to moving out, you and Mom spent over a year traveling the world to promote your debut novel. To say that you have any idea what it's like in the real world as an adult would be inaccurate."

Her words stung. It wasn't easy giving up my high school experience to be homeschooled on the road so my publisher could push me in front of crowds and make me sign and smile on command. It wasn't easy coming back to visit home to find out all my friends had turned on me because I'd left. There wasn't any going back and changing what had begun. Between my mom's excitement over my success and my dad's commitment to staying at the inn and looking after my sisters, the world didn't offer me any choices. And I wasn't complaining. That was purely how it was.

Growing up, I'd imagined what it would be like going off to college and making friends. Instead, my late teens and early twenties were spent in a cramped apartment in the city, churning out story after story for a greedy publisher.

If it weren't for the readers, I didn't know where I'd be.

But again, if I were to utter any of this to Lana, she would think I was complaining. And I wasn't. I was grateful every day that I got to write for a living. I just wished I had someone, many someones, to share it with.

I was tired of being lonely, and it had only gotten worse since my mom died seven years ago.

I turned my gaze back to Lana and smiled. "I won't pretend my life is difficult. You're right. Is there anything I can do while I'm here to make your life easier?"

# CHAPTER EIGHT

*Garrett*

Wyatt had gone back to Fireweed, and I was at my parents' house. My father had bought a mammoth hot tub for his back yard but refused to pay for installation.

Apparently, that was where I came in.

As I crawled behind the tight space that barely allowed enough room for my arm, let alone my body, I twisted and turned in an attempt to finish the wiring.

"You're such a good son," my stepmom sang.

A muffled laugh rolled off my lips since I didn't have enough air to respond.

"We'll let you come and use it whenever you want," she added.

"As long as we're not in it," my dad corrected just as I finished the last step standing between my parents and their fun machine.

I snaked out of the tight space and stood up, seeing the glint of mischief in his eyes as he held my stepmom tight.

It was something I was happy to see but simultaneously wished I hadn't.

Even at my age, I didn't like to think about my dad doing anything other than sleeping, eating, and working on some sort of benign hobby in his retirement.

"What's the matter, Son?" My dad extended his hand to help me up. "You seem to be off in another galaxy."

I shook my head and smiled. "Just a lot on my mind."

My dad patted my shoulder. "Always the case, isn't it, Son? The business giving you trouble?"

I took a seat at the patio table as my stepmom went inside.

"No. The business is going well. Almost too well," I confessed, glancing at the miniature apple orchard my stepmom and father started a few years ago.

My dad laughed and took a seat across from me. "I always hated when the business climbed like that."

I looked at my dad in surprise. "Really?"

He nodded. "Because it never lasts. You have good years, and then one bad year can knock you right off your feet while you're still living the life of a good year. But if you stay the course and don't overspend, you can enjoy having your children come over to help fix odds and ends too."

I chuckled as my stepmom came out with a bowl of fruit and a stack of plates. "Thanks for the words of encouragement, Dad. I guess I probably need a wife first to get to the kids."

He winked at me and laughed. "Sorry. Anytime."

"Are you bugging him to settle down again?" My stepmom chuckled and shook her head. "That's my job. Between Wyatt and Garrett, you'd think one of the boys would find a wife and just cool it. Maybe pump out some grandkids instead of just working all the time."

"Not everyone is destined to find love, especially more than once." I pushed down an unexpected lump that had formed in my throat. I cleared my throat and stared at the orchard. "And, might I add, Wyatt would be shocked to hear that you want him to settle down. He just told me a couple of days ago that you were totally against it."

Damn. I'd been doing so good not going down that emotional path of loss. I'd say the last year to year and a half, I'd really progressed, and then this.

Out of nowhere.

Thinking about the future I thought I'd have already.

With Renee.

My stepmom came over and gave me a quick hug. "I'm sorry. I shouldn't have brought that up. It was careless of me. And as for Wyatt, I want him to find love. I just don't want him to break hearts while he does it. But I know you wouldn't do that, at least not on purpose."

I smiled, seeing the kindness in her eyes. She was right. That was part of my problem and why everything was always casual. "I'd think after this many years, I'd be over it."

"Her," my dad corrected. "And I don't think you'll ever be over Renee."

"And that's okay." My stepmom smiled, sitting next to my dad. "She's a big part of who you've become and who you want to be. She'll always be with you."

I let out a deep sigh and looked up toward the blue sky without a cloud to be seen. I often felt she was up there watching me and guiding me. Maybe even rolling her eyes at me.

My dad let out a nervous laugh, and I brought my gaze to his. "On that note, have you still been seeing your therapist?"

I laughed and nodded. "I'm still trying to figure things out, and I'm not sure I ever will."

My dad nodded. "Nothing wrong with that."

"At least I feel confident that I'm helping to send my therapist's kids to college."

"Then at least something good is coming out of it." My dad smiled.

"In all seriousness, I think I'm starting to move on." I steepled my hands together as my stepmom scooped some fresh fruit onto my plate. "It might not seem like it, but this last year or so finally felt almost normal."

My stepmom nodded and took a bite of a strawberry before looking over at my dad. "Working through the emotions of losing someone takes time. Even though the situation I came from in my first marriage was horrible, it took a lot of time for me to sort through everything and get a clear head. Even when I met your dad, I wasn't all completely there. I'm just glad he was patient and waited me out."

My dad laughed. "I knew I'd found a good thing the moment I laid eyes on you."

I grinned and nodded, thinking back to Samantha.

That's how it felt when I saw her. Like a good thing had come into my life.

A good person.

"I have had a bit of trouble getting an invoice paid from Cloudberry Inn."

"Really?" My dad seemed genuinely surprised. "They do good business. I wonder what's going on."

I nodded and plucked a few strawberry slices from my plate and tossed them in my mouth. "I've tried to find out, but it hasn't gone over well." I shrugged. "At this point, it's not even about the money."

My dad scowled. "Then what's it about?"

"I feel like they're being shady."

My dad nodded. "You think they have the money and are holding out on you? Just the principle of that would get me."

I grinned, seeing my dad's gaze light up. He always thrived on a bit of drama, which was why my stepmom was perfect for him. She came with plenty, but I loved her for it.

"I'm not sure if they have it or not." I tapped my foot against the concrete and debated what else to say.

"You're about as clear as a dirty fish tank." My stepmom pressed her lips together, and she swapped a smile with my dad.

"Did you know there are *three* Roberts sisters?" I asked my dad, who nodded.

My dad smiled. "Yeah. One of them hit it big and never looked back, from what I understand."

"Interesting."

"Why?" My stepmom eyed my dad. "Hit it big? What's she do?"

"She's a writer of some sort." My dad waved his hands in the air as if that explained it all.

"Tell me who." My stepmom's brows rose in anticipation. The mere thought that she could know a celebrity perked her right up.

I cleared my throat and tried to maintain coolness when saying her name. If they even detected a slight interest in my voice, I would be doomed.

"Her name is Samantha."

My stepmom's eyes widened. "Samantha Roberts? I've read every single book of hers. She's like a child prodigy turned successful adult."

I laughed. "That doesn't happen often."

"No, it doesn't." My dad laughed. "Have you seen some of those *Where Are They Now* shows?" He grimaced. "She's lucky."

"If I see her again, I'll have to tell her." I thought back to Samantha and hid a smile.

There was so much about her I didn't know. Was she really a child prodigy? Was she as famous as my stepmom thought?

"So, you've met her?" My stepmom was bringing the conversation right back to where she wanted it.

Gossip.

I nodded. "Took her out to dinner, actually."

My dad's eyes widened. "Really. I'm impressed."

I laughed, shaking my head.

"Don't go getting any ideas." I wagged my finger at my stepmom before she had a chance to say anything.

"I'd never." My stepmom chuckled and took a bite of pineapple. "What's she like?"

"Well, she's beautiful." I realized I'd said too much and shut my mouth.

"Beautiful, huh?"

I sighed, needing to clarify. "And smart and very humble."

"That's a rarity," my dad muttered.

"But she lives in New York." I could tell my parents were staring at me. I also knew I'd better keep the rest of the conversation topline. My stepmom was bad enough when it came to me finding someone to settle down with, but my own mother was downright obnoxious. "So, no need to go fill in my mom."

I stared at my stepmom.

I probably failed to mention that the two women became best friends, which in the beginning made my dad nervous, but he quickly got used to the idea.

It made the holidays less messy, and once my mom remarried, the pressure was off all parties to be riddled with guilt.

My mom and dad had always been very honest about their marriage and falling out of love. They'd met in college, fallen in love, and felt it was the next step. They ignored the fact that there wasn't passion, never a spark between them, and no interests they could even share.

But they did what a lot of people do. They stayed together and thought it would all fall together.

Instead, it fell apart.

I often wondered if that would have been Renee and

me. We both loved each other fiercely. But we'd never had a spark, just a friendship that turned to something physical.

I never knew if that was enough.

Never got the opportunity to find out.

"Anyway, the reason I bring up Samantha and Cloudberry is that—" I looked over at my stepmom. "This doesn't leave the table."

She grinned widely, loving to be a part of a secret. "Got it."

"Apparently, the sisters have been estranged. I don't know details, but it sounds like Samantha is kind of the odd sheep out." I shifted in the patio chair. "From what I can tell, they don't really talk to her."

My dad shrugged and pulled a stem off a grape. "It can't be that bad. She's out here visiting."

I grimaced. "That's where I think it gets tricky. They haven't seen one another since their mom's death."

My dad whistled and shook his head. "What was that? Six or seven years ago?"

My stepmom nodded. "Something like that."

"But Samantha suddenly got word that they wanted her to visit, so she hopped on a plane thinking something was wrong. When she got here, the cold shoulder continued."

My dad narrowed his eyes at me. "You're wondering if they invited her out here to get money from her."

I clasped my hands together. "It's a thought that crossed my mind."

"Nothing would surprise me." My dad nodded.

"Money can do strange things to people."

"I hope I'm wrong, but when I spoke to Lana about the invoice, she assured me that she'd be paying it *soon*."

"Soon because Samantha is in town?"

I shrugged. "It makes me wonder."

"Are you going to say something?" my stepmom asked.

"I don't know yet. I think she's leaving on Monday. Plus, it's none of my business."

My dad nodded and stood to open the table umbrella. The late-spring sunshine had finally heated the patio to an uncomfortable temperature.

"I'd normally agree, but you are loosely involved." My dad took a seat again. "You've always had good instincts, Son. If it's bothering you, do something about it."

"I just don't like the thought of someone being used."

"I know. It wouldn't be right if that were the case," my dad agreed.

I nodded and took a silent breath when I realized there was more than one reason I needed to see Samantha again.

# CHAPTER NINE

*Samantha*

The smell of cinnamon rolls and coffee wafted through the kitchen. It was Saturday morning, and I woke up early to prepare breakfast for the guests. The house was filled with a peaceful silence. The familiar morning chill was still in the air, and I loved the calm that surrounded me in the bright yellow kitchen.

As I stood at the sink, the stillness of the home let my mind wander to faraway places tucked deep inside my soul that I rarely visited.

I thought about my sisters.

My parents.

My stories.

And how even with all of my writing, they were all intertwined and the very crux of my existence and passion.

Last night, I'd knocked on both Vera and Lana's doors and told them not to bother waking up early this morning. I wanted my sisters to have a chance to sleep in and have a break. We'd gotten absolutely nowhere, even with the case of wine I'd decided to bring home.

So, all I could do was extend an olive branch and offer to help, enjoy my brief time out here, and hope they'd open up before I leave to go back home.

I wasn't holding my breath, though.

My phone buzzed, and I wiped my hands on a red-checkered kitchen towel before picking it up. It was still so early out here in Washington that I expected it to be a text from my friend and editor, Jack, back in New York.

It wasn't him.

It was Garrett Mason.

Just seeing his number on my screen made my body tingle.

I smiled to myself realizing that what I'd written in story after story did indeed happen when chemistry existed between two people.

It was true.

Tingles still happened.

I was alive.

I chuckled just as someone's footsteps pattered up behind me in the kitchen. I expected it to be one of my sisters when an older woman's voice brought me back to my senses.

"Excuse me. Is there any coffee down here? I couldn't figure out how to get the thing to work in my room."

I spun around to see a silver-haired woman with sparkling turquoise eyes dressed in a long flannel nightgown and fuzzy slippers.

"Absolutely." I smiled and reached for a cup out of the

cabinet and poured her a cup.

She happily took the steaming mug, sniffed, and brightened even more. "I love the smell of coffee."

"Me too." I grinned. "I'm a bit of an addict, truth be told."

She winked. "Could be worse. Now, how do I find my way to the parlor? I don't want to go back upstairs and wake up my daughter."

"That's considerate of you."

She chuckled and gripped her mug of coffee. "Not considerate. It's just self-preservation. Ever since she was a little girl, she needed her sleep."

I laughed and immediately felt a warmth from the woman. She adored her daughter, no doubt. I imagined my mom to be the same if she were staying at an inn with one of us.

The pang of sadness ran through me as quickly as the warm memories that flooded next.

The memory of my mom rounding us girls up from the back yard to help hang the wet laundry. She was positive the guests could tell the sheets had been touched by sunshine. Or the many times my mom would watch us take our riding lessons down the road at a neighbor's ranch.

So many things my mom would never get to see me doing with my own daughter.

If I were to ever have one.

I let out a wistful sigh, and the woman's gaze connected with mine before speaking. "Looks like you've got a lot on your mind."

The oven dinged, and I quickly used that as my excuse

to avoid spilling my guts.

I'd always found it easier to talk to complete strangers knowing that they'd probably never see me again or even remember what I'd told them. It had worked in New York at coffee shops all around the city.

And I knew I wasn't the only one. Many a time did a fellow coffee connoisseur strike up a conversation that lasted all morning. People who said New Yorkers were rude didn't spend time in a neighborhood coffee shop.

I pulled out the cinnamon rolls and the woman let out a chirpy whistle. "Those smell delightful."

"I hope so. I took over for my sisters today. It's my mom's recipe, but I'm sure they do them better." I used a spatula to spread the rolls onto a platter. The inn always provided a light breakfast of freshly made pastries, dry cereal, fruit, and coffee. "Would you like one while it's still piping hot?"

"Don't mind if I do. You should have a seat with me."

I plated her a gooey roll, and she trundled to the pine kitchen table. I still had strawberries and a melon to slice, but maybe a quick visit with her wouldn't hurt.

"So, you're one of the famous Cloudberry Inn sisters? I'm Margaret, by the way. We checked in under my daughter, Susan."

"Nice to meet you, Margaret. I'm Samantha, but I'm not responsible much for the inn. I live in New York and just happen to be visiting."

"That's nice. I bet they're so happy to see you." She smiled and took a bite of the cinnamon roll before closing her eyes and chewing. "So good."

"Thank you." I smiled, relieved that I'd made

something edible for paying guests.

"I'm here with my daughter to visit my twin sister for our birthday tomorrow. We're going to be ninety-two."

My jaw dropped open in shock. I thought Margaret might be seventy, at the most.

"I get that a lot. You can close your mouth, dear." She giggled. "You know why I look this way?"

I shook my head.

She chuckled. "It wasn't sugar and spice and everything nice. It was pure determination. Screw growing old gracefully. My husband was the same way until he kicked the bucket last year."

I gasped and she smiled.

"It was somewhat expected. He was a hundred and two," she said matter-of-fact. "But I don't believe he's actually gone. I talk to him all the time as if he were physically next to me, which is why I think my daughter was so adamant about bringing me here to see my sister. I think she thinks I'm losing my mind, but I'm just finding it. There is a whole other dimension out there. Anyway, I think my daughter is planning to dump me off with my sister, Mary. Why having two ninety-two-year-olds together would stabilize our mental cognizance, I do not know." She laughed. "Two heads are not always better than one. I might be sane, but my sister is nuttier than a fruitcake, and not in a good way."

I chuckled and nodded, not expecting that answer from the woman sitting across from me.

"I do yoga most days, swim the others, and I write every single day." She tapped her head. "To keep the wheels spinning. So, contrary to my daughter thinking I'm off my rocker, I don't ever intend to own one."

I chuckled and nodded. "Sounds like the best plan to me. What do you write?"

"Poetry."

"Oh, I love reading poetry. I can spend an entire afternoon devouring my favorites over and over again."

She smiled and nodded. "Do you write?"

"How did you know?"

"The way your eyes lit up when I mentioned that I did."

"I would do terrible in an interrogation." I let out a happy sigh. "I do write, mostly fiction."

"Anything I would know?"

"Probably not." I hated that question. The possible answers either made a person sound egotistical or meek.

"Don't worry, dear. Just keep at it. Do what you love, and happiness will follow."

I smiled and nodded, wishing all that to be true.

There was no doubt that with every ounce of my being, I loved to write. Getting to close my eyes and imagine a world to live in was euphoric. Opening my eyes and actually typing out the story was even more so. I would get so lost in the worlds I wrote about that I'd often forget I wasn't still there by the time I stepped away from the keyboard to make dinner.

Which was another good reason not to date anyone seriously. They wouldn't get my hours and my fascination with a reality that wasn't revealed in our every day, and the level of distraction that managed to drape over me when my mind wandered to those faraway places just tended to wreak havoc in normal conversation.

If I couldn't even maintain a relationship with my sisters, how could I ever find a man who understood me for me?

"It doesn't look like you're buying it," Margaret said point-blank.

"Well, I just think that a person can be happy *doing* something, but then the happiness doesn't necessarily translate to other parts of their lives."

Margaret tipped her head slightly and nodded. "So, you love what you do, but it's not trickling down to the rest of your life?"

"Precisely." I nodded. "In fact, I think because I do what I love, my personal and family life has suffered."

"Hmm." She scowled. "That's not how it usually works."

I shrugged. "Seems to be how it worked for me."

"Well, you have a wonderful family, sisters who love you here." She smiled. "What's better than that?"

I held in a sigh and nodded.

"What's better than that?" I asked myself silently.

"You've got the family part covered, so it must be men that's the issue."

I chuckled. "No issue there. I don't date."

"Why on earth don't you date?" She got a wicked gleam in her eyes. "One thing I failed to mention was that sex has kept me young."

My eyes widened in surprise.

"You know what they say about those retirement

homes, right?" She laughed. "It's true. It's like high school all over again but without the worry of getting pregnant."

Laughter between us filled the kitchen, and I couldn't think of a better way to fill my morning. Margaret somehow made everything seem okay.

"Looks like you've made a friend," Lana said, walking into the kitchen. She'd already changed into a blue floral skirt and a matching blue top.

"Margaret is full of amazing advice," I explained to my sister.

"I don't know about advice, but I'm certainly full of something." She finished the last bite of her cinnamon roll and smiled.

I snickered as Margaret stood up.

"Now, if you'll just point me in the direction of the parlor, I'll let you two get on with your day."

Lana led her down the hallway toward the lobby and showed her the parlor, which was next to the ballroom. There was no doubt that the Cloudberry Inn was a special place.

When Lana wandered back into the kitchen, she smiled as soon as she spotted the cinnamon rolls.

"Those look incredible, like Mom's." She smiled.

"I'm sure they're not as good as yours, but I tried." I drew a breath and watched my sister lift a gooey roll off the platter. She took a bite and let out a little moan.

"Oh, Samantha. These are way better than what I come up with." She took another bite. "And better than Vera's by a long shot."

I chuckled, feeling a bit of the icy façade melt away.

"Thanks. If there's anything else I can do to help while I'm here, please let me know."

Lana stretched toward the ceiling and smiled wider. "Just knowing I didn't have to get up to make breakfast did wonders. I can't even tell you how long it's been since I've just laid in bed."

My stomach tightened. "You know, I could come out here if you and Vera ever need a break. I'd be more than happy to fill in here and there."

Lana pressed her lips together and scowled slightly.

"Or not," I added.

Honestly, it felt like I was sinking slowly in the middle of the ocean, and no one would throw me a life preserver. I wanted to make things better. I wanted to know what I'd done wrong. How I'd hurt them.

"No, it's a nice offer." She shrugged. "I just don't know how feasible it is."

I nodded. "I just wish things weren't uncomfortable between us all."

"I didn't think they were uncomfortable. You're my sister, and I love you. I always will." She smiled, and I suddenly felt like a switch flipped again. "And I'm so happy you're here."

"Me too." I held in a heavy sigh and watched my sister.

"Do you have time tonight to go over something?" she asked, glancing at the clock. "I'd do it now, but I've got a huge list of things to do today. And since you're leaving on Monday..." Her voice trailed off.

I nodded and drew a breath, relief finally spreading through me. Maybe this was it. I'd finally get to piece together what's been going on between us all. I was part relieved and part terrified.

"Absolutely. I'd love to talk."

"Great." Lana gave me a quick hug and spun on her heels as I glanced at the fruit I needed to slice.

The moment she left the kitchen, Garrett's text popped into my mind. I'd totally forgotten about it once I'd started talking to Margaret. I went over to my phone and slid it on to see Garrett's text staring right back at me.

*I know you're leaving soon to go back to New York, but I have something I'd really like to discuss with you.*

My stomach knotted with anticipation at the mere thought of getting to see Garrett again. But what on earth did want to talk to me about? I let my mind briefly wander to several scenarios all at once which somehow all ended with a kiss.

Which was ridiculous.

But the thought was appealing.

A little *too* appealing.

# CHAPTER TEN

*Garrett*

I knew it was a mistake. Here I was about to stick my nose where it didn't belong.

So, why did I want it to belong there?

Shaking my head, I turned on the hose at the back of the house. I wasn't much of a gardener, so I'd hired a landscaper. The same one who was at Cloudberry Inn, ironically.

I wondered if they'd paid him?

I heard my mom's car pull into my driveway, and I turned off the hose before wandering along the side of my house. It was definitely a bigger house than I needed, but I liked my space and I didn't like clutter.

I spotted my mom pulling out two big boxes from her trunk and I chuckled.

"Stan made you a shelf for your guest bath and then a wooden checker set." She rolled her eyes playfully as if she were annoyed with her husband, but I knew she loved how handy he was.

I rushed over to help my mom with the boxes. "That's pretty cool." I gave her a quick peck on the cheek before stacking the two boxes and bringing them inside.

My mom laughed. "He's really gotten into this latest hobby. He's bought all the equipment he could find, you can only park one car in our garage now, and I rarely see him. He's even talking about going to craft fairs."

I chuckled and placed the boxes in my entry. I opened the first box, and while I could tell it was a checkerboard, it was hard not to suggest that he keep his day job of retirement. If I put it on a table, there would be no doubt that it wobbled, but it was the thought that counted.

My mom glanced around my house as if Stan could be lurking somewhere. "Personally, I think he needs to practice a little more." She reached down and pulled the empty box off the one that held the shelf. I opened the box to reveal the shelf, and it, too, had a little bit of a slant.

"He's definitely on the right track." I grinned, holding up the shelf before putting it back in the box.

"Just make sure you have it all out when he comes over next. You can keep it in the garage in between." My mom laughed and followed me into the kitchen.

She pulled open the fridge and poured herself some tea. "So, what's this I hear about you dating a famous author?"

I groaned, realizing I never should have mentioned Samantha to Twila and my dad. It was a rookie mistake and one I'd be paying for dearly the rest of the afternoon.

"We're not dating. I just happened to meet her for dinner and—"

"Whatever you say, darling." My mom winked at me.

"No. Seriously. We aren't dating. She lives in New York and plans to head back there on Monday."

"Haven't you ever heard of a long-distance relationship before?" my mom chided.

I laughed. "I think those kinds of relationships make it hard for you to become a grandma, and that's really what this is all about, right?"

My mom smiled and followed me out to the back patio.

"You can't blame me and Twila for hoping. You have a heart of gold, a beautiful home, a steady job..." She shrugged. "You should have ten wives."

The thought turned my blood cold. I could barely handle one woman. There'd be no way I could handle ten.

"If it's meant to happen, it will happen." I smiled at my mom. She shared the same green eyes I had. "So, how about this weather, huh?"

My mom chuckled. "Fine. I get the message."

A few seconds of silence passed between us.

"Is she pretty?"

"You're as bad as Twila, but she's read her books."

"You know me. I like the movies better."

"I'll be sure to tell Sam that."

"Sam, huh? Sounds friendly."

I laughed and shook my head. The skies had turned overcast, but that wasn't uncommon for Washington. We often had the clouds roll in and stay for days without a hint of moisture.

"I just hope that when you do find that special

someone, you'll feel fireworks like I did with Stan."

I nodded. "You two are a good pair."

"The best." She took a sip of tea. "But I do think you need a woman who will keep you in line."

I scowled. "It's not a woman's job to keep her man in line. That is so ancient."

"I know my son. You're a handful, and from what Twila has told me about your Samantha person..." My mom's brows shot up. "She might just be the one to keep you in your place."

"I do not know how Twila could possibly know much about Samantha considering she's never met her."

My mom shrugged and looked out at my gardens. "She's been reading and sending me all of Samantha's interviews."

She had interviews out there? I shook my head. Of course, she'd have interviews. Why didn't I think of that?

Because I didn't want to be a stalker, unlike my mom and stepmom.

"You know, it's a good thing I don't tell you much about the women I see."

My mom chuckled. "That's because most women you see aren't real contenders. You've hidden yourself away from the prospect of real love since—"

"Since Renee." I drew a breath and let it out.

"Yeah, and as much as this pains me to say, I don't think you two were actually in love."

My throat tightened, and I reached for my mom's tea.

"I think had you gone ahead with getting married, you

would have wound up like your father and me."

"I have to say that I thought we'd be talking about how great my gardener did this year on the perennial beds or something."

My mom laughed. "Since when have we ever talked about flowers?"

I sighed. "Not nearly often enough. Listen, Mom. The truth is that I really like Samantha. I have more fireworks than I know what to do with, and I have just as much guilt spilling into my every thought because of it. I *should* be married to Renee."

"Renee was your friend, your best friend, and she wouldn't want you making yourself miserable and crotchety to prove a point. She's not here anymore, honey. It's okay to move on with your life. She would have wanted you to."

I knew what my mom was saying was true, but it didn't make it any easier. Even though every time I saw Samantha, my world stood still and I wanted to bottle up the feelings she produced in me, I had a nagging feeling of regret. I wasn't sure which would ever win.

"It's why it's easier to keep things casual. Then nobody gets hurt."

My mom suddenly threw herself into a fit of giggles.

"Did you put something in your tea?" I asked.

"No, I just can't believe how good you are at lying to yourself. You're just like me. Exactly how I was with your father."

I scowled. "What are you talking about?"

"Telling me nobody gets hurt when you sleep with women and never actually get involved." My mom rolled her eyes. "The person who gets hurt is you, Garrett. You're missing out on love, on what fills life with hope." My mom shook her head. "Without hope, life is a pretty tangled mess of ups and downs. But hope will get you through. Love will get you through, and they're both very intertwined." She polished off her tea and stood from the table. "So, unless you get yourself unsnarled from your very messy perspective on life, you'll be at a standstill."

I laughed, standing up. "I take it you've had it with me."

She reached over like she did when I was a kid and shook her head. "Not at all. I just hope you can snap out of it before it's too late."

Her words settled over me and I nodded.

"You seeing her again?"

I let out a silent sigh. "Tonight."

My mom winked at me and gave me a hug. "Try not to let life slip right on by."

# CHAPTER ELEVEN

*Samantha*

I closed my eyes in the rose garden and took a deep breath. The sweet smell wrapped around me as if I'd never left home all those years before. Growing up, spending time in the rose garden had been another one of my favorite pastimes living here. I'd wander through the bushes and clip roses to bring back to my bedroom or sit on the bench that was no longer here and sink into books as hours passed right on by.

Being young was so much simpler, especially when it came to navigating sisterhood. If someone had asked me at age ten if my sisters and I would stop being friends, I would have thought they were crazy.

A rustle in the bushes startled me, and I blinked my eyes open to see a brown bunny hopping between the roses. I smiled at the creature as if it would notice before I slowly turned around to head back to the inn.

I'd be lying if I said I weren't nervous. In fact, I was petrified. My sisters had done a phenomenal job of avoiding me since I got here, and I was worried that whatever they had to say would make me wish I'd never expected the invitation.

But I was stronger than that. I wanted to make things right. However long it took.

As I walked up to the powder-blue side door to the inn, a smile touched my lips as I thought about my mom's bright idea to paint each door at the inn a different color to represent her daughters. It was nice to see my sisters had kept them. Powder blue represented Lana. My mom thought she was the calm and levelheaded daughter. I wasn't so sure any longer about that. Vera's door was bright red, and I think my mom nailed that color choice. My mom always felt that Vera was feisty and fearless. My door was yellow, which she said represented my bright spirit and adventurous soul.

Right about now, I didn't feel very adventurous or bright.

Just worn out.

I pulled on the blue door and walked into the quiet inn. All the guests had left earlier in the day to go do what tourists did in a town based on agriculture. I honestly didn't even know what that would be. I hadn't been on a vacation in years.

"There you are," Lana's voice rang through the air.

She was obviously in a good mood like when I'd first arrived, which I desperately craved. I was on the brink of being willing to endure more saccharin smiles from Lana just to have some.

I made my way into the kitchen where I smelled a blend of garlic, onions, and rosemary.

"Mom's famous chicken," Lana said, spinning around

to greet me. "I saw you down in the rose garden. You always liked to spend your time there."

I nodded. "I saw the bench was missing."

Lana chuckled. "I wouldn't call it missing. Wood benches aren't known for lasting a long time in our climate. I think it toppled on itself a few years ago. If you go on down the path, you'll find a nice iron bench. Should span the ages."

I laughed. "My time has slipped away from me. That makes sense."

"It's a good reminder. I always tell myself I should order another one. I'm sure the guests would like to be able to sit down in that area too."

I nodded, glancing around the kitchen. "Is Vera coming to dinner?"

Lana smiled tentatively. "She is, but I can't promise good behavior."

Laughing, I shook my head. "I would never expect you to."

I wandered over to the cupboard and pulled out three plates and began setting the table. "How about I cook for you two tomorrow?"

Lana smiled and nodded before placing the chicken on the platter. "That would be really nice. Do you cook often?"

"Well, even though everyone always talks about New Yorkers using their ovens for storage, I actually use mine. I think Mom would roll over in her grave if I didn't."

"Truer words." Lana nodded in agreement. "And she did such a good job of making sure we knew how to adult."

I snickered, thinking back to Vera protesting her laundry day. She was about fifteen or so and refused to do laundry. She protested and even threatened to run away.

Until Mom mentioned Drew North coming over and how Vera would only have smelly old clothes when he got here. I smiled at the memory and shook my head.

"Does Vera date much?" I asked quietly.

My sister walked the platter of chicken to the table. "Do any of us date much?"

I laughed. "Good point. Although, I've gotten more action since I've arrived back in town the last two days than I've had in years back home."

It was weird that I was calling New York home when I'd never felt more at home than here at Cloudberry.

My sister's eyes widened. "Is that so?"

I shrugged. "It's not going to go anywhere, but I'm having drinks with Garrett tonight. He texted me this morning and said he wanted to talk to me about something."

My sister visibly stiffened, and my heart fell to my toes. "Oh, no." My hands raised to my lips. "You like him. I'm so sorry."

Lana's shoulders immediately relaxed, and she laughed, scowling. "No. Not at all. Have at him."

I wiggled my brows. "He is pretty cute."

Well, way more than cute. He was downright sexy. Whether it was the little dimples he had when he smiled or the gruffness of his voice, he just made me forget the fact that I was headed back to New York.

"Uh-oh," Lana teased.

I rolled my eyes. "He's a good listener too."

Lana's brows rose. "What all could you possibly have talked about last night? You barely know him."

I smiled. "Don't you think strangers are the people who are best to talk to? Like Margaret this morning? It just takes the pressure off."

Lana scowled. "I suppose so."

"Think about it." I walked over to grab the bowl of green beans for the table. "Since I've arrived, we've barely spoken about anything of substance."

Vera walked into the kitchen and smirked. "Should I leave? Sounds pretty heavy."

I laughed and handed Vera the green beans. "Only as heavy as you two will let it get."

Vera glanced at Lana. "What's she even talking about?"

Lana grinned and set a huge bowl of mashed potatoes onto the table as I poured the gravy into a gravy boat.

"Samantha thinks it's easier to talk to strangers than people she actually knows," Lana explained.

Vera nodded. "I can see that. Then there's no worry that whatever you said could come back and bite you."

I brought the gravy over and took a seat across from Vera. "Exactly."

Lana sat at the head of the table and sighed. "I don't know. The whole talking thing is overrated, anyway."

I piled a scoop of potatoes on my plate and glanced at Lana. "Maybe you should be the hermit writer and I should be the one here."

Lana straightened in her chair. "If I could write a story to save my life, I'd switch in a heartbeat."

"Ditto," Vera muttered under her breath.

"Really?" Surprise registered on my face. "I always thought you two liked it here."

A chill instantly settled across the table.

Vera pointed her fork at me. "And that, dear sister, is precisely the problem I have with you."

For the first time since I'd arrived, I didn't feel hostility pouring off Vera.

"Problem with me?" I asked, mindlessly scooping more mashed potatoes onto my plate. "Now we're finally getting somewhere."

Vera flinched, and I realized Lana had kicked her under the table.

"You don't have to kick her. I'm a big girl. I'd like to hear what Vera has to say." I stared at Lana. "And you too, for that matter."

Vera pressed her lips into a fine line and stopped.

Frustration took over, and I let out an exasperated groan. "What is it with you two? It really is easier to talk to a stranger. Margaret from this morning was a good listener."

Vera's soft features puckered into bewilderment. "Margaret? Who's Margaret?"

I waved my hand. "Oh, she checked in with her daughter and came into the kitchen this morning for coffee."

Vera cocked her head slightly and laughed nervously. "We didn't have any mother-daughter duo staying here."

I glanced at Lana and pointed. "She saw her too."

Lana nodded. "I did, but come to think of it, besides the bridal party, there weren't any women who checked in alone or with their mom. We had a few married couples."

I laughed. "So, what are you saying? Some elderly woman just wandered in off the streets for a cup of coffee and a cinnamon roll?"

Vera chuckled. "Wouldn't be the first."

Lana stood up and glanced around the kitchen. "No, seriously. I'm going to go look at the computer."

"The daughter's name was Susan. It was Susan and Margaret," I called after her.

Lana marched out of the kitchen, and I turned my attention back to Vera.

"Okay, don't clam up on me. Spill it. I need to know what you meant when you said that is precisely the problem with me. What is? I don't want to be a problem. I'd like to work on it, whatever it is."

Vera drew a breath and let it out slowly. "You went off and lived your life, never once thinking about what sort of life Lana or I wanted."

"You don't want to be here?" I asked softly.

"I don't know what I want because I wasn't given that choice. It was just assumed that Lana and I would be the sisters who took over the inn."

My heart raced as I thought about what my sister was telling me.

"You're right. It was just assumed." I nodded. "And that's really unfair."

Vera smirked and slouched back in the chair. "Now, it

doesn't even matter what I want because I'm too old to do much about it, anyway."

I gasped and shook my head. "That isn't true at all."

Vera bolted upright. "Really? Who would run the inn? Lana can't do it on her own." She shook her head. "This is the life that was handed to me. You got to *choose* yours."

I didn't know if that was entirely true. I was handed an opportunity at a very young age and was encouraged to pursue it and only it.

Not that I would take any of it back, but I lost friends, relationships, and family. But I knew better than to bring any of that up. Vera's eyes sparked with anger, and we'd barely even scratched the surface.

I swallowed down my sadness. "I'm sorry."

Vera's features softened slightly, and she nodded.

"I really am. I was handed a world that I didn't comprehend, and a lot of benefits have been afforded to me because of it." I cleared my throat, feeling my pulse hammering through me. "I wish I knew how you felt long ago."

Lana came dashing into the kitchen. "Felt about what?"

I didn't want to speak for Vera, so I waited for her to say something.

Vera waved her hands and shrugged. "Nothing."

"Well, good. Because we have a problem."

My gaze flashed to Lana's. "What's the problem"

"There was no woman here with her mother. My memory wasn't failing me." She sat down at the table. "That woman didn't exist. Margaret and Susan were never guests."

An eerie silence fell over the kitchen, but my nervous laughter immediately cut through it.

My hand flew to my mouth. "Sorry. I shouldn't laugh."

Lana scowled. "This is serious, Sam."

My heart stalled for a second. My sister hadn't called me Sam since I was like fourteen.

I kept a straight face and nodded. "I believe you."

"There has to be a logical explanation," Vera tried.

"Tell me what it is." Lana crossed her arms over her chest and stared at Vera while I happily continued eating chicken and mashed potatoes.

"She probably has dementia and wandered in off the street." Vera gave a quick nod. "Problem solved."

Lana sucked in a breath and glanced at me and my nearly empty plate. "How can you eat at a time like this?"

I looked around the kitchen. "At a time like what?"

"We've had an emergency at the inn and you're stuffing your face full of food." Lana shook her head, extremely disappointed in my lack of respect for the situation.

"I don't think it's crazy to think that an older gal came wandering in, possibly a little disoriented, and wandered back out. We have beautiful gardens and a lot of people come to view them who aren't guests of the inn." Vera finally cut into her chicken.

Lana cocked her head slightly and grinned widely. "I knew you'd say that, so I checked our front door logs. No one came in or out until close to nine o'clock in the morning. The door never once opened or closed."

Vera let out a heavy sigh. "Lana, what are you trying to say? Just say it."

My eyes connected with Lana's, and I instantly knew.

"You think that the ghosts Mom mentioned all those years ago are real." My eyes narrowed on my sister.

"Why not?" Lana asked defensively. "Mom wasn't crazy."

Vera groaned. "It doesn't have anything to do with crazy. It's just not feasible."

Lana looked at me for help, but I didn't know what to say.

"I think it could be a stretch," I confessed. "And it might not be good for business."

Lana rolled her eyes and let out a frustrated grunt. "You even write about ghosts. Mom always said there were ghosts here." Lana whispered as if Margaret could hear. "What if that's her, one of them? That woman, Margaret?"

"A ghost who's into yoga and sex?" I shook my head, trying not to laugh.

Lana glared at Vera and then turned it to me. "Yes, I have written about them, but I recognize that it's fiction." I pressed my lips together and stared at my empty plate when a thought occurred to me.

Lana groaned in frustration.

"Although, the first night I was here, it sounded like someone had been running up and down the attic stairs all night, but there wasn't a soul when I opened the door."

Lana smacked the dining table, startling Vera and me. "That's what I'm talking about. We've got ghosts."

# CHAPTER TWELVE

*Garrett*

Just seeing Samantha Roberts step into the coffee shop made my blood start pumping. Her dark hair was pulled back with a bright red scarf, and her matching top skimmed the curves of her body, leaving little to the imagination. She had a white sweater draped over her arm, and she just looked incredible and effortlessly put together.

Yet, I highly doubted she had a clue what that outfit did to the men sitting around the café trying to stay attentive to the people they were with. There was something more than just her looks when she came into a room. She had an energy that commanded attention and the friendliest smile I'd ever seen.

Samantha spotted me and gave a quick wave before heading over to the barista. I tried not to look like I was watching her, but I could hardly keep my eyes away. Everything about this woman was fascinating.

I hid a smile and took a sip of espresso. I didn't know what her reaction would be to my fairly cryptic text, but she replied this morning that she could meet me after dinner, and here we were.

She turned around to catch my gaze on her, and she smiled. Electricity ran between us, and I wondered if it was real or only because I knew she wasn't going to be here long.

My therapist loved to point out that I'd developed commitment issues, so this development would fall right into my therapist's hands like warm putty. I could hear it now, *You're only interested in her because you know she's leaving.*

I didn't want to believe that was true. I wanted to believe what my mom had mentioned earlier, that I could turn things around and stop running from love.

As Samantha turned back toward the barista to pick up her drink and a plate of something from the bakery, her laughter rang through the air. I suddenly felt as if I needed to surround myself with that voice, that sound.

Again, the therapist would have a field day with this.

"Hey, Garrett." She flashed her friendly smile, but I caught something in her gaze.

Intrigue, possibly?

I stood and smiled as she took a seat.

"Oh, please. Men don't do that where I live." She set her cup of coffee and plate down, which had a huge brownie on it, and smiled. "I need this chocolate."

"Looks good." I nodded and sat back down.

Funny thing was that whenever I was around women I'd dated, I felt confident and in control. When I looked at Samantha, I felt like a blubbering idiot. Maybe it was because she wrote for a living or lived in New York.

No... location wouldn't be it. I've dated women from around the world, New York included.

There was a simple sophistication about her, and she was direct.

I liked direct.

"So, you said you wanted to discuss something?" she asked, bringing a piece of brownie up to her lips.

Yup, very direct.

"Thanks for coming," I began, suddenly not wanting to share my suspicions with her.

At least not right away.

First, that would make the night end way too quickly, and second...

Well, I wasn't sure that sharing my concern was a good idea.

I nodded and watched her take a sip of coffee. How she made that look sexy, I'd never know, but she did.

"Did my advice about a girls' night go over well?" I asked. "Wine do the trick with your sisters?"

Samantha scowled and straightened in her chair. "Oddly, no. I wouldn't say it made things worse or better."

I laughed and shrugged. "Oh, sorry. I guess I'm not the best guy to give sisterly advice."

Samantha chuckled. "It's the thought that counts. Besides, I think my sisters might be a little off." She stared at her brownie. "A little quirky, both of them."

"You don't say," I said matter of factly, trying not to show how I really felt about her siblings.

She giggled and shook her head. "I don't know. After

tonight's dinner, I think I might have actually made some headway."

"Really?" I asked, surprised.

"It was nice. It felt good." Samantha grinned. "We actually laughed. Vera even opened up to me *marginally*."

I nodded and took a sip of my espresso. "Wow. I'm impressed."

And I truly was. Vera was not the sister I'd imagine who'd open up first.

"Well, I'm probably getting overly excited and optimistic with as little progress as was made, but I'll take it." She shrugged, taking another sip of coffee.

The hopeful look in her gaze nearly killed me. Seeing the desire to be close with her sisters, to do whatever it took to make them like her, nearly ruined me. She was so confident and intentional with every little thing she did, yet her sisters made her crumble. She probably wouldn't admit it, but I could see it.

She wanted to be liked, not just tolerated.

Samantha's brown eyes were so expressive, and I highly doubted that either of her sisters missed the pain they were inflicting either, which made me wonder why they felt the need to toy with Samantha.

"Anyway, I'm actually thinking about extending my stay a little bit."

Her words brought me back to reality.

"What?" I shook my head. "Really?"

"Yeah. Why not, right? Maybe give my sisters a little break." Samantha shrugged. "I think something's going on and they just won't tell me. I don't know if it's their pride or—" She stopped herself and smiled. "Probably TMI."

I smiled. "For a man who's already seen your most intimate wear..."

Samantha blurted out laughing. "Intimate wear?"

I laughed and let out a sigh, scratching my jaw. "I can honestly tell you that I've never heard that kind of expression come out of my mouth before."

My statement only made Samantha smile wider. "I'm not sure if hearing that is better or worse."

I sat back in my chair and rubbed my palms over my face. I had to get back in the game. If she was staying longer, I might actually have a shot. A shot at what, I didn't know.

"I'm just going to call it like it is." I cleared my throat and looked around the coffee shop. "I like you. I wish you didn't live in New York. And for some reason, when you're around, I can barely think straight."

"Something new for you?" she teased, which drove me even more insane.

"Very." My tone flattened. "I like being in control, but you seem to cause me to be the exact opposite."

"Then why in the world would you like being around me?"

"It's something new."

She chuckled. "Oh, the bright and shiny object syndrome."

I loved how she could flip it right back to me.

I was getting to *love* everything about her.

Yup. The therapist would have a field day with this.

"No such thing."

She hummed, "Oh, yes, there is."

"Well, none of it matters, anyway. You made it clear that we can't date. You might extend your stay a tad, but not enough for me to make any headway."

Samantha's dark brows arched. "Headway?"

"Yeah. You know. Impress you with my manliness or nunchaku skills."

Her beautiful eyes widened, and it took everything I had not to lean over the table and kiss her.

"Nunchaku skills?" She closed her eyes and pretended to be mortified. "Please tell me you don't have computer hacking skills and bowhunting skills too."

I was a goner. She knew the movie *Napoleon Dynamite.*

"No female I've dated has ever known that film."

"So, what you're telling me is that you've used that pickup line before." She cocked her head, and I couldn't help but laugh.

"You're good."

"Just observant." She winked. "It's my job."

It literally felt like I was on a rollercoaster around this woman, and I never wanted to get off. She was mesmerizing, and all I could think about was holding her in my arms, kissing every single part of her, and —

"And on the subject of my job, I'm really good at keeping focused, my eye on the prize and all that. It's how I finish every story I start, which brings me to why you wanted me to meet you here." Her smile about did me in. "So, why?"

I looked into her eyes and saw a woman with a kind heart and a fragile spirit, and I did not want to be the one to break it or put ideas in her head that weren't true.

Right then and there, I decided not to tell Samantha my suspicions about her sisters. If she would be in town a few more days, I could see how it all played out.

So, I blurted out the first thing that came into my head.

"Will I wind up in one of your stories?"

She giggled. "That's why you wanted to see me? You worried I'll put you in a book?"

I smiled, running my fingers through my hair jokingly. "I just want to make sure if you do depict me as the main character's love interest that things are accurate."

"Really." She grinned as her eyes stirred with mischief, the chemistry heating up between us. "And why don't you do me the favor of making my job easy? Describe this character."

"For starters, I'm—I mean, he—is charming."

"Charming?"

My eyes focus on her. "Very."

"I need more."

"And he's pretty easy on the eyes, or so I've heard."

"Should I include dimples in the description?"

"You noticed them?" I smiled, feeling a little victory.

Maybe there was a shot with Samantha.

"Only because they're more prominent on you than most men."

I scowled. "Is that good or bad?"

"In this case, I'd say good." She winked at me, and it felt like I'd won the lottery.

There was no way these feelings welling up inside me were merely because I knew subconsciously that she was leaving town.

Nah. It couldn't be.

I wanted her because she was Samantha Roberts, an amazing woman with a heart that I could care for.

"I can stay on task too. Back to the story." I smiled as her eyes locked on mine and a flicker of desire ran through her gaze.

I was sure of it.

I continued. "The man is a jack-of-all-trades, wealthy because of hard work and dedication." I smiled. "Plus, he's a bit brilliant."

"Brilliant, you say?" she asked, pretending to take notes.

"Extremely." I nodded. "And of course, he's considerate, fiercely loyal, and quite protective."

"Interesting."

"You think?" I asked, surprised.

"You see yourself in such a flattering light."

Stabbed right in the heart. Yeah. I was definitely falling for Samantha Roberts.

"Okay, then. How would you write me?"

She chuckled. "I honestly can't believe you asked me out to discuss something that seemed rather urgent and then this is it."

"Would you have come if I'd told you?" I asked, not

wanting to hear the answer.

"Absolutely." She grinned, sitting back in the chair.

I caught her eyes drifting up and down my body, and my pulse accelerated. I wanted to know what she was thinking. What she was feeling.

She began softly, almost cooing her answer. "I'd describe you as a very sexy..."

My brows shot up. "Sexy?"

She nodded. "A sexy small-town hero who swoops in to save the day when he sees trouble."

"Are you describing Clark Kent or me?" I laughed.

She giggled. "Honestly, I don't see you as a character. I see you as a nice guy I'd probably be friends with back at home."

*Friends.*

"Question." I tapped my fingers on the table, wishing her home wasn't so far away.

"Yeah?"

"Do you ever think about this place being home again?"

Her expression softened and she nodded slowly. "In imagination only."

"What do you mean?"

"It seems so idealistic and fanciful. I have memories of literally running through tulip fields, coming into the inn to eat cookies and sip tea, and curling into my reading nook where I gobble up words until the wee hours. Those were magical memories—magical years—for me. If I try to imagine what it would be like as an adult, I don't even come close."

I nodded. "Probably doesn't help that your sisters aren't exactly warm and fuzzy."

She laughed with a wistful look in her gaze. "That too, but I refuse to believe that side of them doesn't exist."

"Don't hold your breath," I teased.

"Now, that I wouldn't do. I'd either pass out or die waiting." She brought her gaze back to mine. "Speaking of death and dying."

"Another lovely topic..."

She grinned and nodded. "Before I came here, Lana brought up how she thinks the inn has ghosts."

I kept my gaze on Samantha's, but I didn't know if she was kidding or not.

"Did you not hear me?" she teased. "Or did I just give you the perfect excuse to go running away?"

"It would take more than ghosts to get me to question things about you." I shrugged. "I could see it. I mean, the place is how old?"

Her eyes brightened. "You actually think it could be true? There's no way." Her gaze filled with delight.

I didn't want to mention that I'd had a little too much time on my hands this morning and looked up some of her books on the internet. Her debut novel dealt with this very subject.

"No way that I could believe it or no way there could be ghosts at the inn?" I questioned.

She laughed. "Both. Seriously, though..." She let out a slow breath and her features turned serious. "I think my sisters need a break for many reasons."

"You think the ghosts are getting bored with them?"

She chuckled. "Well, they certainly aren't giving the ghosts much in the way of excitement. My sisters are like robots."

I wanted to tell her they couldn't be that bad, but that was kind of how I saw the Roberts sisters as well, so I just stayed quiet.

I smiled sympathetically. "I'm not getting into all that, but I will say I'm surprised you're related to them."

"Thank you. At the moment, I'll take that as a compliment."

I winked at her. "Good."

She glanced at her phone. "I should probably get back home. I'm taking over for them tomorrow morning again so they can rest."

"Do they know you might stick around longer?" I asked.

Samantha shook her head and stood. "I haven't told them yet."

Nodding, I stood, and she stumbled toward me as she tugged her sweater off the chair. My hand brushed against her arm, and I suddenly felt like I was thrown back to tenth grade. Every cell in my body responded to her with a barely-there touch.

She giggled as she steadied herself and pulled her sweater on before turning to face me. We'd somehow managed to be less than six inches apart and neither of us wanted to move. The electricity between us was fierce.

"Well, this is awkward." She brought her gaze up to mine, and my body heated instantly. The thought of holding her in my arms came over me to the point of being paralyzed.

It didn't matter that we were in the middle of a bustling coffee shop. Samantha was a magnet for me.

"Which part?" I asked, looking down at her.

I even loved how she was so much shorter than me.

Samantha glanced around the coffee shop and smiled. "Just things."

"You know, if you weren't just passing through town, I'd kiss you right now even though we're in the middle of strangers." I looked into Samantha's eyes and saw the same longing I felt.

Her cheeks flushed as our eyes stayed locked on one another's.

"And I'd kiss you back."

# CHAPTER THIRTEEN

*Samantha*

"Why are you always so perky?" Vera didn't quite snarl the question, but she was close to it.

I slid the tray on her lap as her fingers slid through her tangled locks.

The weekend guests had checked out, and I thought I'd surprise both of my sisters with breakfast in bed.

Lana had waved, mumbled something, and turned over in bed, so I expected something similar from Vera.

But Vera was already upright in bed reading when I came in with the tray full of melon, granola, and two poached eggs.

I smiled wider, determined to make my sister like me. "Just happy to be here with you two."

The reply only made Vera scowl harder, and I had to keep from laughing. Did she really feel that grumpy inside? Wasn't there something about waking up in the morning that made her happy? Or did she shove the sheets off every morning feeling like a wrinkled prune inside instead of happy to be alive?

"Why are you staring at me like that?" Vera barked, taking a piece of melon off the plate.

"Just wondering if I should have put prunes on your plate."

Vera let out an exasperated sigh. "I'm not backed up."

I chuckled. "Never said you were. And yes, I tend to be a pretty happy camper on most days."

A wry grin spread across Vera's lips. "I suppose when you wake up doing something you want to do, it helps."

I narrowed my eyes on Vera and glanced at an empty floral chair in the corner.

Vera had redecorated the room since I'd last seen it.

Surprisingly, the décor was very cheery. Light and bright pastel colors were splashed on throw pillows and soft organdy curtains hung on the windows to let in the brilliant rays of sunshine.

Yet somehow, not even a fleck of sunshine managed to brighten Vera's demeanor.

Strange.

Very strange.

"May I sit?" I pointed at the chair.

Vera shrugged and took a sip of coffee.

Sitting down, I said, "I'll take that as a yes."

"I assumed you would." Vera rolled her eyes.

"The message I'm getting loud and clear is that you don't want to be at Cloudberry."

Vera cocked her head slightly and smiled. "It's not that

I mind being here. I mean, what else would I do?"

My stomach tightened. I didn't want to make my sister angrier toward me. I felt our relationship was already full up on that, but I wanted Vera to quit looking at me like the enemy.

"Do you like living in Washington?" I asked.

"It's as good a place as any, I suppose." She pressed her lips together for a split second before taking a bite of egg. "Not that I would know. I haven't been many places since our family vacations stopped when we grew up, and I'm how old?"

I swallowed down the realization that haunted the very core of our relationship. Something that I took for granted and never thought twice about ate away at Vera.

Freedom.

I was free.

"I can come back to Washington. Nothing is holding me in New York."

Vera turned toward me and her cheeks flushed. "Why would I want that?"

Her words stung so badly I couldn't think of a thing to say.

I actually wasn't sure why she would want me here.

What did I offer?

I shook my head and glanced at the breakfast tray before standing up.

Vera straightened on the bed. "That came out wrong."

I drew a breath and smiled. "I'm not sure it did, and that's okay."

"No, it's not okay." Vera slid the tray off her lap, but I made my way to the door quicker than she could get to me.

I felt the tears welling up, and I refused to let either of my sisters see me cry.

Vera was right. What did I think I could fix by being here?

I dashed down the stairs and found myself in the sunroom. The sunshine came through the glass and bounced off the crystal vases my sisters had on display. The cut crystal reflected a beautiful prism on the wall, and I stopped to stare at it as I willed myself to keep the tears in.

The geometric design reminded me of my complicated relationship with my sisters. Everything was compartmentalized and frozen in its place. Emotions were in one facet, actions in another, reality and fantasy at odds, feelings on the far edges, and secrets at the center.

A tear rolled down my cheek that I quickly brushed away. There was no reason to cry. Nothing had changed since I'd arrived.

My relationships were firmly grounded in the same place they were before I got here.

So then, why did I feel even worse?

I closed my eyes and let out a deep sigh.

Because I wanted to live in the fantasy part of the prism.

More silent tears fell, and I collapsed on the suede couch near the window.

It didn't matter if I were to stay or go. My sisters had their lives here, and I had mine elsewhere.

What would our mother say about us now?

Prior to her death, we'd already grown apart, but the distance after my mom's death was cataclysmic.

If something amazing happened in my life like a book deal, a bestseller list, or just a good day, my sisters weren't who popped into my head to share it with.

I leaned back on one of the millions of pillows and looked around the sunroom as I pulled one of the pillows on top of me.

"So, this is the room that Garrett built," I whispered, taking in the beautiful details. The addition wasn't a typical sunroom thrown together by a kit or a couple of guys over a few weekends.

You could feel Garrett Mason's touch. Every piece of glass was beveled, all the wood trim cut with precision, and the features only added character to the old inn rather than taking anything away.

I smiled as I thought back to Garrett.

He was good-looking.

Funny.

Smart.

Successful.

Curious.

And in the wrong state.

Such was my luck. I closed my eyes and thought back to Vera.

Did she finish the breakfast?

If I were in her shoes, I wouldn't have. I would have put the tray aside and ran after me.

Actually...

No, I never would have put my sister in that position in the first place. I wouldn't have been mean to a person who brought me food. Home-cooked meals were like waving the white flag of surrender. I thought back to the chicken dinner last night that Lana had cooked. Maybe that was her white flag.

I scowled and nodded my head in agreement with myself.

The one thing I'd gotten very good at over the years was talking to myself or, really, with myself. It wasn't one-sided. In fact, I could get really deep, peel back the layers and all that. One of the perks of being an introvert.

Now, Garrett didn't remind me of an introvert. He reminded me of the life of the party.

Not that it mattered, anyway. I wasn't sure why he kept popping into my head other than the reasons I'd listed for myself a few seconds ago, but he did turn around my spirits.

"Hey, there." Vera's voice tossed me out of my speculative mood, and I bolted upright from the couch. Our eyes connected and she forced a smile. "I'm sorry. I honestly don't know why I can't be nice."

Surprised laughter rolled off my lips, and I shrugged. "I've wondered the same thing."

Vera grinned and walked into the sunroom even though I wasn't sure I wanted her in here with me. I'd already decided several minutes ago that this was going to be my sanctuary for the remainder of the trip, whether the trip was ending tomorrow or another time was still up for grabs.

"For years, I've played out all these different scenarios if you came out here." Her voice trailed off as she took a seat in a wooden rocking chair. "And now that you're here, it's not working out how I imagined."

I nodded, wondering if Vera was actually going to open up again or close up on me the moment I opened my mouth.

I decided to stay silent.

She began again, "I'm not trying to punish you for your success."

I so badly wanted to tell her it felt like that was precisely what she was doing, but I stayed quiet and just nodded.

"But..." She paused.

There was *always* a but in these types of conversations.

I'm sorry, *but* you never should have done this or that.

I never meant to, *but* I had no choice because you did this or that.

That wasn't what I intended, *but*...

You get the idea.

I stared at my sister, knowing if I said even one word, she'd probably spin right around and never finish this conversation.

She cleared her throat, and I briefly moved my gaze to the wall that no longer had the colorful patterns dancing across it. "But I just wonder when my time will come. Why I'm the one stuck here."

I knew better than to get into the logistics of things. What I wanted to know was what she'd rather be doing.

Drawing in a slow breath, I focused on my sister. "Vera, I won't apologize for where my life has taken me, but I will offer an ear to listen whenever you want to talk about where you want yours to go."

I prepared for Vera to storm out.

Instead, her shoulders slumped and she nodded slowly.

"I don't know where I want it to go. I'm in my mid-thirties and I don't have a clue." She bit her lip, and my pulse raced.

I never dared to imagine that Vera would actually open up to me like this, but I knew it was a fragile moment.

"Do you want to know something really dumb?" she asked, blowing some stray hairs from her face.

I smiled. "Nothing you could say would be dumb."

"I actually thought that by this time, I'd be married with kids toddling all around like Mom had at my age." She shook her head. "Maybe living here at the inn or just down the street with my husband. So dumb. Why would I let my entire view of myself and my goals center around that?"

I took a deep breath and looked out the window. "Did all that imagining involve one person?"

"His brothers were here not too long ago," she confessed. "For some engagement party."

Lana had already filled me in, but I certainly didn't want to have Vera thinking we were talking behind her back.

She laughed.

A true, genuine, infectious laugh.

"And if Drew North aged half as well as his brothers, I

have really missed out."

"Is he married?" I asked, knowing the answer.

Vera shook her head. "No, but I'd imagine being a bachelor and owner of a world-renowned ski resort has made his life pretty fulfilling, especially when it comes to women."

I shrugged. "You never know."

She smiled. "I've heard."

"You can't believe everything you hear."

"I know it's all ridiculous, pining over some kid I met at a summer camp and being pissed that I haven't done anything with my life."

My jaw dropped and my chest ached. "Vera, that's baloney. How could you say that about yourself?"

"Seriously?" She looked around. "What have I done? I inherited an inn that even our father didn't want to bother with."

I knew it wasn't that simple for my dad. Cloudberry Inn was as much a part of him as it was of Mom. But being here was literally killing him. Memories flooded him every morning he woke up and suffocated him every night before he went to sleep.

Arizona was an escape that I helped him to achieve, and maybe there was a way I could help my sisters too.

"You've run a successful inn that has visitors from around the world. You and Lana should be proud of that. It's a big deal."

"Says the woman living in some swanky apartment in New York City and writing for a living." She looked at me, and I saw the ice begin to form in her eyes.

"Vera, I wish you'd have visited me when Mom did." I shook my head. "You'd realize the image you have of me is very different from the reality I live in."

"Spare me."

I shrugged and let out a silent sigh. "You're more than welcome to stay with me and tour the city. You'd be amazed at how unimpressive my life is and how dull the city can be. Believe me. I can make New York City as dull as if I were living in Death Valley on the verge of dehydration and certain death with vultures just circling."

Vera's brows shot up. "You are so weird."

"It's true. I love my life. I'm not saying I don't, and that's probably not something you want to hear, but it's not exciting. It's just comfortable."

There was no denying that I'd been very lucky early on in my career. Writing certainly afforded me luxuries if I would have wanted them, but I seldom wanted much of anything. I had a beautiful apartment, but it was modest because when I first purchased it, I was afraid my first book would be a one-hit wonder. I had no car, and while I took vacations, I didn't have anyone except my editor to share them with.

"I know Mom wanted the best for me, but I don't know if she knew how lonely I'd be with the life I've chosen to lead." I shrugged. "But I couldn't imagine living any other life, if that makes sense."

Vera nodded. "I can't imagine living any other life either. Cloudberry is all I've ever known, but it still feels like I'm missing out on something. When I think of your life, it just makes me antsy over mine."

Her words rattled around me like a bowl full of jumping beans. I'd never thought much about my life or job or how either would be perceived. Sure, my publisher wanted me to do more on social media, build a presence, but I honestly didn't have much to say.

My food wasn't pretty enough to photograph. I didn't have any cat or dog videos to post. There were no glistening lake photos with my legs kicked out in front of me with my laptop typing *The End*. And I certainly didn't feel like having someone take grinning photos of me standing somewhere with my books. I just didn't look that interesting.

Now, maybe if I had some friends that could spice me up a bit, sure! Or a family with cute little kids and diapers falling off, or pets rolling around in the snow that my witty, pretend husband could capture, I might give it a go.

But I really didn't feel like letting the readers see into my life, which consisted of empty take-out boxes at midnight, an unmade bed, and a life that didn't have time for hobbies because I was too busy enjoying the process of making up stories.

But I didn't have any of that, so my publisher just had to learn to live with my mostly blank social media content.

Even though my apartment was a lot quieter than my very first one in the middle of it all, no glass could entirely keep out the city noise. There were days when the constant honking, yelling, and smells were just too much. So, I did what any good introvert would do and I stayed inside and ordered takeout.

"My life shouldn't make you antsy. It should make you grateful."

She scowled.

"I hate to bring him up again." I wiggled my brows, and she rolled her eyes. "But what you experienced with Drew is something I've never experienced. Ever. Everything I write about when it comes to love is observed, not experienced. I envy you."

Vera snorted. "You shouldn't. The last time I experienced it I was like twenty. There's been a drought since then."

I laughed. "Hey, one good one can last a lifetime."

"Yeah. Maybe if they're with you a lifetime. I can only think back to Drew's kisses so often." Vera's cheeks blushed.

"Imagine if you never had those kisses to think back to." I smiled. "We all have things in our lives that others wish they had."

Vera chuckled. "Shouldn't I be the one giving you this talk? I am your older sister."

"With age does not necessarily come wisdom," I teased, tossing a pillow in her direction.

She laughed. "And you wonder why I don't talk to you?"

"Ouch."

A comfortable silence fell over the sunroom, and I glanced outside, feeling a pull to wander the gardens.

I looked back at my sister and saw her gaze stirring with emotion.

"That's not the only reason you don't like me, is it?" I asked rather matter-of-factly.

"It's all I can handle for today." She tried to be funny, but I could tell she wasn't kidding.

"Well, it's good that I've decided to extend my stay then." I smiled.

Vera's mouth dropped open, but she didn't say a word as I wandered outside toward the rose gardens.

It wasn't until I made it to the bench that I finally felt the buzzing from a recent text.

When I saw who it was from, my heart skipped a beat.

Garrett Mason asked me out to dinner tonight. It was a shame I'd have to tell him no.

I looked up at Cloudberry Inn and realized that there were indeed ghosts lurking in the hallways and corners of the grand old house, but they were mostly our own, and the only hope we had to save our family was to let the ghosts come to life before we buried them away for good.

# CHAPTER FOURTEEN

*Garrett*

I didn't know if this was another one of God's cruel jokes or if karma had decided to make another appearance in my life, but accepting the dinner invitation from the Roberts sisters could be either.

When I shot off the text this morning to Samantha to have dinner with me, I was thinking it would be just the two of us—not the four of us.

And what was I supposed to say when Samantha invited me to dinner with her sisters?

No?

I didn't think that would go over well.

So, here I was with a bottle of wine, a bouquet of flowers, and wicked doubts flooding my every thought as Samantha opened the door.

She smiled her beautiful smile. "I wasn't sure you'd actually show up."

I laughed and shook my head. "I'm never one to miss

a challenge."

"My kind of man."

I handed her the flowers and the bottle of wine as Lana and Vera wandered into the foyer.

Lana's gaze landed on mine, and it stayed there as I smiled.

"Good evening, Lana. Nice to see you again."

She cocked her head slightly and narrowed her eyes on me as Samantha wandered down the hall toward the kitchen.

"Nice to see you." Lana pursed her lips together as Vera attempted to cut through the tension.

Vera chuckled. "Hope dinner is just as relaxed as this is *right* here."

I laughed and nodded. "Yeah. It's *great* so far."

Lana walked over to me. "Why are you seeing my sister?"

Again, I wasn't sure if this were karma or a cruel joke. I was beginning to think both for extra fun.

I shook my head. "Wow. That is direct."

"Geez," Vera muttered as she wandered down the hall after Samantha. "Better save your guest, Samantha."

"I'm spending time with your sister because she's a lot of fun. She's refreshing and brilliant." I smiled wider. "Not that any of that is actually your business. Unless, of course, that is what you're worried about. Your business."

"Don't scare him off until he's had dessert." Samantha's voice rang down the hall, and Lana plastered one of her plastic smiles on her face and spun around to see her sister come back into the room.

The moment Samantha came into the room, it thawed like twenty degrees, and I realized that my suspicions about her sisters, or at least one of them, might be right.

"I put the flowers in water. I hope Lana didn't say anything too embarrassing," Samantha teased.

I laughed, holding back a grimace. "Oh, no. She was as amusing as ever."

"Not that I actually had many boyfriends growing up, but Lana and Vera were never overly friendly to anyone I brought home."

Lana rolled her eyes, and I laughed.

"You don't say. Your sisters seem like such lovely people. I wouldn't have thought that started way back in high school."

"Ha-ha." Lana pushed by us and made her way up the stairs. "I'll let you two have some alone time."

"We don't need it," Samantha called after her sister. "He's just a friend."

I scowled and let out a low laugh. "Way to take it easy on my ego."

Samantha spun around, smiling. "What? It's true, remember?"

I thought back to the near kiss and smiled. "I was hoping with your possibly spending some more time out here..."

"Don't hope too hard." Samantha chuckled. "You might hurt yourself. Besides, you think I'm nice now, but you have no idea what I'm like near deadlines. I'm completely crabby and unbearable."

"I find that hard to believe." I laughed. "And it never hurts to hope."

Samantha smiled and motioned for me to follow her down the hall to the back of the house, which was where the sisters had their more personal space away from the guests of the inn.

Garlic and onion drifted through the air as we got closer to the kitchen. "Dinner smells amazing."

Samantha glanced behind her and grinned. "Thank you. I made my famous meatballs."

And the woman could cook. I held in a happy sigh and followed her through the kitchen into the family room. It was a warm space, but it didn't look like it had been touched since Samantha's mother lived here. I glanced around the room and realized that much like the house, most everything was like stepping into a time capsule.

Samantha took a seat in a recliner and I sat on the couch.

"You didn't have to bring me flowers." She crossed her legs that were fitted in a tight pair of jeans, and I did my best to keep my gaze on hers.

"Oh, I brought those for Vera."

Samantha giggled and drew a deep breath. "I really wasn't sure if you were going to come over or not. I know my sisters can be a lot."

"If it meant getting to see you one more time, I'd do just about anything."

Samantha looked surprised and dropped her gaze to the floor. "That's nice of you to say."

"It's true."

She brought her eyes back to mine, and it felt like the world stood still. I could see so much going on behind her gaze, but I recognized none of it.

For the first time in a long time, I wanted to peel back the layers. I wanted to get to know a woman. I also wanted to see how her sisters interacted with her after a few days of togetherness. I didn't want to believe that Lana and Vera would use their sister for her money, but I wouldn't put it past them.

From the looks of it, the inn was fully booked for the night, like every other night I've driven by or stopped by when working, so I really didn't understand what could be going on.

Which was why I'd hoped I was wrong.

Samantha lowered her voice. "Vera started opening up to me. Big time."

Surprise must have registered on my face.

"I know. Can you believe it?" She grinned as pure happiness radiated from her beautiful mouth.

Oh, how I hoped I was wrong.

"I can't, but I'm happy for you."

She nodded. "I know I've only scratched the surface, but I'd started to think the surface was impenetrable."

I leaned over and propped my elbows on my knees. "I don't know what to say other than I'm impressed."

"I brought her breakfast in bed, which didn't go over quite like I expected," she informed me as if we were old friends catching up. "And I nearly ran out in tears."

My heart stalled hearing that she'd been hurt, and once again, I wondered why Samantha's sisters were so intent on beating her up.

"But I went to your sunroom." She paused. "It's beautiful, by the way."

"Thanks." I nodded.

"And it gave me a sort of clarity. It's a lovely place to spend time."

Hopefully, Lana and Vera felt the same since they hadn't finished paying me for it yet.

"Vera came down a little later in the morning and we talked." Her usually full lips pressed into a thin line as she was thinking hard about something. "I think I haven't been as compassionate to their needs as I thought. I'm not sure my sisters want to be here."

"At the inn?" I asked, surprised.

I couldn't imagine what else they'd want to do. They both seemed like fixtures of this old place.

Samantha nodded. "There are definitely some misconceptions about what they think my life is like, but I was able to really listen to Vera."

I nodded as a timer went off. "Enough family drama for the night. Dinner is ready."

Samantha sprang off the couch, and her light pink sweater inched up above her waist, revealing just enough of her fair skin to drive me wild. I was definitely losing it around Samantha. All it took was a brief touch or a glimpse of some bare skin and all I could think about was sleeping with her.

Maybe my therapist was right.

I was doomed unless I changed my ways.

Or my mom was right and I needed to cling to hope.

But *maybe* I could change my ways with Samantha.

As I followed Samantha into the kitchen, she turned around and nearly bumped into me. The near miss made my body tighten with desire. The thought of holding her in my arms swam through my mind in a completely nonplatonic way.

Her hand was at her mouth. "I totally forgot to offer you something to drink. Would you like wine, beer, soda, or water?" She dropped her hand and grinned. "Coffee in case my sisters and I bore you to death?"

I laughed and shook my head. "Something tells me this dinner will be anything but boring."

She nodded. "Probably true. I think I'm going to have a beer. Want one?"

I smiled and nodded, looking around the kitchen. "Sure. I'll take one."

The table was already set and a salad had been placed in the middle, along with water for everyone. Samantha peeled back plastic wrap from some French bread and placed it on the table.

"Is there anything I can do to help?"

She pointed at the fridge before grabbing some plates from the cabinet. "How about you be in charge of the beers after all?"

"That I can handle."

I walked over to the fridge, which was twice the size of a normal refrigerator, and scanned for some beer.

"Think your sisters would want any?" I asked, bending over to get two bottles of summer ale.

It suddenly felt like Samantha was watching me,

which made me smile to myself before standing up and shutting the fridge.

I spun around slowly and caught a glimpse of Samantha's gaze quickly moving away from me.

So, Samantha was checking me out when I bent over.

I twisted off the caps as Samantha texted her sisters that dinner was ready.

"Where should I sit?" I asked.

Samantha shrugged. "I give Lana the head of the table and Vera sat there last night." She pointed at the chair near the door. "You can just sit next to me and we can play footsy under the table." She laughed, and I let the warmth cascade over me.

It felt good.

Until the scowling sisters wandered into the kitchen.

I took my seat next to Samantha and prayed that the dinner would go well.

Once Lana had taken her seat and Vera popped the cap off her own beer, Samantha lifted the lid of the main course. The meatballs were the size of tennis balls, and the garlic linguine in the pot next to the meatballs would scare away the hungriest of vampires.

Samantha really did plan on keeping the night platonic.

Vera smiled. "Amazing dinner. Wow. You just might have inherited the role of chef."

Samantha beamed, and I could see the love she had for her sisters emanate from her very core. She wanted to please them. She wanted to be a part of their unit. But I wasn't sure they even wanted to be a part of their unit.

"Works for me." Samantha smiled wider and scooped two meatballs onto Vera's plate before turning her attention to Lana, who raised her plate and got two as well.

She turned her attention to me. "Two or three?"

"Will you think less of me if I say three?"

Samantha laughed and managed to place three meatballs on my plate without any of them rolling away.

"This is mom's recipe with some modifications," she informed us all.

Lana took a bite and closed her eyes. "Even better than Mom's."

"Really?" Samantha's eyes widened, and I just wanted to reach out and hug her. The need she had to be accepted by her sisters nearly killed me.

But maybe my suspicions were wrong about Lana's intentions.

Samantha drew a deep breath in and glanced around the table. "I've been thinking about staying a little longer, if you'll have me."

I dropped my gaze to my plate and cut into a meatball as silence settled around the table.

Not quite what I expected after the praise for the meatballs.

"Don't you have a book to finish?" Lana asked, her gaze staying on Samantha.

"I actually have a book to start, but I don't really have it all hammered out yet." Samantha glanced in my direction and pointed. "This guy wants to be the main male character, but..."

"Hero," I joked.

Lana flashed a smile that couldn't quite be believed and nodded. "And staying here won't get in the way of your work?"

I could feel Samantha's disappointment roll through her. I think she expected them to at least act a little excited about the idea of her staying.

"Well, I think it would be great." Vera nodded and took a bite of linguine.

"Really?" Samantha's eyes sparkled with hope, and I wondered if that was what filled the inside of her books.

Compassion, hope, love, turmoil, anger... sadness.

When I looked into Samantha's eyes, it was like seeing all of those emotions swarming into one mass of creation waiting to be delivered.

Vera smiled at her sister, and I realized that Samantha was right. Vera might have turned a corner. "I think it would be nice."

It was like these two sisters did a role reversal on Samantha, switching one from good cop to bad cop just to keep her off balance.

"I don't have to stay." Samantha looked uncomfortable, and I slid my hand to hers under the table. The emotions clashed and fought inside me, growing with every passing second into a raging swell of anger.

Samantha gave it a light squeeze and smiled at me.

"No. It would be nice." Lana took a bite of pasta and turned her attention to me. "So, it seems you two have hit it off."

"He's a fun guy." Samantha grinned and nodded. "He seems to be very handy, and I love his work. I could live in that sunroom every single day." She looked over at me. "It's too bad you don't travel out of state for projects."

"I might make an exception."

Samantha giggled. "Having something added to an apartment in New York probably isn't very feasible."

"Probably not."

"How long are you thinking about staying?" Lana asked, and the tension immediately returned to the table.

"I haven't thought that through too much." Samantha shrugged. "I was thinking about leaving it open-ended."

Lana smiled and laughed. "Well, we have to move you out of the bridal suite. We have a couple coming who reserved that room in a few days."

Samantha chuckled. "No problem. I can sleep in my old bedroom."

"It's stuffed full of boxes," Lana explained, and Samantha nodded her head.

"I know. I snuck in there earlier today, but I can just shove some aside."

Both Vera and Lana looked surprised and I wondered what kind of misconceptions they had about their own sister. Samantha seemed liked the most down-to-earth woman I'd ever encountered. She was warm, open, and forgiving to a fault.

I thought back to my stepbrother, Wyatt, and how lucky our family was to have come together the way it had. I really didn't understand what Vera and Lana's problems were, and it was hard to keep quiet.

Samantha frowned. "What, you didn't think I'd sleep in there?"

Vera laughed and shook her head. "You're some big

hotshot writer from New York. I didn't expect that you'd even want to stay at Cloudberry."

Samantha's eyes widened. "This is the most beautiful inn in all of Washington. I'm lucky to stay here. I'd be happy in a closet just to be able to spend time with both of you."

I turned to Samantha and saw the look of determination in her eyes.

"If you say so." Lana grinned and finished the last bite of pasta on her plate. "I will confess that it's nice having you here, and the last two mornings off have been..." She let out a sigh. "Incredible."

Samantha nodded enthusiastically, which made me like her even more. "Anything I can do to help out while I'm here, I'll do. I'm more than happy to."

"In between seeing me now and again," I added.

Samantha laughed. "Oh, you're still here?"

Vera and Lana laughed, and the tension finally began to ease as everyone finished their meal.

"I love the gardens." Samantha smiled. "I still have dreams about those. I miss being able to wander out the back door and wind through perennial gardens in the summer or the orchards in the fall."

"Tired of all the concrete?" I asked.

I'd been to New York a few times. It was an interesting place to visit, but I wasn't sure I'd want to live there. I liked being able to roam the outdoors and smell fresh air, not hot dogs and sewers.

She nodded and ate the last bit of salad. "This sounds horrible, but I don't go outside that much, especially when I'm writing. Yet, I miss the idea of going out and not having to run into a million strangers on the sidewalk next to me."

"Makes sense," Vera agreed.

I noticed the scowl that usually outlined Vera's features had softened, but I didn't want to count on it meaning something it didn't.

Lana cleared her throat. "Hey, Garrett. Would you mind coming with me to the office?"

I looked at Samantha, and she shrugged, nodding.

"Sure." I nodded and slid my chair out from the table and followed Lana out of the kitchen.

When we'd gotten inside the office, she shut the door.

"I'm hoping that you've been discreet while with my sister," she started.

My head cocked slightly as I narrowed my eyes on Samantha's sister. "About what, in particular?"

Lana walked over to the desk and opened a drawer, pulling out a check. "The amount we owed you. I told you I'd come up with it, and here it is. I'm hoping this payment delay from Cloudberry stays between us."

My heart pulsed at the thought of keeping a secret from Samantha. I didn't know what the purpose was, and I still didn't feel comfortable with how things were being handled.

Instead of answering, I took the check from Lana Roberts, folded it, and stuffed the check in my back pocket.

# CHAPTER FIFTEEN

*Samantha*

Garrett and I excused ourselves from the meal after he returned from the office with Lana. Thoughts were flying around my head at a crazy pace. Maybe there had been something between Garrett and my sister.

A shudder ran through me, and Garrett wrapped his arm around me, which made every cell in my body warm instantly. I had never experienced a reaction like that merely from a hug.

"Cold?" he whispered as we walked along the lighted garden path.

I didn't want to lose the rush running through me, so I just nodded, and he pulled me in a little closer as I pretended to be bothered by a chill in the air.

"I have to be honest with you, Sam."

Hearing him call me *Sam* did all kinds of crazy things to me.

I looked into his eyes and smiled. "Yeah?"

"That was one of the weirdest dinners I've ever had."

I burst into laughter. "Not quite like the family dinners you're used to?"

His lips skimmed the top of my head, and I swore I felt him gently kiss me, but I also knew I had an incredible imagination.

I wrote for a living.

"Not even a little bit," he confessed.

I didn't even have to look at him to know he was smiling. It was etched in his voice.

"Well, our dinners didn't used to be that..." I twisted my lips into a pout as I thought about what our dinners had become. "Stilted."

"Ah, yes. Stilted." Garrett laughed. "You're so a writer."

I had no idea what he meant, but I laughed and nodded. "Anyway, we used to have amazing dinners. My parents loved cooking together and love just poured out of the kitchen. It wasn't until I was a little older that my sisters kind of started to distance themselves."

"From the family?" he asked. "Or just you?"

We stopped walking near a bench, and he dropped his arm to his side. I instantly missed his touch.

"In hindsight, I think me." I shrugged, sitting down. "I don't know. The more I go over everything in my head, the more I can pinpoint the change in the family dynamic to when I got a book deal. Well, really, before that moment when my mom was sending out my manuscript to a million agents. It was before agents accepted emailed projects, so she was constantly stuffing pages into huge envelopes and trudging to the post office." I smiled at the memory. My mom's determination was the only thing that made me believe in myself and my writing.

"What was the story about?" Garrett asked, sitting next to me.

I pretended to shiver again, but I probably just looked like I had a spasm of some sort.

He graciously scooted closer and draped his arm over my shoulder.

"Simply put, it's about the ghosts that haunt the living. Really,      our      own      personal      ghosts. I smiled. "But I was a teenager, so I had to put in actual ghosts and a couple of fae."

Garrett's brows shot up. "Fae?"

I laughed. "Sorry. Fairies, but not like you're probably thinking. These were nasty, mean, fight to the death types of fairies. And the ghosts were fairy ghosts. It was a unique concept at the time."

He looked stunned. "And you came up with it when you were a teen." He shook his head. "I was busy chasing girls, playing baseball, and chasing girls."

I laughed. "I didn't have a ton of friends, so I either read my weekends away or wrote."

Garrett nodded. "I looked you up online and noticed you kind of dealt with the paranormal a little bit. I actually ordered a few of your books."

My cheeks flushed, and I suddenly got hot. What if he thought my writing was horrible? What if he left a bad review and it was signed ~ *Garrett*?

I drew a breath and grinned. "Well, I hope you like them. They aren't everyone's tastes. In fact, I don't think my sisters have read any of my books besides the first one I wrote." I laughed. "And that was only because our mom made them."

Garrett's head tilted slightly. "Really? You don't think your sisters have read your recent stories?"

I pushed my lips into a frown and shook my head. "No. I'd be surprised, but I wouldn't expect them to. In all honesty, in my inner circle, I bet it's just my editor who's read them all, and he's paid to do it."

Garrett shook his head. "Wow. If Wyatt wrote, I'd read every single piece he published. I'd *want* to read it. I'd beg to read it."

"But that's because you would purely be seeing if Wyatt wrote about you as a character," I pointed out. "To make sure you looked good."

Garrett laughed. "Nice one."

My shoulders relaxed, and I leaned into Garrett a little bit more.

Why were things so easy with this almost stranger?

"My later books haven't dealt too much with paranormal or fantasy, but I do have an urban fantasy series that I finished several years ago, and my agent couldn't sell it to save her life. My publisher didn't want to take a chance on it and no one else bit, either." I shrugged and let out a sigh. "But I like it. That's the thing about what I do. I like to do it."

"I'd love to read that series someday."

"Really?"

Garrett nodded, and his gaze fell to my lips and I couldn't help but smile. "Yeah."

"We'll see." I grinned. "If we're still talking to each other in six months, there might be a shot. You'd be only one of a handful of people to see it."

"Then I'd be honored." He smiled a genuine smile, and I wondered how he could be single all these years.

I pulled away slightly. "Can I ask something kind of personal?"

"Go for it."

"Have you had any serious relationships?"

"That was from left field." He smiled wryly. "Is this for research on your latest book?"

I laughed. "I'm far more subtle than that."

His gaze softened. "The answer is yes. I've had one serious relationship. Have you?"

"Only if you count book boyfriends."

Garrett looked perplexed, and I shook my head.

"Sorry. Nerd humor."

"There's no way you're a nerd."

I laughed. "Oh, but I am, and proud of it."

"I'll have to look up the book boyfriend thing." Garrett smiled, and I wished I could bottle the look and take it back with me to New York.

I loved every single thing about how his dimples deepened, and the left side of his mouth curled a tad higher, while smile lines spread along his features in a completely rugged way. I seriously wished I could write what I was experiencing, but the feelings were surreal.

The stir in my belly as his eyes stayed fastened on mine only intensified, and breathing in deep became nearly impossible.

I wanted to know more about the one relationship he'd considered serious, but he didn't offer details, and we'd only met a few days ago.

"This might be kind of out there, but..." Garrett stopped himself.

"What?" I asked, skating my hand to his knee.

He smiled widened. "I'd love if you'd come to Fireweed tomorrow. I have to drop some stuff off at Wyatt's, and I wouldn't mind some company."

"You mean, as in the island?" My eyes widened in surprise.

Garrett nodded. "As in the island. Unless you have something else planned."

I glanced toward Cloudberry Inn. The faint glow of the guest rooms illuminated the night sky. It felt like home. I let out a slow breath and nodded, turning my gaze back to Garrett's.

"I'd like that. It would be fun."

"It will be." He slid his hand over mine, and heat swam through me as his gaze fell to my mouth. My pulse pounded as I prayed for a kiss while simultaneously hoping he wouldn't attempt one since I hadn't been kissed in forever.

He squeezed my hand lightly and brought it to his mouth, kissing my knuckles. It was one of the sexiest acts and yet so simple.

Garrett placed another kiss when he knew I had no intention of pulling away.

My eyes closed as he brought his mouth to mine.

Every ounce of worry slipped away as our kisses

deepened.

Garrett's mouth parted just enough as his arms looped around my waist and he pulled me onto his lap. It felt like a scene right out of my stories as his tongue slowly slid along my mouth. His lips felt incredible, and my mind was already in an emotional tug of war. The closeness wrapping around me as our kiss deepened only confused me more.

I wanted to let myself forget all my worries and stay in Garrett's arms, but I knew these types of things worked better between the pages of my stories. I wasn't good at relationships, or at least I imagined I wasn't.

Garrett ran his fingers under my top just along my spine, and I let out a little moan of pleasure. He smiled as he kissed me again, and my pulse raced with something I'd never truly felt.

Desire.

My breathing turned more erratic as we continued to kiss, and I knew I couldn't have dreamed of something any better under the moonlight, in my favorite garden, with a man who made all other men look like they'd crawled out of a hole.

I giggled, and he slowly parted his lips from mine, smiling.

But I was in a complete fog with everything Garrett Mason as I looked into his beautiful green eyes.

His mouth ghosted my ear, and he whispered, "Do your book boyfriends kiss like that?"

And I knew I was done for.

# CHAPTER SIXTEEN

*Garrett*

I picked Samantha up at the inn around ten o'clock in the morning. I came bearing a salted caramel latte and a croissant. After leaving the inn last night, I barely slept. I couldn't stop thinking about the kiss we'd shared.

It was incredible, and now, seeing Samantha's smiling face as I pulled in front of the inn made me keenly aware of how fast I was falling for this girl. She'd braided her hair and tucked the ends underneath a straw hat with a hot pink bow plastered on top.

When I stopped the truck, she kicked her heel behind her and jumped up. Her energy was infectious, and I prayed I'd never have to let it go as she opened the door and squealed at the sight of the coffee cup.

"Hope you like salted caramel." I grinned as she climbed into the cab of the truck.

"I have a pulse, don't I?"

I laughed. "Indeed, you do."

I handed her the bag with the croissant inside, and

she beamed. "You do know all the right moves."

"To stay in the friend zone." I smiled, and she rolled her eyes.

"Okay, last night went a little sideways." She pulled her short floral skirt inside and shut the door. "Not how I treat most friends."

"Not to toot my own horn, but if I were to write a scene like that, I'd say it was pretty hot."

She giggled and took a bite of the croissant. "Would you, now?

I pulled the truck slowly onto the main road and glanced at Samantha as she happily drank her latte and stared out the window.

"I had a really nice time last night." She turned to face me, and I tried not to grin like a dopey clown.

I cleared my throat and nodded. "I did too."

"And since I'm staying out here for an undetermined amount of time..." Her voice trailed off.

"You threw your rule book out the window?" I teased.

"I'm not saying that." She shook her head, grinning. "I'm just not worrying too much about everything I'd mentioned when I first met you. The conclusion to us isn't as clear as it once was."

I nodded. "So, what you're saying is that there's a chance."

She laughed. "A small one."

"I'll take it."

"Are you always in a good mood?" she asked, and I smiled.

"Not to sound cheesy, but when you're around, I'm in an even better one."

"You have a way with words." She crumpled her empty croissant bag. "My sisters have repeatedly told me I'm too perky. Is there such a thing?"

I shook my head. "Not on my watch. I'd rather be around someone who's happy rather than..." Vera popped into my head, and I shuddered.

"You okay?" Samantha asked, resting her hand on my knee, and I had to hide a laugh.

The one thing I knew I couldn't, shouldn't, wouldn't do was to pick on Samantha's sisters because they'd someday find a way to patch things up, and I'd be the ass who said stuff about them.

"Yeah. As I was saying, I'd rather be around someone chipper than someone who's a downer."

"Me too." She nodded and let out a wistful sigh.

The ride to the ferry was filled with favorite bands, books, and movies. I'd learned she loved eighties movies and nineties music. Her favorite color was pink, and her favorite candy was dark chocolate. She loved diamonds and rubies and never had a dog but wanted one.

By the time we pulled onto the ferry, all I wanted to do was lie down in the back of the truck and make love to her.

I knew perfection didn't exist, but Samantha Roberts was my version of perfect.

Sexy, funny, cute, intelligent, good taste in music and movies, and did I say sexy?

I followed the ferry worker's instructions and pulled behind an old red corvette with the top down.

"Nice car," Samantha said, eyeballing the convertible.

"You like that?" It did seem like a car I could see Samantha driving.

"I do." She laughed. "I don't even have a car in New York. Can you believe it? Everything out here is so car dependent, but back home, I just don't need one."

Hearing her refer to New York as home made my stomach clench. I wanted this to be her home. I wanted her to fall back in love with Washington.

The ferry started to move slowly toward Fireweed Island as the cab of my truck suddenly felt very small. I tapped on the steering wheel and glanced in her direction.

"Did you want to go up on the deck or stay in the truck?"

She twisted her lips into a sexy pout as she contemplated her options. I couldn't help but smile.

"You know what?" She unbuckled. "Let's go up. Who knows when I'll be back on a ferry out here again?"

Her logic was a gut punch, yet another reminder that this, that she, was only temporary.

"You've got it."

Samantha was already out of the truck by the time I met her at the stairwell. The skinny metal door with the small port window had just shut from the last person who'd passed through it. The cold air whistled through the deck as I reached for the door and swung it open for Samantha to jog up.

"It's a bit nippy," she shouted over her shoulder. "I hope I don't freeze to death up top."

I followed right behind her trying hard not to notice

her bare legs and short flouncy dress. The smell of stale coffee drifted our way once we got to the top where the cafeteria and doors to the outdoor decks were located.

"Did you want anything from the snack bar?" I asked.

She scrunched her face and shook her head. "Nah. I'm good."

We walked past the booths with peeling green vinyl seating until we reached the double doors leading onto the open deck. I pushed through the doors, and she grabbed her hat as we walked onto the empty deck.

It was a beautiful sight, nothing but open waters directly around us and the faint shadow of Fireweed Island in the distance. As we walked toward the railing, pigeons circled above.

Samantha chuckled and looked up. "Good thing I have my hat."

"Always thinking of possible conclusions." I smiled and shook my head.

Samantha nodded, clutching her floppy hat, and her hair blowing in the wind. It was hard not to reach out and bring her into my arms.

She turned around, facing Fireweed as her hands alternated between keeping her hat anchored and her dress in place.

"This is more difficult than I thought." She glanced over her shoulder and smiled. "It's beautiful, though. Really beautiful."

I nodded and walked up beside her, sliding my arm around her waist.

Samantha scooted into me, leaning her head on my chest as she clung to her hat.

The view was beautiful, but sharing it with Samantha was special.

"It's times like these I wonder why I stay in New York," she muttered under her breath.

"I wonder why too."

She laughed, and I held her a little closer as she took in the beauty the Pacific Northwest had to offer.

The birds had circled away, heading back to their port as the ferry continued its journey, and I wondered how I would ever be able to convince Samantha to stay.

"If I'd asked myself what I thought I'd be doing in Washington, this wouldn't have been it." She stepped back a little and looked into my eyes. "It's nice."

I laughed. "Are you saying outlining isn't all it's cracked up to be? You know, where you already know the conclusion before the rest of us?"

She shook her head and ran a finger along my chest. "I didn't say that. Outlines are still a good thing. They point me in the right direction."

"They point you in *a* direction, but I don't know about the *right* direction."

She smiled and nodded. "I thought when I showed up at the inn, my sisters would be kinder, but I wanted the story's ending to be that we all understood one another. That I'd recognize what drove them to turn their backs on me, and that they'd appreciate how much I miss them." Samantha shook her head and sighed. "I just thought that it would be easier. That whatever reason they had called me out here for would help soften everything."

Her brutal honesty was like a dagger to the heart because I knew she wasn't sure that would be the ending she'd get.

I brushed a piece of flyaway hair that had escaped from one of her braids. She smiled at the touch.

"What if instead of looking for an outcome that is some sort of conclusion, you look at this trip as just the beginning?"

Samantha's smile deepened, and she nodded. "The beginning instead of the end."

"Yeah. Something like that." I saw Fireweed come into view and sucked in a deep breath of sea air. I didn't want this ferry ride to be over, but any second, the captain would announce our arrival.

"You never cease to amaze me," Samantha said, smiling.

She slipped her hand into mine, and we made our way back to the truck.

Within minutes, I was driving off the ferry and onto Fireweed Island.

"This is such a cute town," Samantha gushed. "I've always liked it here."

"Wyatt loves it, but I think it's more the ratio of women to men."

Samantha laughed and nodded. "That sounds about right."

I turned down Main Street and drove through the heart of town.

"So, why did you have to come to see Wyatt today?"

I looked over at her. "I needed him to sign some papers."

"And you needed an escort for that?" she teased.

The electricity ran between us as I hung on her every word. It was as if I were trying to memorize every second with her.

I had it bad.

"Oh, there's even a candy store." She pointed out the window, and I just couldn't believe how adorable every little reaction Samantha had was.

"Even a candy store," I mimicked, and she laughed.

"If we have time, I just might make you stop there on our way back to the ferry."

"Your wish is my command."

As we drove out of town toward Wyatt's home, I let my mind wander to what it would take to get Samantha to stay.

Would it be mended relationships with her sisters? Falling for a guy she barely knows? Reminiscing and yearning for Cloudberry Inn?

I wished I knew.

"It's a beautiful day," I said, suddenly at a loss for words.

The mere thought of losing her before I'd ever even had her made my heart race, my mind wander, and exhaustion hit.

Somehow, I needed to make her see why she needed to stay.

"Are you getting any extra inspiration for your writing out here?" I asked, glancing in her direction. A smile surfaced on her full lips.

The very lips I wanted to kiss this second.

"I am." She nodded. "There's something about this place that's magical. There's a freedom here that I don't have in New York."

I nodded, knowing that same freedom.

"But the ache of loss is stronger too." Her voice softened. "It's not like I can ever get over the loss of my mom. The pain is always at the surface, just waiting to be scratched into a new memory or burn into an old one. The hurt just never really leaves when you love someone, does it?"

I kept my eyes on the road and shook my head.

That ache is something my soul touched every day. I knew all too well the hot and fiery ache buried deep in my chest that eventually led to the dull twinge of sorrow brought out in the sameness of every day.

"I never knew which was more difficult." I looked at Samantha. "The initial sharp pain from losing that person or the dull ache of knowing you'll never have them back."

Samantha's eyes connected with mine, and she let out a deep breath. "It's been seven years, and I miss my mom as much today as the day she left us. You're right how the pain changes."

I nodded, realizing I hadn't ever talked about this with anyone before. It was always surface level, even with my therapist.

"It's one of the things that have made me hesitant to move back. My dad couldn't handle it, so I found a house for him in Arizona that he loved and moved him down there. But it makes me wonder if that could happen to me too."

I nodded. "You did?" I had no idea she'd bought a house for her dad.

"Yeah. I could just tell that staying in Cloudberry wasn't good for him." Her shoulders sank. "But, I don't know. When I'm there now, it feels cathartic. It's like I don't want to leave, but there's nowhere for me to stay."

# CHAPTER SEVENTEEN

*Samantha*

Hearing Garrett describe loss so intensely told me he'd experienced something very profound, but I knew his parents were still alive, and as far as I knew, his grandparents were too.

I thought back to the brief mention of a relationship. He'd had one. I looked over at Garrett as he turned down the road.

I didn't want to ask. It wasn't my place.

"Do you like your job?" I asked, trying to bring the conversation back to something neutral.

His lip curled into that sexy smile that made me melt, and he nodded.

"I do. I can be creative with the projects I take, and I really enjoy growing the business. It's been a lot of fun, a good distraction."

"A distraction from what?" I asked just as he turned into a driveway.

"We'll talk about it later. Wyatt's already wandering out the door."

I brought my eyes over to his brother who was waving at us with a huge grin.

"I apologize for anything my brother says in advance." Garrett winked at me, and I didn't want to be anywhere else.

I chuckled. "Sounds like dealing with my sisters."

"Except Wyatt's nice." Garrett's eyes widened when he'd realized what he'd just said.

I knew I could toy with him a little bit, pretend to be offended and all that, but I couldn't do that to the poor guy.

"I tend to agree." I climbed out of the truck and straightened my skirt as Garrett walked over to Wyatt and hugged him.

It was nice to see such a carefree relationship between them. It was something I'd often hoped for, but I had no idea if it was something my sisters and I could ever achieve again.

"I'll grab the papers." Garrett pointed back to the truck.

As I made my way to Wyatt, Garrett was rummaging around in the cab of the truck and Wyatt chuckled under his breath.

"He convinced you to make his trip out here less boring, I see." Wyatt had the same mischievous twinkle in his eyes as Garrett. I knew they weren't related by blood, but they certainly seemed to both have that cocky sense of self and a fun-loving spirit.

"I don't know if I did that or not, but it was a fun trip." I smiled, rocking back on my heels. "It's nice to get away from the inn every now and again."

"Especially with your sisters." Wyatt had the same look on his face as Garrett did, and I laughed.

"Boy, Vera and Lana certainly know how to make an impression."

"Sorry. I shouldn't have said that," Wyatt apologized, glancing at Garrett who was walking over with a stack of papers.

Garrett shook his head. "Already? I can't leave you alone for a minute."

Wyatt scratched his chin and laughed. "I know. I'm a complete loser."

I watched the two brothers tease each other for a few seconds and soaked up their good-natured banter.

"You two are infectious." I took a step closer to Garrett. "Have you always been this close?"

Garrett nodded, looking over at Wyatt. "I'd say so."

"Yeah. When I first met him, I wanted to beat him up, but he turned out to be pretty cool," Wyatt informed me.

Garrett laughed, throwing his hand into the air. "Beat me up? What are you talking about?"

Wyatt shrugged. "I'm just being honest. You were a real arrogant ten year old."

"I see not much has changed," I muttered, and Garrett's grin widened.

"Whose side are you on?" he asked.

"I didn't know I had to pick a side. Umm." I pointed at Wyatt. "Umm. His. Wait, no. Yours. No, his."

Garrett shook his head and clutched his chest. "I

didn't know rejection hurt so much."

Wyatt rolled his eyes. "Please, this isn't the first time you've been rejected. Women choose me over you all the time." Wyatt laughed. "You just don't know it because they're discreet."

I slid my hand around Garrett's free hand, and he turned to look at me. "Feeling guilty?" he teased as electricity shot up my arm. Just merely touching this man made me forget about my problems.

I giggled. "Marginally."

Garrett brought his attention back to his brother. "Where do you want to sign?"

"On the patio table around back is fine. It's a nice view." Wyatt's eyes connected with mine. "And my kitchen is a mess, so..."

"Your housekeeper hasn't come today?"

"Whatever, dude." Wyatt laughed. "I can do my own dishes."

"Then why don't you?"

Wyatt turned to me. "See what I have to put up with?"

I nodded and glanced up at Garrett as we started walking around the side of the house. "He's a handful. Truthfully, I don't like doing dishes either."

"Exactly." Wyatt pointed at me right before he opened the wooden gate letting us into his back yard.

The moment I stepped through the gate, it was like a magical place unfolded in front of me.

"And no, I don't do my own yard either," Wyatt explained. "But neither does Garrett."

"Oh, I haven't seen Garrett's place." I let go of Garrett's hand.

Wyatt's brows arched. "You haven't?"

I shook my head and looked over at Garrett. "Come to think of it, why haven't you invited me over?"

Garrett laughed. "How about you come over tonight?"

"Oh, tonight, I'm busy." I smiled. "But maybe another night."

"And that's why I haven't." Garrett laughed.

"You two are both handfuls." Wyatt walked over to the table where Garrett had spread out the pages for signature.

I wasn't sure why or for what Wyatt's signature was needed, but I assumed the family business. Although, I wasn't sure whether Wyatt actually worked with Garrett or not.

"We'll get to work on the place this fall. Some of the tenants might not be happy," Garrett explained, which immediately perked my ears up, "but we'll try to work on any issues that might come up."

"Sure thing." Wyatt nodded, penning his name wherever Garrett pointed.

I wandered away from the men and walked along some perennial gardens until I reached the back of the property where I could see the water.

The dark blue water was still as a couple of sailboats gently bobbed up and down in the far distance. Washington was a really special place. It didn't matter if a person lived on the coast, an island, inland, or near the mountains, there was something unique about every space.

I didn't hear Garrett wander up behind me until his hand slid on my shoulder.

"Incredible view, huh?" Garrett asked.

I nodded, spinning around slowly. "It is."

"A bit different from the city?" Garrett's green eyes locked on mine and a thrill of the unknown ran through me.

"Extraordinarily so."

Garrett touched my chin, and I smiled. "I've wanted to kiss you since you climbed into my truck earlier."

"Then why haven't you?" I asked, noticing his eyes become darker.

Might as well just go for it. Let him have it. Tell him where I stand on the issue.

He smiled and stepped closer, narrowing the gap between us.

I wanted to squeal in pure joy. I couldn't have written this scene any better. The wind was ruffling my skirt. The sexiest man alive was inches away, looking into my eyes as if I were the one he'd always been waiting for.

Every part of my body tensed with anticipation. I wanted to be kissed again by Garrett Mason so badly it hurt.

A good hurt.

He slowly moved his hand along my back, up to the nape of my neck.

Garrett's gaze dropped to my mouth, and I sucked in a breath, praying he would kiss me already.

"Here's the deal, Samantha Roberts." He bit his

bottom lip briefly and looked over my shoulders at Puget Sound before bringing his eyes back to mine. His beautiful green eyes were filled with a quiet determination. "I like you. I like you more than I think you realize."

My heart hammered in place as he continued to watch me for a reaction, but I stood still and emotionless on the outside while my insides were going crazy with anticipation. Never had I wanted to hear words so badly.

Garrett drew in a deep breath and slowly slid his fingers through my hair, sending tingles through my scalp and every other part of me.

"I see the start of something here, but I don't want to waste your time or mine." He pressed his lips together for a split second. "Because when I fall, I fall hard."

I licked my lips slowly as I thought about his words.

"You certainly know how to toy with me." He smiled, and I cocked my head slightly in confusion.

And then I got it and flashed a wicked grin. "Oh, the whole lick my lips thing."

He smiled. "Yeah. That whole thing."

I laughed, trying to figure out what to do or say. Since the kiss last night, I started imaging all kinds of scenarios where we took whatever this was one step further. But then I thought I was being foolish since we'd only known one another for a handful of days, and last night was nothing more than a kiss.

An extremely amazing kiss.

I brought my gaze back to Garrett's and tried to steady myself, but being this close with his fingers in my hair and the anticipation of another kiss made my knees completely weak, and my thoughts ran all over the place.

"I like you too, Garrett." I drew in a deep breath. "But I can't make any promises. I don't know what the future holds. As I see it now, my old life in New York is still waiting for me."

He took a step back and nodded. "And that's why I'm going to wait to kiss you again."

My jaw dropped open, and I went to say something but zero words came out. The man had left me hanging, and by the look in his eyes, there was no changing his mind. He was going to make me wait for a kiss.

"So, no kiss?" My voice sounded a little too raspy for my own good.

"No kiss *yet*." He looked at me as if he were taunting me, daring me to persuade him otherwise. "But I think I'll be able to change your mind."

I crossed my arms over my chest, trying to regain some sort of composure—possibly some dignity too.

"About what, in particular?" I asked.

"Everything." He smirked. "You. Me. New York. Your sisters."

"What makes you so sure?"

"I have a hunch," he said flatly, smiling.

"If you think you can fix everything..." My voice trailed off as Garrett shook his head.

"I didn't say I'd fix everything," he corrected. "I just said I'd change your mind."

I laughed. "Are you saying crazy can't be fixed?"

"Your family isn't necessarily crazy." He grinned as his hand slipped over mine, and we began to walk toward Wyatt, who was working at his laptop on the patio table.

"I don't know. I'm starting to wonder." I took a deep breath. "My sister is really set on the whole ghost theory."

Wyatt scrunched his brows and looked up at us. "You two doing something a little shady over by the water?"

I giggled and shook my head. "No. Not even close. Your brother refused to kiss me."

Wyatt's eyes widened, and he looked at his brother, who seemed to be signaling for his silence.

"But as for the ghosts, ever since Margaret and Susan showed up at the inn uninvited, my sister thinks it means we have ghosts," I explained.

Wyatt tilted his head and scratched the day's stubble along his chin. "Margaret and Susan?"

I nodded. "Yeah, Margaret was staying at the inn with her daughter, Susan, before they celebrated Margaret's birthday with her twin sister."

Wyatt and Garrett exchanged glances.

"That's so weird," Wyatt muttered under his breath.

Garrett agreed. "It's a little odd."

"What's weird? That we had guests, or my sister thinks they're ghosts?"

Wyatt shrugged. "It's probably just a coincidence. They're common names."

Garrett nodded and sat across from his brother. "Totally."

"Would you just spit it out?" My hands flew to my hips. "You're worse than me when trying to build anticipation in a story."

"You tell her." Wyatt pointed at me.

"My great-great-grandmother's name was Margaret and my great-grandma's name was Susan." Garrett glanced at his stepbrother.

"Keep going," Wyatt prompted.

"And they did stay at the Cloudberry Inn back in the day when it was less of an inn and more of a" —Garrett grimaced— "boarding house, I think it was?"

I nodded, feeling a chill coming over me.

"The story goes that Margaret lost her husband and wound up staying at Cloudberry with her daughter, Susan, while they tried to hunt down Margaret's twin sister who had quite a bit of money."

I opened my mouth and then shut it.

"At least that's how the story goes." Garrett shrugged. "Whether these are the same folks or not?"

"Do you know how long they stayed at Cloudberry?" I asked.

"I think it was like a year or something." Garrett glanced at Wyatt. "I only know it because my grandma always used to tell us about how her mother's favorite place was Cloudberry Inn."

"Even though it was a boarding house at the time?" I asked.

"*Because* it was," Garrett corrected.

I knew at the turn of the century, the home had been used as a boarding house of some sort, and then off and on for the next thirty years or so, it became many things to many people, but it had always stayed in our family, which was why I knew how important it was to my mom to have us girls keep it in the family.

"Wow." I scratched my braids and adjusted my hat. "I'm not sure I want to tell Lana that or she'll be calling the *Ghostbusters*." I grimaced.

"It would be kind of cool if Margaret and Susan were visiting the inn." Wyatt looked generally impressed.

Garrett and I looked at him strangely.

"Well, for starters, that would make ghosts real," I pointed out.

"Who says they aren't?" Wyatt looked confused.

"Who said they are?" I turned it around, not sure why it mattered.

"It's not like they died there," Garrett added. "Aren't ghosts supposed to haunt the last place they took their final breath or something?"

My brows scrunched as I thought about it. "It depends."

Garrett glanced at his brother. "This sounds like the perfect project for you and your sisters to work on together. Maybe you'll even come out of it liking each other."

I scowled at the brothers. "It feels like a setup."

"Sounds more like a challenge to me." Garrett smiled.

# CHAPTER EIGHTEEN

*Garrett*

It was nearly impossible not to kiss Samantha at my brother's. I'd wanted to do more with her than that, but I didn't want this to be casual.

I could tell that unless she figured out everything with her sisters, she wouldn't stay. Even if she missed Cloudberry, loved the area, and wished she could live here, she wouldn't. Not if she couldn't mend fences with her sisters.

And that had suddenly become my job.

Sure, I didn't think her sisters were the sweetest females on the earth, but there had to be some degree of kindness after all the layers were shed. I'd hate to think they were just rotten onions no matter what was peeled back.

I shook my head. There was no way they could be related to Samantha and not have substance and kindness hidden in them somewhere. Just impossible.

I stared at my full inbox and decided the messages

could wait. I didn't know how long Samantha was going to be in town, and I didn't have time to waste.

I'd only known her a week, and my entire life had shifted. Even my way of thinking had changed. I felt freer. I wasn't worried about who I was going to sleep with next or how to break it to them that I wasn't in it for a relationship.

I didn't have to worry about any of that because I only wanted one woman.

Now, I just had to make her want me back.

Make her want Cloudberry back.

I turned off my laptop and grabbed my jacket.

I had to come up with a plan of attack and execute it flawlessly or she'd be back in New York ordering late-night takeout and forgetting I ever existed.

I couldn't let that happen.

She belonged here whether she knew it or not.

I grabbed my jacket, walked out of the office, and got into my truck.

Within minutes, I was pulling into the library's parking lot.

There had to be something about the inn when it was a boarding house. I had no idea about the whole ghost thing, but finding out that some old ass relatives of mine might have suddenly turned up at Samantha's family inn was intriguing. The fact that they were dead was even more so.

I looked around the parking lot as if someone could have heard my thoughts and might call the looney bin.

I wouldn't blame them, but love did crazy things.

Shaking my head, I laughed as I pulled on the library door.

Love?

Not even close.

Crazy for thinking it.

Crazier for wanting it.

"Howdy, Garrett." Leslie, the town librarian, gave a quick wave. "Long time since you stepped in here. Guess building all those apartments cuts into your reading time."

She was one of the old-timers that didn't approve of my project.

I nodded. "It has indeed, ma'am."

"Well, I have to say that our patronage is up quite a bit. Seems like you brought a lot of readers to our town."

I laughed, and she whipped her finger to her mouth to motion for my silence. She walked over to me.

"Is there something I can help you find?" she asked.

"I'd like to look at the old historical records. Do you have any info on the old Cloudberry Inn when it was a boarding house?"

"Do we ever." She waved her hand for me to follow her to the back of the library where a microfiche machine sat.

She walked over to a row of file cabinets and started pulling out drawers. "Have at it. There's the microfiche over there."

I didn't want to admit that I had absolutely no recollection from high school how to look this stuff up, so I just smiled and nodded when a thought occurred to me.

"Hey, do you have any books by an author named

Samantha Roberts?"

Leslie scowled. "Does this have to do with why you're looking up the old inn?"

I smiled. "She's visiting her sisters. I ordered some of her books online, but I haven't gotten them yet."

"I think a few are checked out, but I can go see what's available." She walked toward the front of the library while I stared at the file cabinets wondering where to begin.

I bent over and saw the file cabinets seemed to be catalogued by date. I opened the first drawer and figured out how to narrow it down by the local newspaper articles.

When Leslie came back over with a pile of books, she saw me about where she'd left me and started chuckling.

"Why don't men ever ask for help?" She put the books on the table near the microfiche machine and wandered over to where I was standing. "Any particular time period you want to narrow it down to?"

"Maybe between 1900 and 1930?"

Leslie shook her head. "You'd be here all spring and summer."

I laughed. "Maybe I'd better do some research before I try to look at anything here."

"Might save you a bit of time." She nodded. "Anyway, here's what we have in stock. She doesn't seem to write in series, so you can really choose whatever story interests you."

"How many can I check out at once?" I asked, suddenly feeling like I was back in high school. Except in high school, I tended to avoid the library.

"Four."

I stared at the stack of seven books and grinned. "Would you loan me all seven just this once?"

Leslie frowned. "No exceptions. I'll meet you up at the counter once you've made your selection."

Guess the old Garrett charm wasn't going to work with this one.

Since I knew I'd love anything that Samantha wrote, I grabbed the top four in the stack and walked over to the counter where Leslie was waiting.

I slid them over to her.

"Library card?"

"Shoot. I don't have it on me."

"Okay, fill this out and we can look it up."

I stifled a chuckle.

Leslie was by the book.

After scribbling down my information, she entered everything into the computer and looked at me.

"You owe a fine."

"For what?"

"Three dollars and ten cents or I can't let you take these."

"Okay, fine." I honestly had no idea why I'd owe a nickel, but I didn't have time to worry about it. I slid her my debit card, and she shook her head.

"We don't take debit cards if the charge is under five."

I let out a sigh. "Can you just charge me five bucks for when I'm late next time too?"

She shook her head. "Can't do that."

I glanced around the library and out the window to across the street where there was a little shopping market.

"Can you just keep these for me? I'm going to dash across the street and get some cash."

"So, you want me to place a hold on these?" she asked.

"No. I'll be right back. I just want to run across the street. It will take me ten minutes, tops."

Leslie shook her head again. "Can't do it. We need to place a hold if you want them, but I can't place a hold until you clear this up."

I tried not to glare at her, so I smiled. "Then I will have to take my chances that someone won't check them out while I'm gone, won't I? But I'll be back."

Leslie nodded as I nearly ran out the door to get cash.

This whole thing was crazy, but I'd worked with government bureaucracies before. I just never thought our little library was one of them.

The small shopping market had a few carts out front, so I grabbed one and pushed it inside. The smell of the floral department and bakery hit me immediately, followed by the fried chicken in the deli. I scanned whatever was closest and saw a large bunch of sunflowers. They'd be nice for Samantha. I dropped them in the cart and wandered over to the produce section.

I bagged a few bell peppers and a bunch of carrots. Might as well get some shopping done since I was here.

About all I had left in the fridge were a couple of beers, a wilted bag of lettuce, and mayo.

As I wheeled down the milk aisle, I heard a laugh that sounded like Samantha's, and excitement ran through me. I forgot about the milk and drove my cart to the sound, only to see absolutely no one.

Great! Now I was hearing her voice. I already felt a little odd for reading her books, like I'd get a real sense of who she was without her ever actually revealing things to me, but now? To be hearing her when she's nowhere to be seen? I had to get a grip.

I shrugged and wandered over to the pasta aisle and picked up some lasagna noodles and spaghetti noodles before grabbing some sauce off the shelf.

"Garrett? Is that you?"

I spun around with the sauce in hand to see Samantha and Lana standing behind a full cart of groceries.

"Hey, fancy meeting you here." I grinned, feeling like the biggest dope in the world. I didn't understand what it was about her that completely put me in a tailspin.

Lana rolled her eyes and marched away with the cart, leaving Samantha and me in the aisle.

Her eyes dropped to the flowers in the cart. "Planning on wooing someone special, or do you like to dress up your kitchen with flowers?"

I grinned. "Wouldn't you like to know?"

Samantha laughed. "I kind of would, actually."

"Does it matter?" I asked, seeing her eyes narrow on me. "We aren't *really* seeing one another."

She snickered. "So, I'm still being punished for being truthful."

I cocked my head and bit my lip.

Was that how she saw this? As punishment?

Maybe I was a better kisser than I thought.

"You've got a lot going on with your family and the inn." I shrugged. "Sounded like you had a book to finish—"

"Start," she interrupted, smiling coyly.

"Anyway, you said that New York was waiting for you, and I don't really see this as punishment. Just the logical thing to do."

She smiled wider and folded her arms over her chest. "So, you pride yourself on being logical."

I laughed. "Very."

"Then, *logically,* you should get those flowers in some water soon, so I'll let you go." She spun around but flashed me a wicked smile before tracking down her sister.

My day instantly felt lighter just from running into Samantha in the store. Imagining what she could do to me if we were ever to be in a relationship was tantalizing.

I wandered over to the checkout, remembered to get cash, and carried the bags of groceries over to the library's parking lot and put everything in the back of my truck.

By the time I got back inside to see Leslie, probably about twenty minutes had gone by. I walked up to the counter, and not a Samantha Roberts book was to be had, but Leslie was waiting with her hands folded together.

"I'm back with my cash." I pulled out my wallet. "Where are the books?"

"I told you I couldn't put them on hold for you, and I certainly am not going to let them clutter up my counter." She smiled as I handed her the five dollars. "I would have preferred exact change, but this will do."

I tried not to laugh and just nodded. "Sorry."

"You can go grab the books. I put them back on the

shelf."

"Of course you did." I wandered off toward the R aisle and spotted the freshly shelved books, which I pulled back off the shelf and took up to the counter.

As Leslie slowly checked out each book, I glanced out the windows hoping to see a glimpse of Samantha.

No such luck.

But once I got home and realized the sunflowers were nowhere to be found, I realized right then and there that Samantha had and always would have the upper hand.

# CHAPTER NINETEEN

*Samantha*

"You stole those flowers," Lana muttered, standing in the doorway of my old bedroom. I'd started the arduous task of cleaning out the room so I'd have a place to stay, and the sunflowers were a nice addition.

"I didn't steal them. They were meant for me, anyway."

Lana shrugged. "You can't be sure."

"What do you mean?"

"The guy gets around."

My stomach tightened. I knew Lana didn't say it to be mean. Coming from her, it would be more of an informational tidbit than a stab. Now from Vera, it would be an entirely different story.

"Have you actually seen him get around, though?" I asked.

Lana smiled and took a few steps into my room. "No, I haven't. I've just heard things."

Now, my interest was completely piqued.

"What kinds of things?" I sat on the edge of my full-size bed.

"That he's good at what he does." Lana flashed a wicked grin.

"And who did you hear that from?"

She glanced around the room as if someone might hear. "Violet."

My brows shot up in surprise. "They never did anything."

Lana frowned. "Says who?"

"Says Garrett."

"How did she even come up?"

"When he took me out to dinner, I ran into her. We exchanged numbers."

"And you believe him?" she asked.

"I have no reason not to." I glanced at the wall of boxes. "And it's not like it really matters. I live in New York."

Lana smiled, and softness etched her features like when we were younger. "That could make it more fun."

"I suppose." I let out a sigh and put my hands behind me and leaned back. "But then it could get messy."

"It doesn't have to be that way. You could just look at Garrett as a fun attraction out in Washington."

I laughed nervously and shook my head. "That's the problem. I'm not sure I could."

Lana narrowed her eyes on me, studying my features. "You kissed him."

My cheeks flamed and I shrugged.

"You did."

"It might have happened, but only once."

Lana moved into my room at lightning speed, shoved a pile of clothes off a chair, and took a seat.

"And you're just now telling me?" She looked completely exasperated and so much like the sister I grew up with.

A seed of hope sprouted inside, and I grinned. "I didn't want to jinx it."

"Jinx it?" She shook her head. "How could you possibly jinx a kiss?"

I laughed. "I don't know, but I'm sure if it can be done, I could do it."

"Was he a good kisser?"

"Beyond..." I glanced at the sunflowers I'd stolen from the back of his truck and smiled. "It's probably a good thing that I'm headed back to New York."

Lana drew a deep breath and bit her bottom lip. "When do you think you're leaving?"

"Trying to boot me out already?" I smoothed the comforter with my hands and looked up at my sister.

She let out a sigh and shook her head. "No, I'm really liking your company. It gets dull spending time with Vera all the time."

"Don't let her hear you say that," I teased.

"I'm sure she feels the same way." She shrugged. "It's just kind of tough, you know? I never thought I'd be this age without a family and my own life. Yet, here I am."

"You feel stuck?"

She brought her gaze to mine. "Sometimes, but I know this is the best place for me. It's not like I'm completely without men." She chuckled. "But there's never been The One, and I'm beginning to think there might never be."

I nodded, knowing exactly how she felt. "I think about how much Dad and Mom loved each other and this inn, and I don't think I could ever replicate that with someone." I smiled. "But I do love the inn."

She let out another heavy sigh. "Most of the time, I do too."

"I'm glad you invited me even if I don't think it was purely to visit with your long, lost sister."

Lana dropped her gaze.

"What?" I prompted.

She brought her gaze to mine. "I—" Lana stopped and pressed her lips together until they formed a thin line.

"Things just haven't been going quite as great as I want them to."

"What do you mean? It seems like people love it here, and there are always bodies filling the beds." I realized how creepy that sounded and laughed. "It's probably good that I'm not your marketing person."

Lana smiled. "Well, we've kind of gotten some negative reviews online over the last couple of years and I think it's finally hurting us."

My eyes widened in complete shock. "What? Cloudberry? It's perfect. How could anyone say anything bad about it?"

"It's not about the inn. The guests always rave about the rooms and the breakfast and the gardens and..." She threw her head back and groaned. "This is so embarrassing."

"Spit it out or I'll go look online." I was actually shocked that it never occurred to me to look online at Cloudberry Inn, anyway.

"Some of the guests have complained about *us*."

My brows wrinkled. "As in you and Vera?"

Lana nodded. "She can be a little bit snarky, and I think when she's miserable for whatever reason, she doesn't realize that she makes everyone else miserable. Guests can feel it."

"They've actually written this stuff in reviews?"

"Well, it's only Vera and me here and the reviews talk about *the woman checking us in* or *the woman who served breakfast*."

Considering both of my sisters did both jobs, I wasn't sure why Lana was so quick to point the finger. I'd seen some unpleasant sides from both of them recently, but I certainly wasn't going to say that.

"What does Vera think about everything?" I asked.

Lana shook her head. "She seems to think that the guests can find somewhere else to stay."

I chuckled and nodded. "Sounds about right."

"When I wrote that letter, it was because we needed help."

I tilted my head and watched my sister. She was fidgeting with her skirt and her left knee kept bobbing up and down, which didn't exactly give me the warm fuzzies about what would come out of her mouth next.

"I'd like to think it's because of my dazzling smile and charming ways, but..." I didn't finish my sentence.

Lana tried to plaster the superficial smile on her face, but it slid right off. "Partially."

"Then what's the other part?"

Lana let out a slow breath. "Has Garrett said anything to you about anything?"

I crinkled my nose. "Well, he's said a lot of somethings, but unless you're more specific, I couldn't really answer that."

"I'm just going to come right out and say it."

I nodded.

"We're behind on last year's taxes."

The moment the words slipped out of her mouth, relief spread through me. Now, this was something I could help with. I also imagined if they were behind on last year's taxes, there was a high possibility that they would be behind on this year's as well.

My brows shot up. "Really? That's it?"

"What do you mean, *that's it*?" Lana stood from the chair. "We could lose everything. If they put a tax lien on the inn, then it would all be gone. Generations of the Roberts' hard work gone because the wrong sisters inherited it."

I shook my head and stood up to try to hug Lana, but she quickly took a step back and nearly fell back in the chair.

"It's okay. I can help with whatever needs to be brought up to date." It couldn't be that much money, could it?

"Just like that. You don't even ask how much or what happened?" Lana's voice was alternating between being incredulous and bursting into tears.

Yet again, it felt like a trick. She told me so I could help and then she got mad because I wanted to help.

"I just want to offer what I can. I want to make things right between us all."

Lana sucked in a deep breath. "I'm telling you why I initially invited you out here, but I'm not telling you this so you give us money. Once you got here, I decided against asking for a loan."

"First of all, it wouldn't be a loan." I cleared my throat, hoping my sister would bring her gaze back to mine. "And second of all, I'd do anything to help you. You're my sister."

Lana started toward the door and turned around, resting her hand on the doorknob. "It must be nice to have no worries and be free like that. Not a care in the world, plenty of money in the bank, and a job you love."

"I—"

Lana left my room before I had a chance to finish my sentence, but I wasn't going to let it go down like this.

I needed answers.

I wanted to show understanding and support.

By the time I'd found her, she'd managed to plaster a smile on her face and busy herself with new guests who had just walked into the inn minutes after everything went down. If Vera and Lana were having any kind of discussions like that when guests were around, I can imagine how uncomfortable that could make the guests feel.

But that was the least of my worries.

Once Lana had shown the couple their room and

they'd wandered out to the gardens in back, I tracked her down.

She was sitting on the couch in the family room acting as if nothing had happened.

"We're not done talking about this," I started, but she quickly tried to shut me down.

"Oh, yes. We are very much done." She grinned at me as if I would go away like everyone else who received that would do.

"No, we're not." I sat down on the couch. "There are so many things wrong with what you just told me that I don't even know where to begin. If I start by tackling the money issue, that can be solved, but the fact that you think of me with such little regard... that hurts."

Her eyes focused on me. "I would love to have your problems for one minute." She held up her index finger. "Just one minute. Instead, I'm left running an inn I can barely keep afloat with a sister who'd rather be anywhere than here. You show up and think all it takes is for you to whip out your checkbook and everything will be solved."

I glanced around the room and tried not to blow up. I was only trying to help, but I was being blamed for having money, yet my sisters wanted the money to help them.

*Except they don't.*

Or at least Lana didn't. I wasn't sure where Vera stood on the subject or if she even knew much of anything.

"Listen, we can only work on one problem at a time." I tried a different approach. "Why don't we discuss what is owed and we'll work from there?"

She cocked her head slightly. "Well, we don't have to worry about paying your precious contractor anymore. I wrote him a check when he was here for dinner."

"That's why you pulled him away?"

She nodded.

"Why did you pay him instead of putting it toward the taxes?"

"What?" Lana smacked her hands on her lap. "You want to criticize everything I do now?"

I closed my eyes. "That's not what I meant. I was only trying to point out that he probably could be a lot nicer about a payment plan than the IRS."

She shrugged. "Well, I didn't want to take the chance. I was worried he was going to tell you that we hadn't paid him yet."

"I guess that didn't go according to plan."

And now I wondered why Garrett didn't say something to me.

The whole situation was just messed up.

"Let me help with the taxes. It's the least I can do since I'm not here to help you guys on a day-to-day basis and haven't been since I left home."

"It's not your responsibility." She shook her head. "Do you know what haunts me at night?"

"I don't."

"The fact that I can't keep this place together the way Mom and Dad did. Everything was so effortless for them. They didn't have a gardener. They did that themselves. They didn't have help with housekeeping or outside laundry services. Mom hung the sheets outside." My sister stood. "Do you know how inadequate I feel every single morning when I wake up?"

Tears welled up in my eyes, and I quickly brushed them away. "You're anything but inadequate, Lana. You've done an amazing job. Things have changed since Mom and Dad owned it. You have to market differently. You're competing with all these websites that offer rooms all over the place. You've got reviews to deal with and websites to keep up with." I drew a breath and let it out slowly as Lana wiped away tears as well.

Years ago, my mom had asked me to keep a secret, and I'd vowed that I would.

But as I looked into my sister's eyes, I knew I had to tell her.

"Do you want to know why Mom tried so very hard to get me published?" I asked softly. "Why she spent night after night locked away from us all as she sent out my manuscripts to people who'd never even open the envelope, just... hoping?"

Lana nodded. "She knew you had a gift."

I let out a deep breath and smiled. "No, she knew I could save the inn."

# CHAPTER TWENTY

*Garrett*

There was something about the fact that Lana stole her flowers right out from under me that completely made my day. It didn't matter that I had an inbox full of emails I still hadn't read, or my task about finding out info at the library on Cloudberry Inn never happened, or that I still hadn't come up with a surefire way to make Samantha fall for me.

All it took was for Samantha Roberts to leave her mark on me—on my day—to make the world a better place.

I stared at the third chapter of her debut novel, and it was impossible for me to believe a teenager had written it.

Her words were so very soulful, the concepts she elaborated on completely above my head, and her writing was effortless.

So much like the woman I'd come to know.

But as I read, I couldn't help but feel like a bit of an intruder. It was one thing to read an author and love the words and feel them coat you as your own, but it was completely different when you knew that person.

It felt more personal.

Then suddenly, a turn-of-phrase meant something more or I could imagine her lips uttering these very words to me across the table.

It brought the whole experience to a completely different level.

An intimate level that Samantha had no idea she was part of, which made me completely uncomfortable and gave me the perfect excuse to go visit Samantha and her sunflowers where everything was out in the open.

By the time I was at the inn, I'd already started talking myself out of the visit until I heard what sounded like eighties music blaring from one of the garages at the rear of the property. It was faint from where I was sitting in my truck with the window down, but I knew it had to be loud for me to even hear it.

I glanced at the old mansion and smiled. The parking lot was empty, which meant the guests were out and about, and something told me it wasn't Vera or Lana listening to that music.

Turning off my truck, I prayed I was right about which Roberts sister was out back and started to walk along the garden paths. I'd always liked how Cloudberry Inn's landscape had so many architectural features and hardscape throughout it. Winding paths, burbling fountains, and gazebos gave the property a character of its own. I had a long way to go before I got my yard looking like this one, but at least I'd hired the right landscaper.

As I made my way toward the music, I saw one of the garage doors open and a woman in booty shorts bending over near a bucket of suds.

It had to be Samantha the way the shorts cupped her butt. Her dark hair was in a messy bun with wet pieces of hair falling along her shoulders. Her booty was shaking to the beat of the music, and I couldn't help but take it all in.

When the chorus came on for the punk rock song, she belted it out and danced like no one was watching.

Which made me feel extremely guilty except that she was so damn cute, and I couldn't turn away.

And seeing the suds roll down her bare legs didn't hurt things either.

When the next song came on, she squealed with delight as LL Cool J's *Back Seat of my Jeep* from the nineties rang into the air, and I held in a chuckle.

Once she started rapping and rubbing the sponge all over the car, I was a goner. Never in my wildest dreams could I have pictured this big-time writer washing her car and singing at the top of her lungs about doing the nasty.

Everything about this moment seemed right.

More than right. It seemed perfect.

She seemed perfect, and the air was electric just watching her. Samantha was like a magnet for me. I didn't want to be away from her.

And yeah, I completely understood that there was nothing perfect out there, but I was starting to feel like she was perfect for me.

Wasn't that all that mattered?

I batted away the ridiculous thoughts as she belted out the lyrics again, and I knew I had to say something. I couldn't keep staring at her.

But I gave it just a few seconds longer as I watched her breasts squeeze against the hood of the car...

The car...

She was washing her *rental* car?

Who did that?

I took a couple of steps forward as she leaned over the hood, stretching toward the center, and a low laugh rolled off my lips.

She didn't even seem startled.

Instead, her doe eyes fastened on mine and a smirk covered her gorgeous features as she turned down the music volume on the boom box with a remote.

A charge ran between us, and all I wanted was a repeat of our last kiss.

"I think you might have something of mine?" I smiled, and she stood with the oversized yellow sponge in her hand, waving it in the air.

Suds rolled down her wrist, and I couldn't believe how she'd made even that as sexy as hell.

She set the sponge on the hood and put her hands on her hips.

"I have no idea what you're talking about." She cocked her head, and the electricity sizzled between us. "Go ahead and search the car for whatever it is you're looking for."

I laughed and shook my head. "You know, I've never seen anyone wash a rental car before."

Her smile widened, and she kicked a pebble with her shoe. "When I'd just gotten my very first book deal, I bought my mom an old '69 Chevy Chevelle that was mostly restored. We used to come out here and wash it.

Sometimes, my sisters would join us, but most of the time, they were out with friends. In hindsight, I wonder if they'd just been avoiding me."

Hearing the longing in Samantha's voice for her mother nearly killed me. I knew what it was like to bury myself in memories just to feel closer to the person I could no longer touch. It was both good and bad. But anger tipped my thoughts about her sisters, and I knew I had to put it aside.

"Where's the car now?" I asked.

Samantha wandered over to the hose and turned it on. "It's in Arizona with my dad. He loves it."

"Do you miss seeing your dad?"

"Surprisingly enough, I see him a lot." She started to rinse off the car and twisted her lips into a pout. "I see him way more than my sisters. I try to fly out to Arizona at least once a year, but I often go out there two or three times."

"I bet he loves that."

She nodded as she rinsed the last of the soap off the hood. "You can't let the soap stay on or it can ruin the finish in the sun," she explained.

"Well, I'm sure Hertz or Enterprise will be very relieved that you took such good care of their vehicle."

She let out a wistful sigh as she turned off the hose and walked over to where I was standing. "You knew about my sisters and the inn."

Never in a million years did I expect that to come out of Samantha's mouth, and since she looked completely expressionless, I wasn't sure how I should take it.

I drew a breath and ran my fingers along my chin, nodding. "I knew that there might be some issues going on."

"And you were worried my sisters were only using me, which was why you've invited me out so many times. You wanted to warn me."

I scowled, wondering what it would be like to be in a relationship with a mind reader.

"But then you thought better of it." She took a step closer, folded her arms over her chest, and she stared at me.

"Yup."

That was it? That was all that rolled off my lips?

"Well, thank you." She smiled. "I needed to hear it from Lana."

I let out a huge breath I didn't know I'd sucked in and nodded, still not wanting to say too much. I wasn't sure what all the sisters had spoken about, and I could really step in it by saying the wrong thing. They might be estranged for now, but I knew blood was thicker than water in just about all cases, and I didn't want to do anything to mess up my nonexistent chances with Samantha Roberts.

"I don't know many details, and it's none of my business." I pressed my lips together and thought about precisely what to say. "I just don't want you to get hurt."

Samantha took another step toward me, narrowing the gap even more. There was something different about the way she was looking at me, less guarded maybe, and all that made me want to do was protect her even more.

Her innocent doe eyes looked up at me and heat rolled through my body. My emotions were getting shredded like I was in the middle of a hurricane just from one look.

I knew by looking in her eyes that she had no intention of staying, but she wanted me. I could see that, and I wanted her more than anything.

She slowly parted her lips and licked her bottom lip as she looped her arms around my neck.

"Thank you for the sunflowers, Garrett. They're beautiful in my bedroom."

I smiled as she pressed her body against mine.

"I don't remember giving them to you."

She laughed and nodded. "Well, who else would you be getting them for? Unless you had a hot date that I didn't know about."

I stared into Samantha's eyes and saw a delicious wickedness that I wanted more of.

"I find it hard to believe that you don't have a line of men back in New York."

She threw her head back, laughing as she kept her arms looped around my neck.

I slid my arms around her waist and pulled her in as she brought her gaze back to mine. It felt like my entire body was on fire for this woman.

"I could say the same about you." She glanced over my shoulder. "But I've heard you're not hurting in that department."

I shrugged. "More talk than action, I assure you."

Her teeth disappeared behind her lip as she sucked on her bottom lip for a split second. The move was so quick that had I not been trying to memorize every little thing about her, I wouldn't have caught it, and the sweet little gesture nearly put me over the edge.

I wanted to be nibbling on those sweet lips.

"I don't care either way." She grinned and let out a wistful sigh. It was as if her heart were lighter than before. "I'm just happy to be here with you now."

It took everything I had not to kiss her. "Really?"

"Mmmhmm."

She nearly purred her response, and I shook my head. "You're going to be the end of me."

Samantha winked and unlooped her arms from my neck before taking a perky step back.

"I've decided to stay until midsummer."

My heart started pounding in my chest from that little statement.

There was a chance, an actual chance that I might be able to persuade Samantha Roberts to fall in love with Cloudberry Inn again.

And maybe even me.

Not wanting her to get even a glimpse of the crazy emotions raging inside me, I nodded slowly and replied, "What changed your mind?"

*Please say me.*

*Please say me.*

Samantha glanced toward the inn and let out a slow breath. "A lot of things, really. I want to mend my relationship with my sisters, and for the first time since arriving, I think I have a shot. And I like it here. I miss it." She shrugged. "Plus, since I've arrived, inspiration is just hitting me from every direction."

I smiled, and Samantha chuckled.

"I didn't say *you* were the inspiration. You can wipe that smirk off your face."

I took a step back and tapped my chest. "Who, me?"

"All I'm saying is that for the first time in a long time, I'm excited to write. Ideas are spilling in from everywhere, and I feel... invigorated."

Seeing her excitement made me excited. Samantha just had a way of making the world come alive, and I just wanted to be a part of it.

I reached out and took Samantha's hand in mine. "Humor me and let me take you on a walk, because I don't think I'm ready to be away from you."

Her cheeks flushed, but she didn't pull away as my hand cupped hers.

"You know, Garrett." She glanced at me with a spark of something new in her gaze. "Your character is getting more and more complex the longer I get to know you."

"That's a good thing, right?"

Samantha laughed. "A very good thing."

# CHAPTER TWENTY-ONE

*Samantha*

Sitting on my bed, I had my laptop open in front of me, a notepad next to me, and a cup of coffee tucked between my thighs. I'd been writing for two weeks straight. The words wouldn't stop coming, and I'd spend hours each day staring at my screen and writing.

When I did break away to eat, shower, or chat with my sisters, all I could think about were the characters in my head and the story begging to come out.

And of course, Garrett Mason.

He was on the tip of every thought, word, and feeling of this story.

When I'd explained the premise of the book to my editor, he nearly jumped through the video chat and kissed me. I could see the excitement in his eyes for my new project, which sent relief clear to my soul.

Now it was up to me to put everything swirling around in my head into some semblance of order, and I really hoped I did the story justice.

After walking around with Garrett, I'd realized how much of life I'd been missing.

Like truly been missing.

Every time his hand would touch mine, an incredible sensation would run through my body. Whenever his eyes locked on mine, it felt like the world drifted away and it was only the two of us left in the universe. And that smile! Garrett's smile made me feel like I was the luckiest woman on the planet.

Now, I'd like to believe that he reserved that special smile only for me, but I wasn't entirely sure yet. All I knew was that I ate up every second with him, and by the time I went to bed that night, a story came flooding through me like never before and I wound up staying up all night writing.

I texted him the next day and told him I was going to be on a writing binge, so I might not be able to see him for a little bit, and he was okay with it.

He didn't make me feel guilty or like what I had to do wasn't important.

Two very important traits that I'd come to appreciate and search for since some dating fiascos in my early twenties. I'd learned a lot since then, like not to put too much value in finding someone special.

But that didn't stop the fact that I couldn't keep the vision of his gorgeous green eyes out of my head.

Or the way his lip curled slightly when we flirted.

As I stared at the screen, I reread about the first kiss shared between the characters, the fiery heat running between them.

*The first kiss between Garrett and me.*

I always loved writing about that first kiss in books.

Writing about it was so special because it told everything about the couple. Were these two really meant for one another? What emotions were felt? Could it ever be experienced between two others?

*I'd never shared a kiss like I'd had with Garrett.*

My characters were destined to fall in love with one another. It didn't matter what life threw at them. I knew in my heart that they'd see it through.

I smiled thinking back to Garrett's kiss. It was so sensual, so pure, and I wished a million times over that we could recreate that moment, but you only get one *first kiss.*

Just like my characters only get one *first kiss.*

I let out a happy sigh, read the kissing scene again as my mind drifted to Garrett, and closed my laptop. It was close to dinner, and I'd promised I'd make cheeseburgers on the grill to go with the potato salad I'd made earlier.

Cooking was one of those things that always cleared my head. Whenever I was stumped on a story, I'd wander into the kitchen, pull out the cutting board, chop some veggies, and whip together some creation on the stove.

Usually, by the time I'd washed the dishes, I had the plot holes all figured out.

It was a handy technique.

And it worked today too.

Until Lana had come into the kitchen to make lunch. Then I completely forgot what it was I was thinking about, but I didn't care because at least Lana was smiling in my direction without quite the saccharin charm reserved for strangers.

I'd often wondered if others saw through the façade too.

But at least she'd been excited to see potato salad waiting for her when dinner rolled around.

Baby steps!

I picked up my coffee and slid off the bed before I glanced at a stack of boxes in the corner. I'd been meaning to go through them all, but I hadn't had the time. It looked like a whole bunch of old photographs and newspaper clippings of the inn and our family had been in the one and only box I'd opened.

It might be fun to look back to see what my family had kept. I hadn't really mentioned anything about Margaret or Susan being relatives of Garrett's.

How would I even bring that up?

*Oh, by the way, the guy I'm seeing has a couple of dead relatives who match the description of our mystery visitors.*

Not gonna happen.

My sisters already had enough reasons to keep me at arm's length.

I glanced at the one remaining sunflower from the bouquet Garrett inadvertently gave me and walked down the hallway with a smile on my face. I spotted a couple rolling their suitcase off the miniature elevator. They looked absolutely oblivious and completely in love.

It would be really fun to get to hear our guests' stories.

And that was when an idea popped into my head.

We could have a little journal in the parlor that allowed guests to write messages or little snippets about themselves for others to read. It would be so much fun.

By the time I reached the kitchen, I was fully exhilarated and proud of my bright idea, so when I accidentally bumped into Vera, I barely noticed her grumble.

Wait.

What just happened?

Vera and I had come a long way since our sunroom chat a couple of weeks ago. She'd stopped slinging quite a few of her mini digs and even started a few conversations.

It was progress.

So, this grunt-grumble took me by surprise.

"Hey, you okay?" I asked, sliding by her to reach the refrigerator. I'd set my coffee on the counter, and my sister merely shrugged.

I laughed. "That's not exactly selling it."

One thing I had noticed since I'd arrived at the inn was that my sisters both had a habit of sneaking off. They always made sure one or the other of them was at the inn, but more times than not, it really was only one or the other at the inn. I had no idea where either of them went since they still hadn't really opened up to me. It wasn't like they'd come home with shopping bags full of stuff they'd bought, so I was always a little curious when one of them would show up right before dinner without a word about where they'd been or what they were doing.

"Just a bad day." She sighed and poured herself a cup of coffee.

I shook my head. "You weren't here." I thought about it for a second. "Were you?"

Had I become that oblivious while writing?

Vera laughed and rolled her eyes. "Glad I make an impression. No, I had some errands to run."

I nodded, studying my sister. She didn't look like she was hiding anything, but she wasn't exactly forthcoming, and I wasn't sure what all could go wrong while running errands.

"Must have been some doozies for errands." I smiled, opening the fridge to pull out the seasoned patties I'd already prepared.

Vera scowled. "You're nosier than Lana."

I laughed as I held the platter of burgers to take outside. "I'm curious about her too."

Vera stopped scowling, but her eyebrows stayed furrowed. "What do you mean?" She opened the doors for me to wander onto the patio. I set the platter down on the table and turned on the grill.

"I don't know." I tried to act like I hadn't been keeping track of them, but it was probably too late for that. "It just seems like you two both spend as much time away from here as possible. I mean, I get it. You both work your tails off here and probably need a break."

Vera pulled out a patio chair and sat down. "I never really thought about it."

"Really? It seems like either you or Lana are always somewhere out and about."

"Could be." She glanced at the grill and yawned.

"Oh, am I boring you?" I teased. "So, what errand pushed you over the edge?"

"You're really persistent."

I chuckled and nodded. "I can't help myself."

"Fine. It wasn't exactly an errand that got me all riled up."

I pointed at her. "A-ha. So you admit it."

She grinned and nodded. "I got a call from Drew."

My mouth dropped open. "As in *the* Drew North?"

She nodded.

This was completely fascinating.

Writers lived for this type of this thing.

I sighed. "Summer camp Drew North. The one that got away."

I couldn't wait to hear what happened next. My fingers got the special tingly feeling as I craved the keyboard and thought about the incredible story this could make. Long, lost loves who met at an innocent summer camp, separated by... I scowled, not sure what separated them.

"He wasn't the one that got away." A little smile crept onto her lips.

"Okay, so he called you. What did you guys say? What did Drew say?"

This had to be good! After this many years?

Excitement drilled through me.

Vera's expression dropped to the patio. "I don't know. I haven't called him back yet."

I straightened in my chair, completely shocked. "Why not?"

"I don't know what to say. His message was vague, and

I don't want to sound as ridiculous as I feel."

I shrugged. "Oh. Well, it can't be that bad. He obviously wants to talk to you. I wouldn't keep him waiting. When did he call?"

Vera pressed her lips together and glanced at the grill. "Shouldn't you put the meat on?"

"The burgers can wait. When did he call?"

Vera's cheeks flamed. "A month ago."

My eyes widened. "A month ago and you haven't called him back? Does Lana know?"

Vera shook her head. "No, and please don't tell her."

I let out a low, steady groan. "Fine. I won't say a word, but I think you should call him tonight."

Vera appeared horrified.

Then she looked like she wanted to vomit.

"Are you okay?" I asked, standing up.

She nodded. "I shouldn't have said anything."

I walked over to the grill and put the burgers on the grate. "Fine. I won't pressure you, but why let this opportunity get away? What if you've always been destined to be together?"

Vera wandered over to the grill and stood next to me. "You're only saying that because you write stories about love and romance and all that."

I laughed, nodding. "Sometimes, I do."

She snickered. "No, you always do. It doesn't seem to matter if you're writing about ghosts, mad men on the chase, or some historical piece set on the prairie. Love always sneaks in there."

My heart stuttered and nearly stalled in my chest. "You've actually read some of my books?"

She nodded. "I've read them all. Why wouldn't I? You're my sister."

I was dumbfounded. "I just... I thought you could care less."

Vera smiled and shook her head. "Not even a little bit. I love to read, and you're amazing at what you do."

Emotion swelled up inside me like a tidal wave, but I didn't even know what was thrashing around in me more—happiness or relief. Maybe my relationship with Vera wasn't as dire as I thought.

"Wow. I had no idea." My voice softened, and I felt my cheeks flush. "I just thought you guys kind of wrote me off, no pun intended."

Vera chuckled. "The pun probably was intended, and I can't speak for Lana. I don't know if she's read them."

The sizzle of the burgers crackled between us as I drew in a breath. "You guys don't really talk much, do you?"

"No." Vera shook her head. "Not really. We may live under the same roof, but we aren't that close. Actually, we aren't close at all."

My heart hurt for my sisters, for my family.

If my mom knew how we'd all gone our separate ways, she'd be crushed.

I unwittingly glanced up toward the sky, realizing my mom already did know and that was why I was here now.

It wasn't about my saving the inn.

It was about the inn saving us.

# CHAPTER TWENTY-TWO

*Garrett*

Two weeks and counting, and I still hadn't seen Samantha since she'd been all sudsed up.

How long could it take to write a full book?

Would she make me wait the entire time or she'd lose her train of thought?

I'd Googled those questions a million times and had gotten a million different answers.

All I knew was that I missed her. I'd only known her coming up on one month, and I missed her like she'd been in my life for years.

It was maddening.

Maddening and addictive.

I wanted more Samantha. It was like all these little snippets of her were never enough. Every little detail she let me in on about her life only led to my wanting to know even more. It was a never-ending cycle.

And I loved every second of it.

Wyatt was staring at me and shook his head. He'd picked up some salmon from the market on the way to my house, and now he expected me to grill it.

"What is your deal, man? You seem really antsy."

I scowled at him and shrugged. "I'm fine. Do you want me to cook this fish or not?"

"It's not just fish. It's Copper River salmon." He rubbed his hands together.

"You really need a hobby."

He let out a low laugh. "Same could be said about you."

"I'm not the one getting all excited about an overly gimmicked piece of fish," I pointed out.

"No, you're just pacing back and forth with an insane look on your face while you mutter a word here or there under your breath." Wyatt folded his arms across his chest and smirked.

I laughed. "Better watch it or I'll knock that baseball cap right off your head."

Wyatt narrowed his eyes. "I dare you, old man."

Within seconds, he dashed off the deck and I was after him. It was like we were back in college, but I didn't let him beat me then and I wouldn't now.

I swatted at my brother as he tripped and rolled onto the lawn, his hat blowing away from him.

"Damn it." Wyatt laughed. "I thought you might have lost your touch."

"Never, my son." I winked at my brother and caught my breath as I saw the grill smoking.

"You'd better not burn my salmon," Wyatt shouted

after me as I jogged over to the grill.

The filets were on a cedar plank and everything looked just right. "No worries there," I shouted as Wyatt wandered over.

"Thank goodness." He smiled. "Seriously, though. It's like you've got ants in your pants."

I started laughing. "You're sounding like your mother."

"God help us all." Wyatt smiled but didn't drop it like usual. "Does it have to do with the writer?"

I couldn't help but smile. "Yeah, It might."

"You kind of like her?" he asked.

I nodded but didn't say anything.

"And she likes you?" he asked.

I grinned. "Who wouldn't?"

"You're so full of it."

"I know. It's bad." I shook my head. "But what's funny is around her, I have no game."

"What makes you think you've ever had game?" Wyatt's brows arched.

"I have a certain way..."

Wyatt scratched his chin and shrugged. "I've heard it's mostly talk."

He had a point.

I liked women, enjoyed spending time with them, but I didn't seek them out much. I might flirt heavily when I'm out, but rarely did I take anyone home.

Of course, it's all relative, I suppose. I wasn't monogamous, either.

"What's the deal then?" he continued as I plated the salmon from the grill.

"She's writing a book and needs her space."

Wyatt puckered his lips. "Ooh. The old *I'm sorry, I'd normally date you, but I have to write this book* excuse."

I laughed. "Aren't you on a roll tonight?"

Wyatt grinned and took a seat at the table where he'd placed his beer.

"At least it's not the *it's not you, it's me* excuse."

I scowled, looking down at my salmon. "You think it was an excuse? The writing a book thing?"

Wyatt shrugged. "Well, she's a writer, so I suppose she does need to write, but since she is a writer, you'd think she'd know how to do it while still functioning in other parts of her life."

I poked at the salmon. "You think she made it up then?"

"Which part?" Wyatt was happily eating away on his overpriced Copper River delicacy while I was left stewing and poking.

"Not seeing me so she could write a book?" My brother wasn't helping me out at all. I'd been happily giving her space while in complete turmoil, and then Wyatt came over and made me think I was losing my mind.

And possibly Samantha.

Although I didn't have her to lose.

"Only one way to find out," Wyatt suggested.

"You think I should just barge in on her? What if she's right in the middle of a chapter? What if she loses her train of thought and blames me for the rest of her life about a book that went sideways?"

Wyatt nodded. "True. It could be the book that jumps the shark."

I shook my head. "What the hell does that mean, anyway? You always say it. Ever since college."

"Film class. *Happy Days* reference." Wyatt took another bite of salmon. "Look it up sometime, but I can guarantee you Samantha wouldn't be happy if that happened to her."

"So, on one hand ,you're taunting me to go there and on the other, you're telling me I could destroy the woman's entire writing career?"

Wyatt nodded. "Your call."

I laughed and shook my head. "I wonder what she's doing right now?"

"Probably having dinner on her patio."

"You think?"

Wyatt laughed. "Shoot, dude. I don't know. Call her and find out."

I took a bite of salmon. "Dang. This is good."

He nodded, forking another bite in. "What did I tell you?"

I smiled and took another bite.

"Are you gonna call?" he prompted.

"Shouldn't I finish dinner first?"

"Do you want to know the inevitable or not?" Wyatt let out a deep sigh. "No wonder you're still single."

I laughed and wiped my mouth with a paper towel. "You're impossible."

"That's what the ladies tell me."

"Why do I think you're talking out of your—"

"Hey, now. Do you like the salmon or what?" He waved his hands at the grill and table. "This cost like two hundred bucks."

"It did not."

He shrugged. "Just call the woman, please."

Merely thinking about Samantha, I let out a deep sigh and smiled.

Maybe she was sitting on the patio with her sisters like I was chilling with my brother. Maybe she'd made some breakthroughs with those two. A couple of weeks was a long time. A lot could happen in two weeks. I glanced at Wyatt. I couldn't imagine not being close to my brother. It was hard to understand what had happened between the Roberts sisters. I still didn't trust their motives around Samantha, but it wasn't my business.

Wyatt waved his hand in front of my face. "You have the weirdest expression on your face right now."

I stood up and pulled my phone out of my pocket. "Fine. I'll call."

Wyatt threw his arms into the air. "I didn't say a word."

On the second ring, Samantha picked up, and the sound of her voice threw me for a loop.

"Uhh." I cleared my throat.

Where'd my words go?

"Is this Mr. Garrett Mason?" Samantha chuckled, and

all was right in the world.

"It is. Sorry. Wyatt's here and he distracted me."

"Not true," Wyatt shouted in the background.

I could feel her smile over the phone. "So, what's up?"

"Just calling to see how your book was going."

"Amazingly well," she gushed. "The words keep flowing. But I did stop for dinner today. I'm about to flip the burgers."

"Yeah? I just grilled some salmon."

"Fancy," she teased.

"Actually, it kind of was. Wyatt spent way too much at the fish market downtown."

"Let me guess. The old Copper River trick."

I laughed. "Indeed, it was."

"I need the night off from writing. You free?"

I stared at Wyatt and pointed at myself while mouthing, *Am I free?*

He nodded his head and rolled his eyes.

"Yeah, sure. That sounds great. Should I bring dessert?"

"Perfect. I'd better go before I burn dinner. See ya soon." She hung up, and I stood staring at my brother. It was like the earth was continuing its orbit and life was moving on, but I was stuck.

Wyatt walked over and patted my shoulder. "I'm surprised you didn't say something lame about Samantha *being* dessert."

"I'm not that bad." I laughed, glancing at my brother.

"Could've fooled me." He picked up his plate. "Mind if I crash here tonight? I don't feel like the long drive, followed by a ferry ride."

"No sweat."

"Think you'll be back tonight?" Wyatt wiggled his brows like we were in high school.

I laughed, following my brother into the kitchen with the dishes. "Who needs enemies with a brother like you cheering me on?"

"While you're pining over a woman who lives out of state, I'm going to stretch out on your sectional and catch the Mariners."

"You do that." I glanced at the pile of dishes we'd just brought in.

"I'll take care of them. Just get out of here. You have to stop at the store for the dessert you promised her."

"Thanks, man." I dashed upstairs, changed my shirt, brushed my teeth, and grabbed my keys before heading out the door.

I'd managed to stop by the grocery store and get to Cloudberry all under thirty minutes. I could tell even Samantha was surprised when she opened the door.

"Come on in." She motioned into the foyer. "We're just finishing up. You want a burger?"

Her hand brushed mine as I handed over the coconut cream pie. All it took was that little touch to make me crave her even more.

"I'm good. Thanks, though."

She tore her gaze from mine and looked at the pie. "This looks sinfully delicious."

*Not as delicious as Samantha looks.*

Oh, no.

It was like Wyatt crawled into my mind and gave me cheeseball thoughts. He was the worst imaginary wingman possible.

"You're sure I'm not interrupting anything? Your writing? Sisterly time?"

Samantha's laughter filled the room as we wandered down the hall to the kitchen. "Not a chance."

I spotted Vera and Lana sitting at the table outside, concentrating on their burgers.

"Do they always seem that lively when having dinner together?"

She let out a low chuckle and turned around to face me. "Yeah. That's about all you get in the animation department."

Samantha let out a deep sigh from her soul. It was heavy with so much unsaid and yet to be discovered.

"Things are not at all how I imagined them to be here at Cloudberry."

"Better or worse?" I hated to ask, afraid she'd leave sooner than I thought.

"Both, I suppose." She leaned against the counter and folded her arms over her chest.

Without thinking twice, I moved closer to her and instantly felt the tension between us pull taut like a thread about ready to break.

Not seeing her for two weeks brought everything to the surface. It was almost like I was meeting her again for the first time.

Her chocolate brown eyes settled on mine as she smiled slowly. "Why do I think you've got a dirty mind?"

I laughed, shaking my head. "I was just thinking about how beautiful your eyes are."

Her cheeks flushed, and she dropped her arms down. "Well, thanks. They work well."

I nodded. "That's good to hear."

Samantha looked up into my eyes, and I couldn't help myself.

I had to kiss her again.

# CHAPTER TWENTY-THREE

*Samantha*

How did this man look better and better each time he showed up? The first time I met him, I thought he was the sexiest man alive.

Now I knew they just didn't make any like him anymore.

For real.

Garrett's mouth parted slowly as my eyes closed, and he circled his arms around my waist, slowly drawing me into him. His strong arms cradled me like I was something that needed protecting, and maybe at this particular moment, I did. I'd spent so long on my own, I didn't even know what I needed anymore.

Maybe he recognized how fragile everything in my life was with my sisters.

Or maybe he was just really good at kissing. A little hum escaped my lips as our kisses deepened.

Yeah. He was just an expert in this field.

A little shiver ran through me as my mind went to that next step.

It wasn't until Lana cleared her throat that I even remembered I was in the kitchen at Cloudberry Inn. For all I knew, I was at the South Pole, worlds away from everything and everyone except Garrett Mason.

My eyes blinked open and I quickly took a step back.

"Garrett brought dessert," I blurted.

Lana's brow arched. "By the looks of things, I'd say you were dessert."

Garrett laughed and shook his head. "I've heard that before."

"I bet you have." Lana shook her head.

"No, I mean from Wyatt," Garrett explained.

I cocked my head slightly and grinned.

"Sounds like an interesting sibling discussion." I bumped him with my hip, and he laughed as I pulled dessert plates out of the cupboard.

Lana nodded in agreement.

"He thought I should have made some corny comment like that when I was on the phone with you earlier. You know, like you were the dessert. Just like Lana said."

"Great minds think alike," Lana teased.

I laughed and nodded. "Well, there's a reason Wyatt is still single."

Lana walked over and helped cut the pie as Vera wandered into the kitchen. She glanced over at me and hid a grin I'd recognized. One that told me she caught me doing something, but I wasn't caught doing a thing.

"What about me?" Garrett asked. "Do you think there's a reason I'm still single?"

Vera twisted her lips and looked at all three of us and laughed. "Garrett, do you really want us to answer that?"

Garrett shook his head with a spark in his eyes. "Probably not."

"You know," I began as I took two plates of pie from my sister, "I think you're all talk and no show."

Vera beamed, taking a plate from my sister. "Should we be listening to this?"

Garrett's low gravelly laughter echoed into the kitchen, and it warmed me right up.

"Is that so?" Garrett's brow arched.

I nodded with Garrett following me to the outside patio. "That's how I see it."

"I'm just trying to take it slow." His voice was so low I almost didn't hear it, but his words sent a delightful tremble through me.

I set our pie plates down and took a seat as my sisters came outside.

"Do you want some time alone?" Lana asked, noticing the look in my eyes that I'd tried to shake off.

I glanced at Garrett and decided to torture him a little. "Nah. We're good. Come on out."

Lana and Vera sat down across from us and slowly began eating the pie.

"So, Garrett." Vera eyed him. "What keeps bringing you to Cloudberry Inn? I haven't seen you come by here this much since you built the sunroom for us."

Garrett didn't miss a beat and laughed.

Vera was definitely fishing for something.

"I like your sister," he said matter-of-factly.

"So do we." Lana nodded. "Which makes me concerned about your intentions."

I laughed and covered my mouth. "Lana, seriously?"

She flashed a wry grin. "Well, Dad's not here to make him nervous."

"Funny thing is, Lana, you don't make me nervous." Garrett winked at her.

Vera chuckled. "Ouch."

But then Garrett pointed at Vera. "You, however, scare the hell out of me."

We all laughed as I took a bite of pie. "This is so good. I haven't had coconut pie in ages."

"Not a big thing in New York?" Lana asked.

I shook my head. "Nope. It's more about the cheesecake, which Mom actually made better."

I noticed my sisters drop their gazes to the pie, and I realized that just because I could talk about Mom freely didn't mean my sisters wanted to. Garrett must have sensed something because he slowly moved his hand to my knee. I looked up at him and gave him a grateful smile.

"You must be proud of your sister," Garrett said after finishing his pie. He looked up at my sisters, and I stared at them in horror.

Never had I heard my sisters be proud, excited, mad, or happy for me. The thought of any of those seemed foreign with the strangers we'd become.

Lana was the first to crack a smile as she nodded. "Extremely so."

"She has a true talent."

I smiled and shook my head. "I've just been lucky, that's all."

Garrett shook his head. "I've read your words. It's more than luck. It's talent and hard work."

I felt uneasy talking about my career in front of my sisters knowing they weren't thrilled with theirs.

But a funny thing started happening recently. I began to wonder if maybe I was in the wrong place and maybe they were too.

I looked up at Vera, and she grinned. "There hasn't been a book of hers I haven't read and loved, and I have high standards."

Lana chuckled, and I secretly wondered if she'd read any other book than the first one my mom had made them devour.

"They can hit a little too close to home for me," Lana confessed. "But it doesn't stop me from reading them."

My heart instantly warmed as shock registered on my face. "You've read more than that first one?"

With all the silence, distance, anger, confusion, and turmoil, I honestly never expected that Lana had even opened the cover to one of my books. When Vera had mentioned she'd read them the other day, I was already stunned. But this I didn't expect.

"Of course. You're my sister." Lana smiled, and it wasn't plastic or phony.

"Wow. Thanks." I glanced at Garrett, seeing something

in his gaze that made me wish I didn't live in New York.

But I did.

And I couldn't forget that.

My life was there, my publisher, my friend and editor...

Well, one friend, who was my editor.

I wouldn't really be leaving that much behind.

No. I didn't need to start thinking like that.

In fact, I'd probably be heading back there sooner than I thought with how quickly this book was writing itself.

"You know, Garrett." Vera drew in a breath. "You never answered our question."

Garrett slowly smiled and nodded. "You're as astute as Samantha."

"Well?" Lana pressed.

"I like your sister a lot, and I enjoy her company."

My heart hammered in my chest and heat began rolling though every part of me. I had done nothing other than kiss the man, and my sisters were putting him on the spot, which put me on the spot. What else did they expect him to say? That was more than enough.

"Love you both, but I'm actually an adult in my thirties, and it's okay if I have male friends." I grinned and rolled my eyes.

"I wasn't finished yet." Garrett flashed a wicked grin in my direction. "I like her so much that I'm going to try to do everything in my power to make her want her to stay."

Vera whistled. "Now that's romantic."

My cheeks were flaming hot, as was the rest of me.

"But I know Samantha wouldn't just stay for me, so I'm hoping you three will mend your fences and—"

Lana chuckled. "Convince her to stay?" She shook her head and shrugged. "Not gonna happen. Samantha was always wild and free. Getting her to come back home is about as likely as my leaving Cloudberry. Seriously not gonna happen."

I caught a hint of bitterness in her voice, and I drew a quick breath. "Okay, so all I know is that this conversation has suddenly turned very serious."

"I know what might lighten the mood." A coy grin spread across Garrett's features.

"What's that?" I asked.

He winked at me and chuckled. "Have Margaret or Susan visited since the last time?"

Lana's eyes opened wide. "You told him?"

I nodded. "It's not something that's really left me, to be honest. I mean, I spoke to a woman who theoretically shouldn't have existed."

"Oh, she existed." Garrett nodded. "Just not in this century."

"What do you mean?" Lana looked far too intrigued for her own good.

"Yes, do explain," I teased.

"I actually have a distant set of relatives that stayed at Cloudberry when it was a boarding house. They were a mother-daughter duo by the names of Margaret and Susan."

It looked like Lana was about to fall out of her chair.

"And Margaret did have a twin sister, just like the one who visited here."

"I'll be." Vera pushed her lips into an impressed frown of complete confusion.

Lana nodded "You're telling me. This is crazy. Do you have any info on them?"

"Not much. I tried to look up some info at the library, but I got distracted," he confessed.

"Part of me hopes we'll find some pics and they won't look anything alike and that's that." I grinned, knowing there'd be no stopping Lana now.

I also knew Garrett brought his relatives up to break the ice that had drifted over the table only minutes earlier, and the moment he had, the conversation thawed almost instantly.

"It will definitely give me something to research," Lana muttered, and I nodded in agreement.

"Be careful what you wish for." Vera shuddered. "But I think I need some coffee."

I laughed. "You and me both. How about we go make a pot?" I turned to Garrett. "You want some?"

"Absolutely. I need as much as I can get. I'm completely outnumbered here."

Before I realized what I'd done, I bent down and gave him a quick kiss on the cheek. As Vera wandered into the kitchen, Garrett caught my wrist with his hand and pulled me back for another. His soft lips skimmed the top of my head, and desire instantly built into something I could do nothing about.

I dizzily stood and caught Lana's stare as she tried to hold in a fit of giggles. It felt like old times, like when were teenage girls, gushing about boys and pretending we'd done things we'd only read about.

By the time I'd wandered dazed and confused into the kitchen, Vera's eyes were as wide as saucers.

"Damn," she said low enough so her voice didn't travel outside. "He's got it bad for you, Sam."

My eyes darted to hers as she scooped the grounds into the filter.

"You think so?"

"Honey, I swear he'd drop to one knee right now if he thought you'd say yes."

I swatted at her shoulder and grinned. "Yeah, right. We haven't even..." I stopped myself.

"Normally, I'd tell you to be careful of your heart, but I feel like I need to warn him."

I scowled as she poured the water into the coffeemaker. "Warn him?"

She nodded. "I can tell you have no intention of staying."

"Why would you say that?" I asked.

Vera shrugged. "Just intuition, I guess. I'm just not sure he'd let himself see it."

"There's no place for me here." I let out a sigh. "Surely, he knows that. My home is in New York."

"Your apartment is in New York. Your home is here." Vera leaned against the counter.

"You really think that?" I asked, surprised.

Vera nodded. "I do."

"Not to sound weird, but you guys don't really like me."

And I didn't mean to sound pessimistic about our sibling relationship, but it was how it had seemed for years. It wasn't something I wallowed in. I'd accepted it long ago, and coming here had only sealed my thoughts on the matter until recently.

Vera looked horrified. "That's not true."

My brows arched in surprise. "You never want me to visit, you don't return my calls, and you never want to come to New York." I wasn't sure what else to say.

Vera folded her arms over her chest and let out a heavy sigh. "I could see how it feels that way."

I wasn't sure if this was progress or not.

"Listen, I'm not mad about it. I just kind of learned to accept it." I bit my lip for a split second. "When I came back here, my only hope was to find out why, if nothing else."

Sadness filled Vera's gaze and she nodded slowly. "I had no idea, and I'm so, *so* sorry."

# CHAPTER TWENTY-FOUR

*Garrett*

Lana seemed a lot more laid back, which kind of worried me. She had a naturalness to her smile. It wasn't so rigid and forced. She was close to being pleasant.

I glanced toward the kitchen where Vera and Samantha had gone and wondered what was taking so long.

"You seem especially enamored with Samantha." Lana's gaze caught mine.

I nodded and glanced toward the kitchen again. "She's amazing."

Lana sat quietly and nodded.

"I mean truly incredible, Lana." I straightened in the chair. "And I hope whatever is holding you back from connecting with your sister goes away because you're missing out on a kind soul who just wants to be loved."

She drew a breath as part of me wondered if I'd overstepped my bounds, and the other part didn't care if I had. Her sisters invited Samantha out here and then treated her like crap until recently. And I still couldn't fathom their motives.

"I'll keep that in mind."

"I think I'm gonna go check on the coffee." I stood from the table and made my way into the kitchen where Samantha was filling up the mugs. Vera was nowhere to be found, so I snuck up behind Samantha and circled my arms around her waist. She was wearing a flouncy dress and it was hard to resist running my hands where they didn't belong.

"I missed you," I whispered as my lips ghosted her ear. Her body trembled in my arms, and I couldn't help but imagine my lips elsewhere on her body and her reaction.

She giggled. "Coffee doesn't take *that* long."

I tried to memorize the sweet smell of her hair and the curves of her body as she stayed in my arms. It was like I knew on some level that I wouldn't get to have her forever.

But I wanted her to be mine.

Samantha slowly turned around, but I kept my arms around her waist as she looped her arms over my neck, looking into my eyes.

She stood on her toes, which was such a turn on, and she softly kissed my lips.

"I want to show you something." If a woman could purr, I'd swear that was what just rolled off her lips.

"Where?"

Our eyes stayed fastened on one another, and she just smiled.

"Out back."

I unhooked my arms from her waist as she took my hand in hers and led me through the kitchen where she grabbed a folded blanket and pulled me onto the patio. She glanced at Lana and smiled.

"Coffee is on the counter."

"Where's Vera?" Lana asked.

"I think she had to go make a call."

Lana stood. "Oh, okay. I think my latest junk TV show is calling me, anyway."

Samantha kept walking, clutching my hand in hers as we wound through the gardens and made our way past the old garage out back, the greenhouses, and a couple more flowerbeds before we hit an empty field. It was like we were in some video game moving through all these obstacles until we hit our destination.

She stopped at the edge of the dirt and looked off toward fir trees lining the property's corner.

"Where are you taking me?" I asked just as she took off again, this time toward the trees.

"You'll see." She shot me a smile that reminded me why I'd follow her to the end of the earth and back.

I'd do anything for Samantha Roberts.

The moment we stepped inside the wooded maze with towering conifers, the temperature dropped and sunlight dimmed to a shadowy labyrinth.

"I haven't been here for almost seven years," she informed me, pulling me through the woods.

"And where, exactly, is this?" I asked, a step behind her even though she still had my hand in hers.

She glanced over her shoulder, still throwing a world of sunshine in my direction.

I looked up ahead and saw a little mound, but it was what was behind it that made her excited.

"There it is." She nearly squealed with delight when we came up to the structure.

It was probably about six feet tall, had twigs for siding, two open windows made out of tree limbs, and a real pine door in the center of it all.

She turned around to look at me. "My dad made this for me so I had a place to escape and write if I needed it."

"That was nice of him." I could see the love in her eyes.

Samantha nodded and reached for the door. "Hopefully, a family of angry racoons isn't inside."

I laughed and shook my head. "And on that note, let me open the door."

She let out a cute little *aw* and let go of my hand. "I can't believe you'd sacrifice yourself for me."

I chuckled and reached for the wooden knob and pulled it open.

From the outside, I didn't expect much, but when I stepped into the tiny space, I could tell it was built with love. A desk and chair had been built into the side of the building and a bench ran along the back. The floor was hand poured concrete and still very much intact.

I ducked my head and stepped inside with Samantha right behind me.

"It was kind of like a teenage girl's version of a playhouse." She grinned, looking all around as if she'd just stepped back in time.

"It's pretty cool." I nodded, looking around.

"I used it a lot. Sometimes, I'd come out here to write for hours, and other times, I'd come out here to get away from my sisters or their friends and just read." She laughed. "And that was when we got along."

"What was it like growing up here?" I asked, taking a step closer. "At the inn?"

"Wonderful." She smiled as her gaze locked on mine. "It was magical, really. I think that was why so much of my writing has whimsy and mystery."

"I've noticed you play with those concepts a lot. They often lead to main events unfolding in ways I never thought of as a reader."

She immediately looked shy but didn't back away. "You've read a lot of my work?"

I nodded, worrying I'd said too much or too little.

"Thanks. That's more than most people I run into."

I laughed. "I'd like to think I'm more than just someone you ran into."

The shyness rolled through her again, so I narrowed the distance between us.

Samantha nodded. "You are." She sank her teeth into her bottom lip, which drove me insane. I wanted to feel those lips against mine. I wanted to feel her against me.

"I'm falling for you, Sam."

Her gaze dropped to the floor, and my heart nearly sputtered to a stop. Was this where she wanted to bring me to break up with me? Or was there anything to really even break off?

I brushed away the hair that had fallen over her eyes,

and she slowly brought her gaze back to mine.

She drew in a deep, slow breath. "I'm scared that I'm falling for you too."

"Why are you scared?" I traced my fingers along her cheek as I took a step closer.

"I don't want to hurt you."

I smiled more to myself than her and nodded. "I can handle it."

"I'm going home soon." She kept her eyes on mine. "And I obviously don't do long-distance relationships well."

I chuckled. "A relationship with your sisters is a little different."

"I'm just saying..." Her voice trailed off as her gaze fell to my mouth.

Not letting another second pass between us, I covered her mouth with mine, feeling her lips part.

She dropped the blanket onto the ground and looped her arms around my waist as her tongue traced along mine, inviting me to kiss her deeper. I moaned, feeling the heat roll between us as she tucked her hand along my waist, just under my jeans. She pushed into me as my hands slid over her curves. She looped her arms around my neck as she jumped into my arms, circling my waist with her legs.

I walked us backward until our bodies found the desk, and I slowly lifted the skirt of her dress, revealing the same underwear I'd picked up in the driveway.

Her body shuddered against mine with laughter, and I blinked my eyes open to have her smiling at me, breaking the kiss.

"I can't help it. They're comfortable."

For some reason, the panties were a super turn-on, especially when thinking I could get them off.

She let out a low purr as she unbuttoned my jeans, and I kept kissing her, feeling the warmth come through her underwear. I wanted her so much it hurt.

Samantha traced her lips along my jaw as she held on, and I shoved her underwear to the side. The moment I felt her warmth around me, I nearly lost it.

She bit my lip softly as I slid inside her, and she clenched my waist with her legs. She was so tight, and it took everything I had to control myself.

"You feel so good," she whispered by my ear as she traced her tongue along the sensitive areas right behind the lobe.

Everything about this moment was more than I imagined. Her hands were running under my shirt, and she was throwing her head back, her hair falling along her shoulders. Images I'd never let go.

"Garrett," she whispered, her breath catching as our rhythm quickened. "I can't hold—"

The moment those words spilled into the air, I couldn't stop myself. Everything about her body tightened, her breasts heaved, and her breathing quickened. I pushed into her one last time as my entire world spun around me and every cell in my body spasmed into pure ecstasy with her in my arms.

After a few seconds of trying to catch our breath, she brought her head back upright and laughed, glancing down at the floor while she was still in my arms.

"I guess we didn't need the blanket." She grinned,

resting her head against my chest.

And I felt like the luckiest man in the world.

# CHAPTER TWENTY-FIVE

*Samantha*

Not to sound funny, but it was like I had literal springs in my shoes. Now I knew exactly what the term *having a spring in your step* meant. I'd used it in my writing before, but I'd never experienced this much enthusiastic bouncing in my life.

Being with Garrett two nights ago still made my world spin. The world seemed brighter, happier, and in turn, I was filled with hope.

Hope that I'd somehow repair my relationships with my sisters.

That I'd be fine with going back to New York.

And no matter what life threw my way, I'd be okay.

I'd never needed a man to fix me or make me happy, but sex with Garrett was incredible. It wasn't like I was looking toward him to complete me in any way, but he complemented me in so many ways. He listened, he gave advice, and he had my back.

I let out a happy sigh. The way he'd held me in his arms and slowly slid his hands along my body, kissing me in places I'd only written about, made me feel like I was the most gorgeous woman he'd ever laid eyes on. I felt feel alive in a new way.

And we both knew what we were getting into. A relationship that, at its best, would be long-distance and would probably fade away without much drama.

Just the thought of ending this unknown thing with Garrett put a pit in my stomach. I couldn't start thinking like that. As of now, he was a good friend with fun benefits, a vacation fling.

I wasn't very good at lying to myself.

I let out a yawn and stretched from my bed as I glanced at my laptop. I'd stayed up until almost three in the morning finishing a chapter, and I'd be the first to admit that spending part of a night with Garrett hadn't hurt my imagination.

It felt like when I typed, the words carried more emotion, more rawness, and I wasn't sure how that even happened.

But I knew there was so much more I needed to uncover about Garrett. I could see the brief glimpses of pain and loss mixed with the highs of happiness and hope in his eyes, and I wanted to know more. I needed to know more.

As I slid off the bed, I glanced at the stack of boxes that I'd pushed to the corner near the closet. I wandered over and opened the top box to see old black and white family photographs of people I recognized but had no name for. I managed to dig a little deeper and pulled out a few yellowed newspaper clippings about Cloudberry Inn.

A smile touched my lips as I saw an old photo of my grandmother holding my mom as a baby in front of the inn. Everything about the photo looked like such simpler times, but I doubted they really were.

I heard some guests wandering down the hall and smiled.

My sisters had done a wonderful job of keeping Cloudberry Inn going, and I was going to do my best to help the tradition continue.

Lana and I hadn't spoken much about the inn's finances since I revealed the secret that I'd been keeping about helping my parents out so many years ago. I knew trouble was lurking, and I needed to work on a real solution with my sister.

But I also wanted to give her plenty of time to let my words sink in. Both of my sisters needed to understand that times had changed in the hospitality industry. There was more competition and online reviews, and things were just plain more expensive.

I drew in a breath just as someone tapped on my door.

"You up?" Lana asked.

"Come on in." I spun around as Lana came into my room.

She noticed the photos and newspapers spread on my bed and smiled. "So, that's what's in those boxes."

I laughed and nodded.

"I wasn't sure you'd be up as late as I think you stayed up last night."

I smiled and cleared a spot on my bed for her to sit. "Yeah. I was on a roll. There's something about being back at Cloudberry that lets the words just tumble out."

Lana giggled and her eyes fastened on mine. "Or could it be more about Garrett Mason?"

"Well, could be him too."

"You two seemed to have really hit it off."

Lana seemed more relaxed, and I hoped it was because we were making progress.

I nodded and sucked in a deep breath. "I'm just not sure how far it will go."

"Probably as far as you let it." She grinned. "I halfway expected him to be in your bed yesterday morning."

I blushed, thinking back to my little writing shed. "It's not like that."

Lana winked at me. "Whatever you say."

Vera poked her head into the room. "Last of the guests checked out."

"Really?" I asked, surprised. "No guests at all at the inn today?"

"Not until tonight." Lana smiled. "We don't get moments like these very often."

I nodded as Vera wandered into my room too.

"I bet it's really hard feeling like you're always tied to the inn," I said softly.

Lana nodded. "It can be."

Vera moved a towel off the chair in the corner and sat down. "But I also worry I'd miss it if it were gone."

I nodded, knowing exactly what she meant. I always took comfort in knowing that Cloudberry was always out there somewhere. That if something happened in my life, I could come back.

But then again, I wasn't here every single day of the year.

Vera's eyes landed on one of the photos in front of me. "Hey, was that Mom when she was a baby?"

I picked it up and smiled. "Yup. Her and Grandma."

Lana took it from me and smiled at it before handing it over to Vera.

"Look at all that lace on Mom." Vera laughed.

I smiled, thinking about the idea of kids. "I think it would be fun to have a baby girl and dress her up all frilly."

Lana looked over at me in surprise. "You want kids?"

"Well, yeah." I wondered why that was such a surprise, but then again, my sisters and I really had become strangers. "I've always wanted them."

"I just never guessed, you know, living in a big city and all..." Lana grinned.

I chuckled. "You do realize that people have babies and raise them in Manhattan all the time, right?"

She shrugged. "I know, but it just doesn't seem as awesome as here, you know?"

I smiled and nodded. "It was pretty special growing up here."

Vera brought the photo back over and picked up another one. "It really was incredible."

"Remember that one summer the family with three boys vacationed here for like four weeks?" Vera asked, her eyes widening.

I giggled, remembering all too well. "We all had a crush on each of them."

"We'd spy on them when they were outside." Lana laughed, covering her face. "And then we followed them to the lake down the street and pretended like we happened to run into them?"

"Those were the days," Vera gushed, and my heart warmed at seeing my sisters so happy.

"Didn't we blast Cindy Lauper's *Girls Just Want to Have Fun* to get their attention?" I laughed, thinking back to how excited I was to get the attention of the youngest. I think we were both twelve. I didn't even remember the kid's name, but he was my first kiss. I still remember all the feelings that rushed over me the moment his braces-filled mouth smiled when I let him kiss me.

Whoever he was.

"Too bad it's not that easy to pick up quality men now." Lana grinned.

"What?" I laughed. "You're not into swiping on your phone to see some dweeb grinning back at you?"

Vera snorted, which cracked us all up even more. "You know... half the time, I don't even think those photos are real."

My eyes widened. "You've used those sites?"

Vera's cheeks flushed and she groaned. "Desperate times call for desperate measures."

Lana stuck her hand in the air and waved it around. "I've even tried them." She narrowed her eyes on me. "Are you telling me you've never once signed up?"

I rolled my eyes. "I signed up, but it was for research purposes only."

Vera did air quotes. "For a book?"

I laughed and smacked my hands on the bed. "I'm serious. I didn't actually date anyone."

"But did you spend hours looking through the pictures and bios?" Vera asked, grinning.

"I plead the fifth. It was all part of research."

Lana chuckled and winked at me. "Sure it was."

"Such simpler times back when we were kids, huh?" I smiled, feeling happiness wash over me.

"So true." Lana let out a deep breath. "The only worries we had were school starting up again and when winter break would start."

"Do you think we could ever get back to that feeling?" I asked softly, meaning our relationship more than anything.

Lana's eyes connected with mine and she nodded slowly. "I sure hope so."

"Me too," Vera agreed.

I pulled out some more news clippings and couldn't help but feel pride over Cloudberry.

"This inn is such a special place," I said more to myself than anyone in particular.

"It is, and there are so many times that I worry we aren't doing it justice," Lana confessed, and Vera nodded in agreement.

Shock ran through me, and I quickly shook my head. "You guys have done an amazing job with the inn. It's highly rated on all the sites. There are only a couple of somewhat negative comments compared to hundreds of rave reviews. The grounds are gorgeous, the rooms beautiful and clean, and the food's delicious. You need to give yourselves more credit." And the only negative ones were about a crabby worker at the inn, and I didn't want to guess which of my sisters the guests were referring to.

Lana's gaze connected with mine. "Then why do I always feel like it's never enough?"

"All part of owning a business," I confessed. "Even after all the books I've written, I still feel riddled with worry about how readers will react. I still panic that my publisher won't think my sales numbers are enough. I still just worry. Period."

Lana nodded. "I guess it's par for the course."

I drew a breath and let it out slowly. I hadn't brought up the tax issues since our last conversation, and now that Vera was in the room, if she didn't know, she should.

"You know, I want to help you in any way I can. Whether it's coming out here more often to relieve you two or... any other way."

Lana's eyes stayed on mine. "Thank you."

"You've helped a lot since you've been here, actually," Vera added, surprising me.

When I'd first gotten here, if she'd have said that, it would have been pure snark, but I could tell that this time, she actually meant it.

"Even between writing?" I laughed. "I feel so bad spending so much time holed up in my room these last couple of weeks."

"You still have to make a living." Vera smiled. "And I need another story."

Hearing my sister say those words made me feel like the happiest writer in the world.

"Me too," Lana seconded.

"Really?"

"Absolutely." Lana's eyes widened. "And I'm kind of dying to know what you're writing about."

"It's top secret," I teased.

Vera pretended to throw me a dirty look. "I bet your redheaded sidekick knows."

I laughed. "Jack?"

"What's up with him, anyway?" Vera asked. "You said you were just friends, but..."

Lana nodded. "You two do look pretty chummy."

I flinched and shook my head. "He's an amazing friend, but I can't imagine anything other than the friend zone with him."

"You don't get the feels?" Vera teased.

I laughed, shaking my head. "The feels? No, definitely no feels."

"He's kinda cute." Lana shrugged. "But I think my standards might have fallen."

I squeezed my eyes shut and tried to make the images go away. "I just... can't."

"And you don't think he's into you?" Vera asked. "I mean, he seems to text and call you a lot."

I shrugged and glanced at my phone, which happened to have a text from Jack.

"It's usually business."

Lana and Vera didn't look convinced.

"Is he single?" Vera asked.

"Yeah, but it's because he's married to his job. The publisher works him to death, and I'm not his only client."

"But does he give his other clients this much attention?"

I scowled. "Come to think of it, no."

"Very, very interesting." Lana laughed. "Samantha is as oblivious as ever."

"I'm not oblivious. I'm the exact opposite of oblivious. I make a living noticing things and making up stories about them."

"Maybe so, but you've never been really quick on the uptake when it came to boys." Vera was looking through the box of photos as she spoke.

"Well, I'm astute enough to know that Jack is not interested but Garrett is."

Vera let out an evil laugh. "Whatever you say. But does Jack know about Garrett?"

"Kind of. I've mentioned him a bit."

Vera grinned. "I guess time will tell."

I rolled my eyes. "Maybe you should be the writer. You have an overactive imagination."

Both of my sisters laughed, and for the first time in years, I felt like I had my sisters back.

# CHAPTER TWENTY-SIX

*Garrett*

It had been a week since I'd slept with Samantha, and I couldn't get her out of my head, but there was so much I'd been keeping from her. I knew so much about her, but I wanted to know even more, yet I'd been very skilled about leaving details vague about me.

Sure, she knew my family was tight and I loved my stepbrother and parents and stepmom like my own, but I'd pretty much skimmed right over anything to do with my dating life.

There was a reason I'd always let people, even Wyatt, think my dating life was more active than it really was. It was a lot easier to pretend to care than to actually give a damn.

But with Samantha, I more than cared. I wanted to spend every second with her and protect her from the world, even though she didn't need any protecting.

The thing about Samantha was that every discussion, every touch seemed intimate, and after sleeping with her last week, I didn't want to let her go.

When she'd called this morning and asked if she could stop by my house on the way to run errands, I nearly screamed my answer.

I'd since cooled off a little bit.

Literally and figuratively.

I had to take a cold shower and stare at engineering plans of our new apartment complex a town over.

But she kept popping into my head.

And what else popped in was how I hadn't seen my therapist since I'd started seeing Samantha.

I was worried she was coming over to tell me she was leaving already, but I didn't think she would. Not yet. I knew there was still work to be done with her sisters, and I highly doubted that Samantha would leave until the relationship between the three of them at least had hope of being repaired.

My doorbell rang, and I halfway expected Max to start barking and then I remembered.

Max was gone too.

I let out a deep groan before getting up from my desk. There was a lot I had to tell Samantha, and today just might be the day.

As I walked to the front door, I saw her leaning and peeking into the window next to the door. I grinned and waved when she spotted me. She looked completely mortified, which was fun to see since she always seemed so together.

Except for the granny-pants-in-the-pocket trick. That totally threw her for a loop.

I smiled as I opened the door, and she jumped on her

toes and waved. "Hi."

Not bothering to return the wave, I pulled her into my arms.

"Missed you," I whispered near her ear, and she giggled.

"Missed you too." She looked into my eyes, and I was ready to take her to my bedroom.

"Are you always this sexy?" I growled, and she laughed harder.

"I think the small town has gotten to you." She winked, taking a step back as I let her go. "I'm really not all that."

But she knew as much as I did that she was everything and more.

At least to me.

I grinned, thinking back to her legs wrapped around my waist and...

"Hey, no." She laughed. "Get your mind out of the gutter. I know exactly what you're thinking about, and I came over to talk business."

Samantha looked around my foyer and smiled. "This is so you."

I cocked my head and tried to imagine what she was seeing. I had a few family pictures on the wall, a couple of Max, and some of Renee.

*Oh, shit.*

I didn't even remember I'd had some of Renee on my wall.

Samantha followed my gaze to the photos and took a step closer and examined them.

My pulse started going crazy, and I had no idea why.

There was nothing to hide.

I wanted to be open.

Samantha turned slowly and her eyes connected with mine.

"You have a dog?" she asked.

I drew a deep breath and nodded slowly. "I did have one. Max passed away not even a year ago."

Her hands whipped to her mouth. "I'm so sorry. I know how difficult that can be."

I smiled, seeing immediate compassion run through Samantha's gaze.

That was the thing about her.

Samantha always cared.

She was one of those who'd tear up from a sappy commercial coming over the radio. I know this because I saw it happen a couple of times on our trip over to see Wyatt. It was like I got to see right into her soul during those moments.

"Max was a special pup. Always there for me. Completely stole my heart."

"Max sounds like he was a good boy." She grinned.

"Max was a *she*, and yes, she left a mark."

Samantha walked over to me and slid her arm around my waist. "I'm sorry."

I smiled and shook my head. "There are some things I'd like to tell you."

Her brows rose. "Yeah?"

I nodded. "I know I haven't really been all that open about my relationships."

She smiled coyly. "I thought you didn't really do relationships, all just stories and stuff like that."

I knew she was giving me shit, but I also knew she deserved to know.

Sliding my hand over hers, I nudged her down the hall toward the family room that overlooked my back yard.

"I love your home," she said, glancing around the family room that was open into the kitchen.

"Thanks. I worked with an architect to build it. It's too big just for me."

"It's really pretty." She smiled and sat on the couch, and I sat next to her. "A little larger than what I'm used to in New York."

"Yeah?" I asked, trying to imagine Samantha in her own place.

It was probably tiny and packed with books.

She nodded. "I have a nice kitchen by apartment living standards, but it doesn't really have that much character."

"I imagine your place to be filled with books."

"You imagine it?" she asked, smiling.

"I imagine everything about you, Sam." I smiled, feeling like we might not get much talking in after all.

"Is that so?"

I nodded. "In fact, I can't really imagine my life without you in it."

Sam bit her bottom lip and glanced toward my fireplace.

She was still thinking of going back.

No doubt about it.

Was that why she wanted to stop by?

To let me know she was leaving?

"Things between my sisters and me are really starting to change for the better." She smiled.

*Please don't leave yet.*

"That's great."

She nodded. "I think the stress of the inn has been eating at their very existence, and they don't even know it."

"It's a lot to keep something like that up and running."

Samantha drew a breath. "It is, and I've been thinking a lot about what Cloudberry means to our family. My sisters have done so much to keep it going and thriving, really."

"You're proud of them."

"Extremely." She nodded. "I hope they know that."

"I think they do." I smiled. "And I think they'll know even more by the time you leave."

"I just wish I could give them a break."

A thought occurred to me, and I couldn't keep it in.

"What if Wyatt and I take over the inn for a day? Train us on the important things, like checking guests in or whatever, and you three spend some time together."

Her eyes widened. "Really?"

I nodded. "I think it would be fun for you guys."

I had no idea if Wyatt was going to be up for the

challenge, but he had no choice. I needed Sam to connect with her sisters so she'd want to stay here.

"Wow. Thanks." She beamed, sliding her hand to my knees. "I'll talk to them about it."

A couple of seconds of silence sat between us, but she moved a little closer.

"I know it's not my business, but I noticed you seemed pretty close with another female besides Max."

I let out a deep breath, laughing quietly. "You noticed, did you?"

She nodded, her eyes connecting with mine.

Now was the time to tell Samantha everything.

I just prayed I didn't scare her off.

Or make her think she was a rebound relationship, although after this long, I doubted it would qualify.

Or make Sam think I couldn't love again.

Because I could.

I really, *really* could.

"I remember your mentioning that you'd had one really serious relationship," she prompted.

"That was Renee."

Samantha nodded but stayed silent.

"Max was actually our dog together. We picked her out as a puppy."

"So, this was the serious relationship."

My chest tightened, and I nodded. "Very. We were engaged."

"Were?" she whispered, sensing something ominous floating around my words.

I swallowed down the hoarseness in my throat. "Renee passed away."

Samantha gasped, and her eyes instantly filled with tears. "I'm so sorry. I'm..."

I shook my head. "It's okay. I've wanted to tell you about her. I just..."

She didn't say a word. Instead, Samantha was studying me intently.

"I just didn't know how to bring anything up."

"I knew you'd lost someone you loved." She touched my cheek. "I could tell by the way you looked at me when I spoke about my mom."

I shoved my fingers through my hair. "It's so complicated."

"Love often is." She nodded. "That's why it's one of the most written about subjects of all time. It's not easy. It's not hard. It's easy and hard. It's messy. It's clean. It's everything and nothing you want all at once because you might lose it."

I couldn't help but fall even more for the woman in front of me.

Samantha smiled. "Renee was beautiful."

I nodded. "Inside and out. She was my best friend. We were joined at the hip. It seemed like life was all figured out."

"Until it wasn't." Samantha drew a breath.

"I never expected it." I shook my head, feeling the tightness in my chest starting to lessen. "I was talking to

Wyatt a couple of months back about where we thought we'd be by this age, and I thought I'd have the whole thing. Wife, kids, Max."

Samantha cocked her head slightly. "I'm so sorry. I can't even imagine planning and creating a future and having it ripped away like that."

"When we fell in love, I didn't realize it was a different type of love, though."

"What do you mean?"

"It's going to sound awful no matter how I say it."

She shook her head. "It's okay. I won't judge you."

"I didn't realize there were different types of love." I let out a deep breath. "I loved her with everything I had. The ache is always with me, but the love I felt wasn't rolled up in passion and chemistry or even attraction."

Samantha dropped her gaze to the couch, and I'd worried that I'd gone too far.

When she brought her eyes back to mine, I saw tears welling.

She felt what I was trying to explain. I didn't even need words. I didn't need to continue. She knew.

"But the love I had with Renee was what I needed then. It was the kind of love I needed at that moment in my life."

"That's a really beautiful thing," Samantha whispered, wiping away a stray tear.

"It's taken a lot of therapy to realize it." I held Samantha's hand. "And having you waltz into town made me realize the kind of love I need now."

"Which is?"

"The kind of love that's so deep it hurts."

# CHAPTER TWENTY-SEVEN

*Samantha*

My sisters jumped at the chance that Garrett and Wyatt had offered, and Vera and Lana picked a day where most guests weren't checking in until we returned in the afternoon, but they went over everything with the brothers on the off chance that the guests arrived early.

By the time we'd piled into Lana's car, I could feel the tension already gone.

"You ready for a spa day?" I asked. "We'll just drive over to Silver Ridge and—"

Vera whipped her gaze to me, and I snickered. "Kidding."

Silver Ridge was the resort that Drew North owned with his brothers.

"You'd better be. That's downright evil."

I grinned, wondering if she'd ever called Drew North.

"I am totally kidding. Promise. Pinky swear it, even."

Lana drove down the driveway. "Tell me where to go."

"I booked some massages in La Connor at Tulipa Spa and then a late lunch on the waterfront."

"Nice." Lana glanced at me sitting in the passenger seat. "This was a really sweet idea for you to think up."

I chuckled. "I have a confession. It was actually Garrett's idea."

Lana laughed. "Well, you two make a good team."

I nodded. It was hard to disagree with that statement. I really felt at ease with Garrett and the sexual attraction was only getting stronger. To say we had chemistry was an understatement, but the spiritual connection with him was something I didn't even think possible.

I thought back to his words the last time I saw him.

He wanted *a love so deep it hurt.*

I held in a sigh realizing I was on the very precipice of that kind with him, and that scared me. I didn't want to hurt. I wanted to shield myself from that kind of longing, and I'd mastered doing so in New York.

But the desire to be near Garrett burned through me. He was like a magnet that pulled me to him, and if I didn't go, I could feel the pull get stronger and stronger.

"How's it going with Garrett?" Vera asked.

"Amazing," I nearly sang. "I'm really falling for him."

"Does he have anything to do with why you're still here?" Lana asked.

I shook my head. "No. I'm here for you guys. I want to be useful."

"Well, as much cooking as you've been doing for us, I wouldn't call it useful. I'm going to have to order new jeans." Lana grinned, and I rolled my eyes.

"Please. You're as skinny as a rail. I'm the one with the extra pounds."

"I wish I had your body." Vera chuckled. "Instead, I look like a beanpole. Lana and I weren't blessed with curves."

Lana nodded in agreement.

"Well, I'm glad you see them as curves. I look down and see bulges... lots and lots of bulges." I laughed. "But Garrett seems to overlook them."

"Overlook them?" Vera laughed. "More like devours them. I see how he looks at you."

Happiness filled me to the brim. At least I knew Garrett's reactions to me weren't in my head. I always felt like he thought I was the sexiest woman in the world and all I had to do was walk in front of him.

"What do you think he's going to do when you go back?" Lana asked, turning off the highway to La Connor.

A pit in my stomach suddenly appeared. "I'm not sure. I..."

"I mean, I'm assuming you're going back to New York."

I nodded. "Oh, yeah. Totally."

"I think he's going to miss you really bad." Vera sighed. "Like, it's gonna hurt."

I swallowed down the lump in my throat and nodded. "Yeah. It's not going to be pleasant for either of us."

But my life was in New York.

Wasn't it?

I glanced at my sisters. "What if you sold Cloudberry?"

Lana's eyes widened and Vera gasped and they both

shouted, "*Never!*" in unison.

"I know you say that now, but is it really what you want?" I glanced at Lana and her expression hardened.

"I wouldn't know what else to do," Lana said softly. "It's all I have."

"Me too," Vera said from the backseat. "I mean, what are we gonna do in our mid-thirties? Start completely over?"

I tried a different approach. "I'm just not sure it makes you happy anymore."

"Life isn't about being happy. It's about paying the bills." Vera chuckled.

I nodded. "True."

"But seriously. I can't imagine having the inn leave our family." Lana pressed her lips together. "It will all work out. It always does."

I loved Cloudberry with all my heart. The old inn actually energized me. It gave me new ideas, purpose, and joy. When I looked at my sisters and how they interacted with one another and even the inn, I wasn't sure I could say the same.

But I wasn't about to point that out. Our relationships were finally moving forward, and I wasn't about to screw it up.

Lana found a place to park at the Tulipa Spa and Vera squealed in delight.

I hadn't really heard a squeal from Vera since she was a teenager. I laughed and got out of the car as Vera reached back in to grab her purse.

"I can't believe how excited I am for this." Vera

grinned. "I have knots in my shoulders that I'm pretty sure have been there for years."

Guilt flooded through me as I thought about the massage I'd gotten right before I'd stepped on the plane to come to Washington, or the one a few weeks before that. Life really was different for all of us, and I couldn't keep brushing it aside.

Whether my sisters knew it or not, they needed help. They needed freedom to have a life aside from the inn.

Cloudberry Inn didn't have to be a family legacy.

But then, why did I get a pit in my stomach when I thought about the old mansion not being in our family?

I waved toward the tiny Victorian house that had been turned into a day spa. "Onward. We don't want to be late."

"The last time I had a massage was the gift card you sent me five years ago," Lana said offhandedly.

I didn't even know if she'd been getting the gifts I sent. I never heard anything, but I always tried to send a little something on birthdays and holidays.

We climbed the steps and an older woman behind the counter smiled at us.

"The Roberts sisters." She stood and handed us all a robe. "Right down that hall are dressing rooms where you can leave your items, and I'll come back to get you when your therapists are ready for you."

Vera's brows shot up. "Did you trick us into a family therapy session? I thought we were getting massages."

"I don't think there's a therapist in the world who could help us." I laughed. "We're on our own."

Vera and Lana wandered into some dressing rooms

on the right and closed the ivory curtains while I walked into one on my left.

I quickly closed the curtain and undressed, leaving my clothes in a tidy pile.

I didn't actually realize how tense I was since being at Cloudberry. Granted, Garrett helped in that department, but I was still constantly worried about offending my sisters. We'd made a ton of progress. They had both opened up to me more than I'd ever hoped, but I felt like I could still easily destroy the positive steps we'd all made.

"Okay, ladies," the receptionist called. "They're ready for you."

When I stepped out of the dressing room, I saw two female massage therapists and one incredibly sexy male as the female closest to me called my name.

Lana and Vera exchanged funny looks right before the second female called Vera's name. When the man stepped forward, I held in a giggle and glanced over my shoulder to see Lana's cheeks flaming red.

To say he was good-looking didn't give the poor guy justice, and I was pretty sure Lana was going to kill me later, but when I'd made the appointment, they didn't have three females available. So...

"How's your day been going so far?" my massage therapist asked.

"Pretty good."

"What brings you in today? Do you have any special areas you'd like me to concentrate on?"

"My neck and shoulders." I looked at the table and hid a giggle thinking about Lana having to disrobe and slide under the sheet. "I like kind of deep tissue."

Was it payback?

Maybe a little.

"Okay. I'll just step outside so you can get under the sheet. Face down, and I'll be right back in."

I nodded and quickly tossed my robe to the chair and managed to wriggle my way onto the massage table and stick my face into the open head rest as my cheeks got smushed and my nose twisted while trying to work the sheet back over my leg and half a cheek that had slipped out.

When I finally got situated, I heard the door open and let out a blissful sigh.

I heard the oil being spread in the therapist's hands, and I happily prepared for a deep tissue massage to push all the tension away.

When two hands softly touched my bare shoulders, my eyes blinked wide open.

Those weren't female hands.

Were they?

As palms pressed into my shoulders and a little moan escaped my lips, I was certain whoever's hands were on my back didn't belong to the lady I'd just met.

Did Lana switch on me?

I never liked getting massages from male therapists, but this...

This was good.

"How about there?" The moment he spoke, I knew it was Garrett, and every cell in my body lit up.

"You've got some skills," I mumbled as the table

pressed into my cheeks.

"Maybe I should switch professions." He ran his wide fingers along my shoulders and my body trembled from his touch.

"How did you talk your way in here, and who is running the inn?"

"It wasn't hard. They thought it was romantic, and Wyatt's got it under control."

I chuckled. "So you say."

Garrett pulled the sheet lower and moved his hands along my spine. Every touch sent me into another orbit as he moved his hands up and down my back.

"I feel like you've done this before," I whispered.

"Never," he said. "It's my first time."

I could hear the smile in his voice.

"You're hired," I mumbled.

He bent down and whispered near my ear. "Promise?"

"Mmmhmm." Anticipation was building at an unstoppable pace.

Was he going to kiss me, turn me over, and make love to me?

Or just tease me until my time was up?

Just the thought sent goosebumps over me.

"Cold?" he asked, his voice low and gravelly as I imagined myself under him.

It didn't matter that we were in the middle of some spa. All I could think about was being in his arms and reliving what we'd shared only once before.

Without wasting another second, I turned over and let the sheet fall to the ground.

His eyes canvassed my body as heat filled his gaze.

"You're so beautiful," he whispered.

And he made me feel that way.

Garrett took a step back and looked at the table, and I let out a giggle, knowing exactly what the builder in him was trying to surmise.

Would the table hold our weight?

I smiled and sat up, bringing my legs over the side.

Garrett's lips parted ever so slightly as I ran my hands along his sides and pulled his shirt toward me. All I wanted was to taste Garrett Mason again.

He brought his mouth to mine, and my entire world spun into a fantasy I never even knew I had.

My fingers fumbled with the button of his jeans, and I struggled to push them down.

Garrett's kisses deepened as I wrapped my legs around his waist and let him enter as I closed my eyes and leaned back on my hands, his kisses going down my neck to my breasts as we found our special rhythm.

Every piece of me melted into him as my body tightened around him with every thrust, his mouth and hands teasing my nipples, and I knew I couldn't last.

"God," he whispered into the crook of my neck. "You're amazing."

As every part of my body ignited, he cupped my chin with his hands and brought his mouth back to mine.

"I love you, Samantha Roberts."

# CHAPTER TWENTY-EIGHT

*Garrett*

I knew I had limited time to convince Sam to stay. I could just feel it. Even though our connection was strong, we could talk for hours, and we couldn't keep our hands off one another, I knew she was still planning on going back to New York.

I could sense it, even when I'd snuck up on her during the massage. A smile quickly slid across my face as I thought about how that ended.

I'd honestly gone there thinking I was just going to give her a massage, but the girl was full of her own surprises.

But none of it mattered because I knew she was going back to New York.

After all, she already had her entire life back there. She owned a place, had a publisher at arm's length, friends, and everything at her fingertips back in the city.

So, I did what any decent human being would do and

decided to plan a reunion of sorts. From talking with Samantha, she'd had a really strong friend network growing up here, but she hadn't kept in touch with people once she'd left.

I managed to book a banquet room and invite as many classmates of hers as I could find. I even invited Violet. And might I add on a side note, I found it completely odd that Violet still harbored resentment toward me. She'd already moved on and had a family.

I shook the thought away and looked around the room. I'd hired a florist to make the bare space look a little more inviting, but it wasn't that easy when a forest-green rug covered the concrete floor and that was considered the extent of the décor.

There were good and bad things about living in a small town. I highly doubted this equaled anything Sam was used to back in New York where the streets glittered with car lights and the building interiors sparkled with glass and gold.

Nope. Out here, it was more of a do-it-yourself type of operation.

But I'd made sure the café we went to would cater her favorite meal, chicken-fried steak.

I glanced at my phone. I had about thirty minutes before people started arriving and forty-five minutes until Lana and Vera would be bringing Samantha. I personally knew some of the people I'd managed to track down, but a lot of them I hadn't a clue who they were. Hopefully, there wouldn't be any sworn enemies from high school traipsing around soon.

The door clicked open, and I looked over to see Wyatt moseying into the space.

He looked around the room. "Wow. You've gone all out."

I laughed and nodded. "It was what I could find on short notice."

"Why not just do it at Cloudberry?" he asked.

*Why didn't I think of that?*

Wyatt narrowed his eyes on me and laughed. "Dude, you're kidding. You didn't think of that?"

I laughed and shrugged. "Samantha would have figured it out."

"I doubt it. They have functions there all the time."

"Whatever. This is a good neutral space."

Wyatt looked around. "That it is. You really think she's going to head back to New York soon?"

I nodded, feeling the tightening in my chest again. "I do. What's out here for her?"

"I'd like to say *you* at this point." Wyatt smiled.

"Thanks for throwing me a bone, but I'm not enough."

Wyatt folded his arms over his chest. "You never know."

The caterers started setting up the buffet as a bartender took his station.

"I've got a pretty good idea." I smiled.

"Hey, have you seen her editor online?"

I hadn't really looked too much up other than her writing. I saw a couple of interviews pop up, but I didn't want to stalk her online. I was actually enjoying the natural discovery, the old way of falling for someone.

I shook my head. "No, what's up?"

"Probably nothing." Wyatt glanced at the bar.

"Then why'd you bring up nothing?"

"He just looks really..." He twisted lips into a scowl. "Protective."

I didn't know her editor was a *he*.

Not that it mattered.

But I did know that Samantha considered her editor one of her few friends back in New York.

I tried to brush it off. "They've worked together for a long time."

Wyatt nodded. "I know. Almost since the beginning. He's a few years older than her, from what I can tell."

"Did you get his address? Can I go beat him up?" I joked, and Wyatt grinned.

"You may want to with the way he hovers around her. His name is Jack Olson."

"Dude, are you seriously going to burst my bubble right now?" I slid my phone on and quickly typed in this character's name.

Sure enough, as soon as the photos popped up, I could see what Wyatt was talking about. He was all over her, and Samantha looked clueless, completely oblivious.

She had to have some idea.

Right?

"He just looks all up in her business." Wyatt laughed. "I mean, I don't know. Maybe it's nothing."

I turned off the screen and shrugged. "Can't worry

about it too much."

"No, I was just curious if you knew about him, that's all." Wyatt noticed that the bartender was a cute blonde. "I think I'm thirsty."

I chuckled. "Leave it to you to drop a bomb and move on to the next topic."

"What can I say?"

Wyatt wandered over to the bartender, who seemed completely enamored with her first customer, him.

I glanced out the window to see a couple of cars pull up.

It was getting close. I rubbed my hands together in anticipation, but now all I could think about was Samantha's editor.

Wouldn't she have mentioned him if she were in a thing with him?

And by *thing*, what did I mean?

Was I even in a *thing* with her?

We'd only had sex twice, and we didn't spend every waking minute together.

But I thought about her every second I wasn't with her.

Yeah, I had it really bad.

I walked over to my brother who was trying some pretty lame one-liners that were completely working on the bartender.

Wyatt smiled. "This is my brother, Garrett. Garrett, this is Amanda. Isn't that a pretty name?"

I nodded. "Beautiful."

"Is there something I can get you, sir?"

Wyatt leaned over the bar. "He'll have a Blue Sapphire martini. Straight up."

I laughed and shook my head. Wyatt knew me well.

Amanda shook the alcohol and ice before pouring it into the glass and handed it to me.

"At least the place has glass, huh?" Wyatt winked at me, and I laughed.

"It's a classy joint."

I noticed several cars pull up and relief started spilling through me. I'd planned this pretty last-minute and the worst thing that could happen was to have a reunion for Samantha and then have nobody show.

I spotted Violet, but I didn't see her family, which made me a little nervous, but I was happy to see several other people I recognized, mostly through my business endeavors.

When the guests started arriving, heading to the bar, and gathering appetizers while they mingled, the party felt like a success.

Now, hopefully, the guest of honor would think so too.

It could go either way, but I remembered how excited she got seeing Violet. Maybe Samantha just needed a little boost in the right direction to jog her memory, remind her that this was home.

My phone buzzed, and I saw a text come over from Lana. She and Vera were on the way with Samantha.

I smiled at Violet, who looked a little less annoyed with me as she walked over.

"How's it going, Garrett?" she asked, taking a sip of

wine.

I nodded. "Pretty good. Thanks for coming. I know how excited Samantha was to see you."

"She's a great gal." Violet nodded. "Wouldn't miss it for the world, and I wanted to apologize."

Shock must have registered on my face because Violet laughed.

"Don't get used to it," she assured me.

I looked around the room, seeing so many people file in to support Samantha, and my heart knew she belonged here, if only she'd see it.

I laughed. "Believe me, I won't."

"Samantha may seem bigtime now, but she's got a heart the size of a watermelon. I think that's why she wrote. Dealing with people was too much and emotions were too powerful, but in her stories, she has control."

My gaze darted back to Violet. "Wow. I never even thought about it."

She smiled, nodding. "I knew her all through school, and she was the sweetest person. It's why she was so popular. Although, I doubt she even remembers she was well-liked."

"Thank you, Violet. That explains a lot."

Another text came over from Lana. They were rounding the corner.

"I'd better round up the troops," I told Violet. "The Robertses are almost here."

Before I even had a chance to gather the group, Violet was already wrangling the troops, shouting orders and telling them to look pretty and get ready to surprise

Samantha.

I chuckled, thanking God that I hadn't somehow wound up with Violet. I wasn't ready for that kind of order.

I saw Vera's car pull into the parking lot with Lana in the front passenger seat and Vera driving. The back door opened, and out stepped Samantha, looking as beautiful as ever.

She was in a pair of jeans and a billowy top that the sunlight made nearly transparent if it weren't for the white tank she had underneath.

I couldn't help but smile as I watched her stretch toward the sky while her sisters piled out of the car. She really didn't have a clue as to what was coming her way. As the sisters made their way to the door, Samantha laughed, and her sisters looked like sisters should.

Happy.

The moment Samantha stepped inside, the crowd yelled, "Surprise", and she looked like she was about to fall over. Her hands flew to her mouth, and she turned to her sisters, who both pointed at me in the crowd.

She dropped her hands to her side and whispered a quick *thank you* before old friends and classmates descended on her.

Seeing Samantha's eyes light up as old acquaintances and friends laughed and chatted with her told me I'd done the right thing.

Even if she decided to leave and go back to New York, she knew she had friends out here.

"You really love her, don't you?" Wyatt asked, standing behind me.

I drew a breath and nodded. "I really do."

As the night slowly came to an end, Samantha's phone rang, and she quickly picked it up. Her expression went from relaxed to concerned to exhilarated all in the span of ten seconds. When she hung up, and her gaze found mine across the room.

I knew.

Samantha was going back to New York.

# CHAPTER TWENTY-NINE

*Samantha*

Even though I thought I was somewhat ready to go to New York and exciting things were waiting for me there, I didn't want to leave Cloudberry Inn.

Or my sisters.

Or Garrett.

But I knew this day was coming.

I'd only planned on being in Washington for the weekend, which turned into a couple of months.

I let out a sigh and zipped my suitcase. Since I had my rental car, I'd planned on driving myself to the airport even though my sisters and Garrett offered several times. It was for the best. I'd probably tear up and make a mess of myself before I boarded the plane.

Lugging a suitcase off the bed and down the hall, I heard my sisters in the foyer busily checking in two groups as I made my way down the stairs. I tucked my suitcase in the corner and wandered down the hall, through the kitchen, and to the study.

I pulled out a personal check made out to my sisters and placed it on the desk.

I knew my sisters wouldn't ask for help, but I couldn't turn my back on them.

As I walked out of the study and into the kitchen, I poured myself a cup of coffee and took a few sips before Vera bounded into the kitchen.

I hadn't seen that much exuberance from her...

Ever.

"What's got you all excited?" I rinsed out my cup. "That you're finally getting rid of me?"

"Not even." Vera rolled her eyes but the smile remained. "I'm going to miss you. Big time."

"I feel the same. It's going to be really weird going back to the city. It's so peaceful here, and I was so much more productive. I'm almost done with my book."

"You're always welcome here," Vera said softly. "I hope you know that."

I nodded, sensing that for the first time in a long time, I actually was. "It's been a good trip."

Lana came into the kitchen and walked toward me, opening her arms for a big hug.

"I wish you didn't have to go back so soon," she said, squeezing me tight.

"Same." My mouth was by muffled her shoulder, and she laughed.

"Squeezing a little tight?" Lana stepped back and smiled at me as if she were looking at me through a new lens. "Don't be a stranger."

"Same goes for you two. I know it's tough leaving the inn and scheduling and all of that, but if you ever need help, I'll be here on the first flight out."

Lana held my hand. "I believe it."

"It's true."

The dull ache in my chest sharpened as I thought about leaving this place, but I knew I had to go.

I cleared my throat. "I'd better get going."

Vera nodded, and my sisters followed me to pick up my suitcase before I walked out the front of Cloudberry.

They both stood on the porch and waved, hugging one another as I wandered over to my rental car.

Maybe this trip wasn't just good for me. Seeing my sisters actually hug meant the world because when I showed up, I was pretty certain they'd given each other enough sideways glances and eye rolls to last a lifetime.

I opened the trunk and shoved the suitcase next to the other one I'd already put inside earlier.

It was weird to think that by tomorrow morning, I'd be back in the city. Now, hopefully, I could sleep on the plane and make use of the red-eye flight.

"We love you," Lana hollered as I climbed into my car.

I bit back the tears that suddenly surfaced and let out a deep breath.

This was the right decision.

The moment my editor called telling me that I had multiple offers for film rights on my yet-to-be finished book, I knew I had to fly back.

Well, Jack told me I had to fly back.

So here I was, about to leave everyone and everything I loved behind.

"Love you too," I shouted back before closing the car door. It wasn't long before I turned on the car, drove down the drive, and my sisters soon looked like tiny ants in the rearview.

By the time I got to the airport, I was a wreck. I dumped off the rental car, hauled out my suitcases, and made the trek to the terminal.

I missed Cloudberry.

I missed Garrett.

I missed my sisters.

It was like every part of my body was screaming for me to stay off that plane, but I had to go. I punched my information into the screen to check in for my flight when I thought I heard something behind me.

I grabbed my ticket and put the label on my bag to check before shoving it toward the waiting attendant.

"I couldn't let you leave without saying goodbye one more time." Garrett's voice wrapped around me like a warm embrace that I desperately needed to feel.

I slowly spun around to see Garrett smiling and tears touched my lids.

"Just as beautiful as I remembered." He grinned, and my heart skipped a beat.

What was I doing leaving this man behind?

"You're not so shabby yourself." I grinned, tapping his chest as I pulled myself together.

He let out a low hum and shook his head. "I've really gotten used to having you around town."

I smiled and nodded. "But I'm only a phone call away."

Garrett kept the smile on his face as he nodded. "But I won't be able to do this."

He slowly brushed a few loose strands from my shoulder and brought his mouth down to mine.

God, I would miss these kisses. I let out a little hum, and I felt him smile as he kissed me deeper. After a few seconds, he took a step back.

"You go back there and knock them dead." Garrett smiled, exposing the dimples.

I smiled. "Keep watch over my sisters."

Garrett nodded. "As best as I can, but I'm pretty sure Vera can handle herself."

He pressed his lips to my forehead, and I drew a deep breath, closing my eyes and memorizing every single detail about Garrett Mason.

"I'd better go."

Garrett took a step back and nodded as I rolled my carry-on suitcase behind me. I stopped one more time before getting in line and turned around to see Garrett still watching me.

It wasn't until I'd gone through the security check, purchased some random magazines and snacks, and had fallen into a chair by my gate that the first tear tried to escape. I sniffed and dabbed my eyes with my sleeve, willing myself to get over it.

This was exactly why I never should have gone to dinner with Garrett Mason. Now, my heart hurt, my stomach was knotted, and I felt nauseous all because I missed him so badly.

By the time I boarded the plane, ate my snacks, and put on my headphones, I fell asleep dreaming about the life I'd almost had.

When the captain's voice boomed into the cabin rousing me from my sleep and rambling about arriving at JFK three minutes early, I was panicked. The moment I realized where I was, my heart sank and I knew I'd made a huge mistake.

Once the plane landed and I waddled down the aisle with my carry-on and found my way to the baggage carousel, I forced myself to concentrate on my surroundings.

This was New York.

My city.

My state.

It had given me so much, and I didn't need to go and start thinking the grass was greener.

I spotted my suitcase and hoisted it onto the ground when I heard Jack, my editor, calling behind me.

Usually, hearing his voice brought me a sense of calm and peace, but this morning, it did the exact opposite.

I wanted to run.

Far away.

"Surprise," Jack called jokingly as he came up behind me. "New York missed you."

I forced a laugh and nodded, wishing I could say the same thing.

"It felt like a short trip," I confessed.

Jack nodded and grabbed my suitcase, but I noticed

something different about his expression. "I thought you might like me to pick you up so you didn't have to Uber your way to your apartment."

I smiled, wishing that was precisely what I got to do.

"So, did you charm your sisters?" Jack asked.

And that was when the pit in my stomach only grew.

Things here just felt fake, artificial.

My relationships with my sisters, as complicated as they may be, were sacred. I didn't want to just joke about them as some abstract concept, laugh the troubles away, and move on.

I didn't want to move on.

I wasn't kidding when I said I didn't have many friendships, but as I walked behind Jack making his way to the car, I realized I wasn't so sure this relationship was much of anything either.

Sure, he showed up to the airport, but really, most of the time, he got to show up for fancy dinners, publishing galas, and road trips for my signing tours.

And of course, the occasional vacation.

Why wouldn't he want to be my friend?

I shook my head, scolding myself for suddenly turning cynical. It wasn't my nature. I didn't like the feel of it, but as I watched Jack rolling my suitcase in front of me, I had to wonder.

The car ride was a whirlwind, and I was beyond thrilled when he finally pulled up in front of my building.

"Need help getting in?" Jack asked.

A shudder ran though me.

"Nope. I got it, but it really was nice of you to wake up at this godawful hour to pick me up."

"It's what I do." He smiled, and I nodded.

That was when it hit me.

He was a paid friend.

"Well, regardless. Thank you." I opened the door, crawled out of the car, and made my way to the trunk which Jack had remotely opened.

I chuckled to myself thinking back to Garrett. He would have gotten out of the car.

A smile touched my lips as Garrett swam through my mind.

I wondered what he was doing right now.

Probably still sleeping, with the time difference.

I rolled my suitcases onto the curb and gave a quick wave to Jack before heading inside.

It was good to be home.

When I opened the door to my apartment, it felt oddly cold. I took a step inside and let the door shut behind me when I noticed a floral arrangement on my kitchen counter.

My apartment wasn't one of those big, fancy ones everyone always imagined when living in Manhattan. Mine was the type where once you stepped inside, you could see pretty much everything from that vantage point. The kitchen was to the right with an eating bar. On the other side of the eating bar was an eating nook where I had set up my desk instead of a dining room table, and then to my left was a family room and a door leading to my bedroom.

But it was mine, and for that I was happy.

I left my bags behind me and wandered over to the flowers. When I tugged on the envelope sticking up from the arrangement, I got a weird feeling. The only person who had a key to my place was Jack, but it was reserved for emergencies, and I'd never had one.

When I opened the envelope and read that Jack had sent the flowers, it seemed intrusive. Why would he come into my apartment? I set the card down and slowly looked around.

Had Jack snooped?

All the books on my shelves seemed in place, the throws and pillows on the couch were where I'd left them, and my bedroom seemed untouched.

It should have brought me calm, but it didn't.

I'd promised I'd send a text to Garrett when I got to my apartment, so I shot him a quick note and a heart emoji and wished I could be there waking up next to him. I sat on my bed and saw the flowers from where I was sitting.

Jack had written *Congrats* on the card, and what was about to happen was no doubt a big deal. This wasn't just one of those times where you sold away movie rights and the movie never happened. This was a big deal.

My story was going to come to life.

I looked around my empty bedroom and let out a sigh.

"And I have absolutely no one to share it with here," I spoke aloud for extra punch and collapsed onto my bed, knowing I'd made a mistake.

# CHAPTER THIRTY

*Garrett*

Two weeks had gone by since Samantha left, and I couldn't take it any longer. Texts and video chatting didn't cut it. I needed Samantha in my arms. I wanted to feel her warmth, her curves, hear her voice.

Just be near her.

Which was why when I stepped off the plane at JFK, I knew I'd made the right decision. She'd just signed the biggest deal of her career, and all I saw was loneliness drifting in her gaze. She deserved better. She deserved friendships and love and everything in between.

When I punched in the address on my rideshare app, I tried to imagine what Samantha's apartment was going to be like. I'd gotten glimpses of it from the video chat, and it looked cozy, like Samantha. Books were lined on bookshelves and stacked on end tables, and papers were piled on her desk, which I think was in the dining room, and a bouquet of flowers was placed prominently on her kitchen counter.

Those flowers had me worried.

It wasn't like a mixed bouquet.

They were roses.

*Red roses.*

I'd tried to press a little bit about Jack, more as the role of her editor, but she closed up pretty quickly, which wasn't the reaction I was used to with Samantha. She was usually pretty open about everything.

When the car pulled up to the apartment building, I was surprised.

The building was rather unassuming. There wasn't a doorman or even an awning. It was just a regular building stuck in the middle of other regular buildings.

I climbed out and grabbed my bag before looking up to the sliver of sky between the towering structures. It was so weird to me to think that the great expansive sky was a commodity in a place like this. I wasn't even sure if you pressed your cheek to the windows in some of these places that you'd even see it.

I walked over to the entrance of Samantha's building and looked for a buzzer, expecting to see an intercom or something. A woman walked right up behind me, basically shoved her hips in front of me with an air bump, and walked right in. I followed right after her and found an elevator.

The woman went down a hall and into a salon, and I realized the reason there wasn't a buzzer or lock on the front was that the first few floors were mixed use.

As I stepped onto the elevator and pushed the button for Samantha's floor, I realized how very unsafe this building was.

I completely understood that Samantha didn't understand how vulnerable she was, but that was probably because she grew up where and how she grew up. I rocked on my heels and let out a slow sigh.

It wasn't my place to tell her how to start living, but I really hoped it wouldn't matter soon.

When the elevator opened on her floor, my pulse soared. I'd taken the same red-eye flight as Samantha and now I hoped it would be my last, that I could somehow convince her how missed she was.

And it was true. I'd even been getting texts from Lana and Vera checking up on their sister.

It was how life was supposed to be.

I stepped onto the floor and checked which way the numbers went and started toward Samantha's apartment.

When I rounded the bend, I saw Jack standing in front of an open door as he went in for a kiss, and my world completely went into slow motion.

I'd come up with a lot of scenarios on the plane ride here, but this wasn't one of them.

But it all made sense.

The flowers.

Samantha's reactions.

Wanting to live in New York.

I drew a deep breath and about turned around to go to Seattle until I saw Samantha's arms fly out from the apartment and push Jack away.

The dude tripped over his own two feet, and he fell backward just as I came up on the two of them.

Samantha looked horrified as she saw me towering over Jack, and I didn't know if she was afraid I'd beat him to a living pulp or if she was worried I saw the almost-kiss.

Jack scooted back toward the wall and up like a creepy little lizard.

"Who's this?" Jack growled, pointing at me.

My pulse soared as the redhead looked at me like I didn't belong.

Oh, I belonged.

"My boyfriend, Garrett Mason." Samantha gave her editor a cool smile. "The man I've been telling you about since I visited my sisters."

"You barely know him." Jack's voice got louder, which didn't sit well with me. "You've known *me* more than half your life."

Samantha cocked her head slightly. "You're my friend, my editor."

Jack straightened up and glared at me. "You're a nobody."

I smiled and nodded before looking over at Samantha.

"And so are you." Jack pointed his finger at Samantha. "Who do you think talked the publisher into all those deals? Just your agent? No. I sold you. I sold this deal."

My fingers began to tingle with the desire to punch someone.

"You can kiss your career goodbye." Jack stepped closer to Samantha.

*Just one more step.*

*One more step, buddy.*

Samantha straightened and smiled at the man in front of her. "No, I got where I am because of hard work, talent, and a little bit of luck. And I think my agent and publisher will be very interested in hearing about your threats. Remember, I'm the one who brings them *lots* of money."

Samantha glared at the tiny man in front of her, and I couldn't help but let out a low chuckle.

Jack's eyes landed on me, but all I could do was smile wider.

Samantha didn't need my help at all.

She was all woman, all the time.

Jack started to say something, but Samantha interrupted. "And the ink is already dry, Jack."

Without another word, he moved past me and trudged down the hallway without another word.

My eyes connected with Samantha's and I smiled. "Surprise."

She started laughing and shook her head. "I can't believe that just happened, and I really can't believe you're here."

Samantha quickly wrapped her arms around me and pulled me, kissing me like I'd never been kissed before.

"I needed this so badly," she whispered between kisses. "I needed you."

When she parted her lips from mine, I smiled and nodded. "So, this trip was a good idea."

She rested her hands on my chest and smiled. "You have no idea. Come on in."

I grabbed my suitcase and followed her into her apartment. Samantha wasn't kidding when she was being modest about her apartment. It was tiny and cute and everything I loved about Samantha wrapped up into a very New York way of living.

"You like?" she asked, spinning around with her arms up and showing me everything from her front door.

"I do. I can imagine you writing bestseller after bestseller from here." I glanced around the space, seeing all the books and spiral notebooks lying around. "No distractions."

Samantha smiled and curled her hand over mine. "I think I'm kind of ready for some distractions."

"Is that so?"

She nodded and glanced toward the kitchen. "Would you like some coffee? I know how awful those red-eyes can be."

I nodded and walked into the family room.

"Have a seat there on the couch. You can just push my laptop away." She poured me a cup of coffee, and the poured one for herself before coming over and sitting next to me on the white couch. She tucked her legs under her and watched me.

"I can't believe you're here." She grinned.

"In the flesh."

She wiggled her brows and laughed. "I've been thinking so much about you and Cloudberry."

"Your sisters have been texting me nonstop since you came back to New York."

Complete surprise registered over her features. "Really?"

I nodded. "Yeah. They've been asking how you're

doing, if you're done with the end of the book, if I knew what it was about. How you're coping back in New York."

She eyed me coyly. "What did you tell them?"

"The truth." I shrugged. "That I didn't know, which was why I had to come see you."

Samantha took a sip of coffee and nodded.

"I needed to hear straight from your lips that you're happy here in New York, that you don't miss Cloudberry Inn or your sisters or..." I bit my lip and glanced out the window to see more of the same apartment buildings across the way. "Me."

She put her cup down on the end table next to a stack of books and let out a slow breath as I braced for the worst.

"I miss everything about Cloudberry and my sisters, and most of all, you." She pressed her lips together and glanced at her laptop. "Honestly, the moment I got back to New York, it was like all my creative juice just left. I felt so revitalized back home."

*Home.*

I nodded but didn't want to push.

"I've even been thinking about the inn." She brought her legs out from under her and hugged her knees. "I love being there. I love visiting with the guests and ghosts."

I chuckled.

"I love getting to write and garden and cook. Maybe it's because I haven't been doing it every single day of my life for the last fifteen years like they have, but I miss it. I crave it."

I nodded, feeling a glimmer of hope arise.

"I know they miss you, and I do too." I laughed and

shook my head. "I thought I could handle being so far away from you."

"Yeah?" She laughed. "Am I just that irresistible?"

I glanced at the flowers. "Yes, and I noticed two dozen red roses had been delivered to you and that got me thinking."

Samantha cocked her head. "Why?"

I laughed and grabbed her hands in mine. "For a woman who writes a bit of romance into her stories, you're not always that great at picking up on the symbology in your own life."

She closed her eyes and groaned. "I had no idea he was such a creep or that he even had feelings for me."

Samantha got quiet and brought her gaze to mine. "I've been thinking of taking over Cloudberry."

My eyes widened in surprise. "Taking it over?"

She shrugged. "Well, not taking it over. My sisters could stay and do what they'd like, but I just want to take some of the pressure off them." She waited a few seconds. "I probably shouldn't mention this, but they actually ran into some money problems."

My heart stalled.

Damn it—so they were being nice to her for her money.

She waved her hands in the air. "I know what you're thinking. They didn't ask for money. I think Lana had thought about it, but she didn't."

I let out a deep breath as I watched the woman I fell in love with defend them so fiercely. I would do the same for Wyatt.

"They wouldn't be the first who ran the inn and needed a little extra help."

My eyes connected with Samantha's and she nodded. "My mom and dad actually almost lost the inn. It's what motivated my mom to send out my stories. We needed a miracle."

I smiled, nodding slowly. I had no idea. "And you got one."

Samantha nodded slowly. "I look at my sisters, and they've done such a good job with the inn, but it takes so much time and energy and money. I have the money, more than I know what to do with, but having a cushion fund like I do takes the pressure off. They don't have that luxury. The inn could be my passion project if I wanted, and they could finally take time for themselves."

I looked at Samantha in awe. Her spirit was so pure and wholesome and just plain kind.

"Do they know you've been thinking about coming back and offering?"

She shook her head. "I left them a check to cover some taxes they owed, but they never cashed it."

"Maybe they didn't see it."

Samantha shrugged. "Doubt it."

"You do understand that the freedom you have now would go away, right?" I asked, trying to be objective.

"I do." She nodded. "But I also know that I can change things a little bit. I can work having time off into the schedule, and vacancies. They can't. They need the money coming in."

"I hate to ask, but how can you be certain that they'd be okay with giving up the inn?"

She shook her head. "They don't have to give up the inn. In fact, I want to either continue their salaries or buy them out, either way. But they need time to figure out what they want to do with the rest of their lives. I've had that luxury. They never have."

"And what if it's running the inn?" I asked.

"Then they can. I'm not trying to push them out." Samantha blushed. "I'm not trying to brag, but I have more money than I could ever spend. Why not put it to good use? The inn is a good use." She glanced around her apartment and laughed. "I mean, even this is worth millions, and it's paid for."

I shook my head and let out a deep sigh, knowing Samantha's heart was in the right place.

"The inn is a beautiful old place." I nodded. "And you do seem so happy there."

Samantha crawled onto my lap and curled her arms around my neck. "Then it's decided. I'm coming back home."

# CHAPTER THIRTY-ONE

*Samantha*

I pulled up to Cloudberry Inn with a sense of pride and determination. This was my home. This was our home. I glanced over at Garrett, who looked like he'd won the lottery since I'd told him I was moving back to town. He held my hand and squeezed it.

"Do you think your sisters will believe it?" he asked, glancing at the truck behind us.

I'd sold all of my belongings except for my clothes and books. I'd decided to hire Garrett, who already told me he wasn't going to take my money, to redo my little writing shack in the woods. I wanted to modernize it with real walls, electricity, heat, internet, the whole thing.

But first, he needed to have his guys build some built-in bookshelves for my collection that took a moving truck to haul across the country. I never would have guessed I could fit so many books in a tiny apartment, but I did.

I parked in front of the inn and nearly jumped out of the rental car. Garrett jogged next to me as we made our way to the inn.

But when the front door opened and my dad and sisters all walked onto the porch, I turned to Garrett, who was standing next to me.

"Surprise," he whispered.

Pure joy welled up inside me as I ran up the steps to give my dad and sisters a hug. It had been so long since I'd felt like I'd had a family, and Garrett had made it happen.

"So proud of you," my dad whispered as Lana and Vera hugged us both.

"Couldn't have done it without you," I said between happy tears.

My dad slowly let go and both of my sisters gave me a huge hug. "We're so happy to have you back."

I glanced back at Garrett, who was beaming, and I followed my dad and sisters into the inn.

Garrett followed us inside and down the hall to the private family room. I looked to see if he'd also told them my plans, which I doubted he had. He shook his head, and I nodded, knowing it was best to just float my bright idea out there.

"I'm so glad you and your sisters came to your senses." My dad chuckled, shaking his head as he sat in his favorite recliner. "Even in Arizona, I could feel the tension, but I knew better than to step my foot where it didn't belong. But I knew you'd all come back to one another and back to the inn."

I looked over at my dad. "How?"

"It's a magical place," he said simply.

Garrett smiled and took a seat next to me on the couch while my sisters sat on a loveseat.

"It is." I drew in a deep breath and sucked on my bottom lip for a couple of seconds as all eyes stayed on me. "And I know running a place like Cloudberry can have ups and downs, good times and bad times."

"Isn't that the truth?" My dad whistled. "But you girls have done an amazing job."

I nodded. "They have."

Vera and Lana fidgeted but kept their eyes on me. "Anyway, being here has given me more ideas than I ever thought possible for my writing. I feel energized and joyful. Cloudberry Inn makes me feel free."

Lana's eyes teared over.

"But I don't think it does the same for you two."

My dad's brows shot up, and he looked over at his two other daughters. "Is that true?"

Lana shook her head while Vera nodded, and we all laughed.

"While being a place full of magic," my dad began, "it can also suck the life right out of you. That's why I hightailed it to Arizona."

Garrett and my sisters laughed.

"And I don't want that to happen to you guys. When I'm here, it's fun for me because I don't have the same worries as you guys do," I started again.

Vera straightened. "What would we do? This is all I've known. The thought of starting over is terrifying."

Lana nodded in agreement.

"You don't have to start over. In fact, you don't have to leave the inn, but I want to help. I want to help run the inn."

Lana scowled. "I don't understand. You want to live here?"

I nodded. "For a while."

Truthfully, I'd worked everything out with my financial advisor. We went over all of the inn's financials, and it actually had the potential to be a good investment. If I was willing to put in the time, and I was.

"What about when you don't?" Vera asked. "I'm not trying to be a downer, but you don't know what it's like having to have a smile on your face three hundred and sixty-five days a year."

Lana glanced at our sister and scowled. "Neither do you."

We laughed and Vera grinned. "Okay, I fully admit that I might be responsible for a couple of the not-so-great reviews, but it's tough."

I nodded. "Let me help. Let me help make it not so tough."

Lana nodded slowly. "Are you sure you'd want to do this?"

I glanced at my dad, who was watching me carefully, and smiled.

"More than anything."

Garrett reached for my hand and squeezed it. "I want to give you both the same gift you've given me over the years—the ability to imagine the life you want to live and getting to live it."

Tears welled up in Lana's eyes, and she quickly dabbed them away.

My dad chuckled. "I knew we'd have a crier sooner or

later."

Garrett laughed, and my dad winked at him, which was highly suspicious.

"Let me give you this. I have enough money to make this work. I have time, and I have the two best resources at my fingertips to help me along the way." I swallowed down a lump in my throat. "This inn saved me when I didn't even know I needed to be saved."

Lana nodded. "Thank you. I just... thank you."

Vera smiled as her features softened and she took a deep breath. "I don't even know what to imagine my life like, but I want to imagine it so badly."

"So, will you take me up on it?" I asked.

My dad chuckled. "Listen to your youngest sister. She has more money than sense, but I'd take her up on it before she changes her mind."

Lana and Vera looked at each other and then at me. "We do, but we'll be here every step of the way."

I laughed. "I know you will. I'm counting on it."

"Hey, by the way..." my dad began. "Have you thought more about making this place a haunted inn? That could be a whole thing. You know, your mom was certain that we had ghosts." He looked at Lana. "And didn't you say something about a woman here recently whom you and Samantha saw?"

I grimaced. I hadn't actually given too much thought to Margaret. She hadn't really come to mind as I was making this decision, and I wasn't sure if the idea of having ghosts was good or bad.

"We actually more than saw her. We spoke with her."

My dad's expression turned ghostly pale. "That's a whole other level."

Garrett nodded. "It is."

"We could just put the place up for sale." My dad laughed nervously.

I waved the thought away. "Nah. Margaret was super nice, and she was a good listener."

And truthfully, she made me believe in the unexplained and guardian angels again. She felt like my good-luck charm.

"I guess those are two nice qualities to have in a ghost." My dad shrugged and eyed Garrett, who grinned.

Garrett stood and looked down at me. "You know, there's something I've been meaning to ask you about."

I looked around the room and frowned. "Uh, yeah?"

"I already spoke with your father." Garrett got down on one knee, and my world began to spin. "And he gave me permission."

I glanced at my dad and then my sisters as Garrett pulled a ring box out of his pocket.

"Samantha Roberts, will you make me the luckiest man alive and spend the rest of your life with me?" His green eyes fastened on mine, and all I could do was nod as tears of joy rolled down my cheeks. "Is that a yes?"

I nodded and nodded until I could squeak out a *yes* as Garrett placed the engagement ring on my finger.

"I want to be here with you, by your side as you build your dreams," Garrett said, softly kissing me.

It wasn't until an older woman's voice interrupted us with applause that I was brought back to reality.

We all turned to see Margaret standing in the family room, happy as a clam and clapping away.

"I *love* love." She beamed, looking at us all and nodding her head. "You know, I'm here with my daughter, Susan, to visit my twin sister tomorrow. It's our birthday."

I thought back to all the research I'd done on ghosts for my books, and it was often said that they were trapped in the same loop until something released them, but seeing the happiness in Margaret's gaze made me wonder if she really wanted to be released.

"Well, happy early birthday to you," my dad said, turning in his chair.

"Thank you, dear. Do you have any coffee? I couldn't get the coffee pot to work in my room."

I glanced at Vera, who looked like she was about to run away and never come back, and I hid a giggle.

I couldn't think of anyone else I wanted to share this haunting with more than the five people in the room whom I loved more than life itself.

As I stood, all of our phones buzzed at the same time, which sent a chill through the room. It wasn't until I'd read what was on the screen and my eyes connected with my dad's that I finally realized what was going on.

My dad stood up and slowly wandered over to Margaret. "Let's get you that cup of coffee, Maggie. How does that sound?"

"Oh, dear. I haven't heard anyone call me that since I last saw my twin sister." She smiled and leaned her head on my dad as he walked them into the kitchen to make a phone call.

Garrett stood and slid his hand over mine and

squeezed it lightly, knowing that while some of Margaret's story had been explained, not all of it had, and maybe it was up to me to finish the ending.

# CHAPTER THIRTY-TWO

*Garrett*

Samantha slid her newest release across the table toward me.

"Come on. Open it up. Check out the dedication." She winked at me, and I wondered if she'd ever stop getting cuter and cuter.

It had been about eight months of secrets and hints until the big release day. I was pretty sure I had an idea about Samantha's story, but I wouldn't know until she showed me, until I read it.

And now was my chance.

I looked down at the cover and saw *The Bond* written in gold scrollwork and my heart swelled with pride.

My wife wrote this book, and before we knew it, millions of people would be seeing it on the big screen. I didn't even know what was inside the cover, but I knew it was going to be epic.

"Come on, hurry up." She motioned for me to open the cover, and I chuckled.

"It's like Christmas," I teased.

The air was charged with excitement, and I couldn't wait to see the words my wife had used to bring a story to life.

I turned the first few pages until I hit the *Dedication* page. A smile covered my lips that I knew I wouldn't be able to shake off for days and months to come.

*To Margaret,*

*For allowing me to imagine a place and time where strangers can haunt our very souls and lead us to explore and learn what it means to love family.*

*And to Garrett,*

*The stranger who haunted me the most, who allowed me to imagine a story so grand and absolute between sisters, the ghosts they shared, and the love that can conquer all. You are my man, forever and always, real and imagined.*

*P.S. The hero within these pages is you.*

Her words touched my very core, and I hadn't even moved off the dedication page.

I looked up to see my smiling wife looking for approval.

"I love you, Samantha Roberts."

She winked at me. "It's Samantha Mason now."

I laughed, shaking my head.

"Do you think Margaret will understand what you wrote?" I asked tenderly, thinking back to the woman we'd come to know and love. The truth was that I was relieved

Margaret and Susan were not my relatives floating the halls of Cloudberry. I doubted I'd ever be able to leave Sam alone if that were the case.

It turned out that day when we'd all received a buzz on our phone, a Silver Alert had gone out. Margaret had wandered away from her care facility.

Samantha shook her head and smiled. "I don't know, but I think her daughter Susan will."

Vera came into the kitchen with a spring in her step and saw the book.

"It's here?" Vera nearly jumped over me.

Sam nodded and smiled, finally letting herself feel pride in what she'd accomplished.

"Is it?" Lana hollered down the hallway and jogged into the kitchen.

I let her sisters read the dedication and they both touched their chests in love.

"What a beautiful dedication," Lana said, smiling. "I still can't believe everything with Margaret. But how does that explain our camera system not picking her up at all?" Lana asked, and Vera shrugged.

"Either time," Lana added.

Margaret never showing up on the camera was something we'd thought a lot about, but sometimes, it was nice to let yourself imagine the answer rather than know it for certain.

"It doesn't, but some things are better left unexplained," I said, reaching for Sam's hand with mine. "Like love. That's the biggest mystery of all."

I turned the page of the book to see how the beginning

of the story began. Samantha started with our conclusion, but I couldn't stop reading to see how the story ended...

*I looked over at Garrett Mason and knew I'd found the right man. Even though I'd spent years conjuring up perfect relationships and imagining men who didn't exist, once I met Garrett, I realized he did.*

*He had always existed in my heart. He was the man I'd always imagined, and it took coming home to find him.*

**

I hope you loved reading about Samantha, Garrett, Vera, and Lana as much I loved writing about them! These two have haunted me (in a good way) since I thought up their story! Plus, the sisters' relationships are complex, and I can't wait to continue exploring them in the next books! Want to read about Vera and Drew North? *Remembering You* is out now, along with the entire series.

Wyatt's story is also out now! His appears in the Island County Series, *Christmas Crush on Fireweed.* Follow this link to view on Amazon or just type in Karice Bolton on the Amazon site.

Have you read about the other North brothers?

If not, check out the Silver Ridge Series.

Keep reading for a look at Finding Love (Island County #1) and Happy Truth (Silver Ridge #2).

Don't forget to sign up for Karice's newsletter to find out about new releases like the next in Cloudberry Inn. Click here or got to www.karicebolton.com! You can also text KariceBooks to 313131 for a text reminder on or near release days. Thanks again!

# HAPPY TRUTH ABOUT LOVE EXCERPT

*it's complicated*

# CHAPTER ONE

Autumn Tucker sat gripping the steering wheel as she stared at her inheritance. The home looked nothing like the photos her late uncle's attorney had sent her.

*Nothing at all.*

If it had, she probably wouldn't be sitting in front of the dilapidated mansion, cursing her impulsiveness.

Instead, she'd left everything behind in Los Angeles—which, admittedly, wasn't much—and moved to the small mountain town of Silver Ridge.

Autumn sucked in a deep breath and glanced in the rearview mirror of her car. Ronald had just pulled up behind her with a moving truck full of her worldly possessions.

He'd insisted on driving the rental truck up the coast for her. She hadn't asked him to make the drive, and she'd secretly hoped he'd bail at the last minute.

But only recently had she begun to notice that life rarely worked out how she hoped or planned.

Ronald Morder was a nice guy, a few years her senior with dark brown eyes and sandy blond hair. In the world of men, he was extremely attractive with a California tan, bright white teeth, and a lean body from biking most places. He looked like everything she should want, even wearing his lavender polo and khakis.

Besides, the dating app said they were perfectly matched, not that she understood why.

He was a computer programmer by day, and by night . . . well, he was still a computer programmer, and that was about all she could get from him. She was pretty certain his idea of a hobby was learning new code, but now she could add driving moving trucks to his short list of activities.

She still couldn't figure out what in the world made him offer to help her move.

They'd gone on several dates over the last few months, and she kept waiting for that spark.

When the spark didn't appear, she'd started hoping for an ember to glow, at the very least, but so far, she'd only been left with an ashy feeling toward him, and yet here he was by her side, helping her move out of state.

Come to think of it, maybe he felt the same way about her.

Maybe this was his way of ending it gently before it ever really began.

She doubted it though. She was seldom that lucky.

Ronald gave a quick wave, and she let out a sigh as he jumped out of the cab of the rental truck, looking extremely eager and ready to take on the world. Her stomach tensed at the thought of having to make small talk, but this was how the beginning of relationships always seemed to be. The encounters were a little clumsy and tricky to navigate until a rhythm set in.

They were obviously still in that getting-to-know-you stage, and she wasn't sure at what point it would ever turn into something with substance, but they could continue toward that goal.

So what if the state of Oregon sat between them? People did long-distance relationships all the time.

*All the time.*

But did this even qualify as a relationship yet?

She grabbed her purse off the passenger seat and climbed out of her red Fiat convertible, top up, and shut the door. Now wasn't the time to worry about semantics. This move was her new beginning, and she needed to fully embrace the positives wherever they led.

After all, the state of Washington was pulling out all the stops to welcome her. It was early evening, and the sky was sparkling blue without even a wispy cloud in sight. The brilliant green weeds in her new yard stretched for the sun with mighty determination. Contrary to what she'd heard about the soggy state of Washington, it seemed beautiful all the way up the coast and even more so once she got into the mountains.

The jagged cliffs, rushing waterfalls, and brilliantly colored wildflowers along the highway leading to Silver Ridge seemed right out of a fairy tale, and the small bit of the town she saw didn't disappoint either. It was just this little hiccup of a house that drilled a bit of fear into her decision to move here.

"This place is something else," Ronald said, sauntering over and giving the house a sideways glance before giving her a quick kiss on the cheek. Even though a warm breeze caressed her skin, his lips felt like a cold, wet fish and a shiver shot up her spine.

"Yes. It's quite something." She cleared her throat and looked up at the house with a glint of unexpected optimism in her eyes.

Maybe the inside wasn't as bad as the outside. She hoped the opposite was true for Ronald. Maybe his insides were as great as his outside. After all, he did drive over a thousand miles to get her here.

Or maybe that was precisely the problem.

*He did drive over a thousand miles to get me here*, she thought.

"Not what you expected?" he asked warily, slicking his fingers through his hair.

She folded her arms over her chest and hugged herself, letting out an exhausted sigh.

"No. Not entirely." She grimaced and shrugged. "But I've never shied away from a challenge before. This will be good for me. It's time I finally set some roots down, and besides, this was meant to be."

"How do you figure?" His brows shot up in a quizzical expression.

"For starters, I'm tired of LA. Not that I've been there much in recent years." She looked up at the two-story Victorian home with the wraparound porch and wondered if she sounded as crazy as she felt when looking at the home. "But how often does a person inherit a bed-and-breakfast from an uncle they've never met? I can't argue with fate."

As she stared at the house, the peeling yellow paint wasn't her biggest concern. It was the porch's slight lean and the wobbly-looking steps leading up to the front door that worried her the most. It didn't help that the roof looked like it was missing more shingles than were nailed down, and the gutters were barely hanging on.

There'd been a small cash inheritance that came along with the home, but she doubted it would cover much if the exterior was any indication of the interior.

"We should go inside before you make your final decision to stay." He draped his arm around her shoulders, and she stiffened, but he didn't notice. "And if you decide to give this a shot, I can start moving your stuff inside so we can get it all in before I have to catch my flight out tomorrow."

She shook her head and untangled from his embrace. "I've got a couple of local guys I hired for tomorrow to unload. You've done far too much already. You need to relax and try to unwind from all the driving."

Disappointment zipped through his gaze and a pinch of guilt socked Autumn in the stomach. She was hot-wired to sense others' emotions, even though she did her best at extinguishing her own.

Her mother had always called it being emotionally intelligent, but she wasn't sure she bought that theory. It seemed like more of an inconvenience the majority of the time, and it was a hindrance when navigating everyday life. The ability often landed her in situations like this one because she didn't want to hurt people's feelings.

She glanced at Ronald, and her stomach twisted into a tight knot. He definitely seemed bummed, and it made her wonder what all he'd hoped to get out of this trip, considering they hadn't even kissed.

"I really don't mind. I planned on helping unload the truck all night." He bit his lip and the pang of guilt resurfaced.

"You're a saint for driving all this way." She reached for his hand to give a friendly squeeze and instantly regretted it the moment he linked his fingers through hers.

Before she had a chance to object, he pulled her into him and brought down an awkward kiss to her mouth. His lips parted, and her eyes immediately slammed shut.

She wasn't sure whether she closed her eyes to block out the kiss or to imagine it better. When he slid his arms down hers, she knew it was only getting worse.

Here it was.

Their first kiss.

And every slobbery second of it made her grateful for the state of Oregon separating them. She silently reprimanded herself for being so cruel. Just because the connection hadn't surfaced yet, didn't mean it wasn't on the horizon, and then she'd regret thinking thoughts like those.

When his lips left hers, she took a step back and looked into his eyes. By all appearances, he should be a good kisser, and judging by the dopey look in his eyes, he was supremely pleased with how it turned out, which only made her feel worse.

"I've wanted to kiss you from the moment we first met." What he just said should be igniting every single cell in her body.

His words were romantic and sweet and absolutely everything she never wanted to hear from poor Ronald. She scolded herself for not pulling him into her and repeating, but she just couldn't, and she really couldn't fathom how the dating app had ever paired them together. Granted, she might have fibbed a little on some of the questions to make herself sound a little more stable and a little less unpredictable than reality, but still.

"I . . . umm." She wiped her mouth and glanced over his shoulder at a hanging sign she couldn't make out. "Wow. Thank you. That was—"

"You haven't seen anything yet." He cut her off and grinned before glancing at the house. He tipped his head as if that would make the place look better and nodded in complete satisfaction.

It was safe to say he had more on his mind than a simple road trip.

Autumn walked to the miniature trunk of her convertible and took out a small suitcase. "I should at least bring this inside before we go to dinner."

He turned to Autumn and his eyes focused on hers.

"Seriously. Are you sure about this? It's not too late to turn the truck around. You don't have to save face around me. We can drive out of town and pretend this never happened. I'm sure a local realtor can put this up for sale and—"

She laughed and had to admit the idea wasn't completely horrible sounding, but this was her time for new beginnings.

Since her parents' deaths several years ago, Autumn had spent most of her time traveling the world. She'd made it her mission to fulfill her parents' dreams, taking them on as her own and checking off every place they'd wanted to see when they retired.

Only, they never made it.

She drew in a silent, heavy sigh.

"Nope. Staying here feels right."

"Then staying it is." He nodded. "That's why being a programmer is the perfect job. I can work from anywhere. We don't have to let distance come between—"

His words were drowned out by a large diesel pickup truck across the street, a few homes down. It sat idling for a few long seconds before a man jumped out of the passenger side and the truck drove away. She turned her attention back to Ronald as he was grabbing her suitcase from her.

"I think at the very least, I should be the one to enter the premises first," he continued. "Make sure there's not a giant-size cockroach in there waiting to attack or something." He brought his shoulders back, and she wasn't sure if he was serious.

"They have roaches here?"

"Don't they have them everywhere?" Ronald shrugged.

"I don't know." Autumn pulled out an envelope with the key inside from her purse and handed it over. "I'll be right behind you, prepared to swing at anything that comes our way," she assured him.

Autumn was certain he looked relieved at that bit of news, which only made her heart sink a little more.

Secretly, she'd always dreamed of dating a truly capable man. One who could swing in and save the day, battle the cockroaches, spiders, ants, and anything else that came their way. She didn't need him riding in on a white horse or anything, but she thought it would be nice if a guy knew how to change a tire, at the very least.

Was that too much to ask?

She glanced down the sidewalk to see the guy who'd climbed out of the truck bending over and pulling a few weeds in the yard. He was too far away to get a good look, but it appeared like he was wearing a cowboy hat, possibly even cowboy boots. Within an instant, she saw the man swinging and swatting at something, and she held in a chuckle.

She brought her attention back to Ronald, who was triumphantly climbing the stairs. The sound of wood creaking and splitting made her stop in her tracks as she watched him lug her suitcase up the steps.

Ronald reached for the lock and began to wiggle the handle.

"Well, this isn't very safe." He turned around, holding the doorknob in his hand. "It might be a sign."

"Nah." Autumn squashed the thought with her hand. "It's just a sign that I need a locksmith. Nothing more."

"Why don't you wait there while I figure this out and go inside?" His toothy grin didn't hide his uneasiness, but she quickly accepted his offer.

As he fumbled with the door, trying to figure out how to unlatch it, she walked over to the sign hidden by thorn bushes. She reached toward the wooden sign and gingerly moved the vines aside to reveal a worn name.

*The Blackberry Patch*
*Bed and Breakfast*

A smile touched her lips as she let go of the thorny vines and admired the name of her new place. Judging by the thicket of vines entwined around the sign, the home was aptly named. Soon, small, juicy blackberries would be dangling from all the bushes, and she imagined herself making batches of jam for the guests. She looked up at Ronald as he stared at the knob in his hand and hoped she'd be able to get inside before it was dark. She didn't want to step on his manhood, but as each second ticked by, she was less certain they'd actually be getting into the home anytime soon.

"Hello, neighbors." A sexy voice from behind her surprised her, and she glanced quickly at Ronald, who turned around still holding the doorknob in his hand.

His expression soured the moment he saw whoever was behind her, so she decided to spin around and see for herself.

When she did, it was like the wind had been knocked right out of her. The man from down the street was only a foot away, and he looked sensational with his sparkling blue eyes, chiseled features, and dark hair peeking out from under his cowboy hat.

Her gaze fell to his feet, and sure enough, he was wearing the boots just like she'd suspected, and they weren't small. A blush crept up her cheeks as she brought her gaze back to the stranger's brilliant blue eyes.

"I'm Joel North, your neighbor from across the street and down a couple of homes." He stuck out his hand, which she eagerly took.

She loved the way his strong grip wrapped around hers as he removed his hat to reveal his dark, mussed-up hair.

"I'm Autumn Tucker." Her admiring eyes couldn't be pulled from Joel's gorgeous grin as he gave a quick nod, turning his attention to Ronald.

She stood staring at the sexy man in front of her, wondering how in the world he happened to be her neighbor, but she also knew never to get involved with the man next door—or on the same block, possibly the same city. The list of *don'ts* could go on.

"And you must be Mr. Tucker?" Joel asked.

"No. I'm not married." Her green eyes were wide with determination to set the record straight.

"Not yet, anyway." Ronald came down the stairs, knob still in hand, and reached for Joel's hand.

"So you two are moving in?" Joel asked. "This is quite the fixer-upper."

"I inherited it from my uncle." Autumn's gaze stayed fixed on this stranger even as Ronald possessively wrapped his arm around her shoulders and brought her in tightly.

"I'm sorry for your loss. He was a good man." Joel gave a quick nod as he slid his hat back on.

"Thank you." She nodded and glanced at the knob Ronald still clutched in his hand. Joel's gaze followed hers, and his smile widened, which made him sinfully delicious.

"That's a hell of a welcome to your new place."

Joel took a step closer and looked over at the front door. "Need some help?"

"I've got it." Ronald shook his head and straightened up as Joel's gaze fell to Autumn's.

"Actually, if you have any experience with this kind of thing..." Her voice trailed off, and Joel couldn't help but notice her beauty. Her auburn hair cascaded down her shoulders, and the playfulness behind her brilliant green eyes intrigued him, and he wasn't easily captivated.

"Believe it or not, I've broken into my fair share of homes around town." Joel laughed, and Ronald pulled Autumn closer. "It isn't as—"

"I've got it handled." Ronald cut Joel off, which only made Joel's smile widen.

Autumn momentarily wavered but took a steadying breath and nodded. After all, Ronald did drive a thousand miles to get her here. The least she could do was humor him. "We don't want to trouble you, but thanks for the offer."

Now fully satisfied with her allegiance, Ronald let go of Autumn and made his way back up the stairs.

"So where'd you two move from?" Joel asked, folding his arms and studying her with his gaze peeking just below the tip of his hat. The way he looked at her sent the missing spark clear to her toes.

Autumn's gaze skirted down his exquisite frame that happened to be wrapped in a plaid button-down and low-slung jeans. He appeared to be the exact opposite of any guy she'd seen in California in the last decade. Present company certainly not excluded.

"California." Autumn turned her attention to Ronald, who was cursing at the top of the stairs, when

Joel bent down and whispered.

"You know, all you have to do is put your finger in that hole, move it to the left a little, and that door will pop right open." His mouth was close to her ear, and the softness of his breath skated across her neck, shocking her senses into a tailspin of anticipation.

For what, she didn't know.

Her mind flicked back to the failed kiss from Ronald, and she couldn't understand how she felt so alive just standing next to this perfect stranger.

"That's it?" she asked, almost breathless, turning to look into his eyes.

"That's the secret," Joel replied before he turned and walked away, leaving Autumn to wonder what had just happened to make her luck turn around.

# Chapter Two

"There are two kinds of men in this world, Oscar." Joel let out a low chuckle for the two of them to share as he scratched his mutt's ears. "There are those who can open the door, and those who can't. You know which camp we belong in."

Oscar looked up at Joel with adoring brown eyes as Joel continued to scratch him in the perfect spot. The golden retriever-chow mix let out a little grunt and slid his front paws in front of him on the wooden floor until he hit the wood with a thud.

"You do know that, right, Oscar?"

Oscar's chops pulled up in complete agreement, and Joel knew Oscar understood every word he'd said. They'd shared a bond for the last seven years that few would understand and even fewer would ever discover.

Joel didn't need word getting out around town that he spent more time talking to Oscar than anyone else. He had a reputation to uphold and certainly didn't want his brothers getting wind of his nonexistent social life.

But the point was that Oscar had an extraordinary vocabulary for a dog.

Joel got up from the couch in the family room and wandered over to the window in the study, which just happened to overlook The Blackberry Patch Bed and Breakfast. He suspected it took his tip to get the front door open, and that made him smile.

The moving truck hadn't moved an inch since he'd left them earlier in the evening, and he figured they'd called it a night.

When he took Oscar for a walk an hour or so ago, he noticed that the little convertible wasn't out front. They'd probably gone out to dinner. Not that it mattered one way or the other. He was never a man to step on the toes of another man, no matter how oddly matched the couple.

And this was one of the most bizarre matches he'd ever seen.

He'd only met Autumn briefly, but her spirit was captivating. Besides her beauty, there was something about her that was light and bright. She seemed excited about being in Silver Ridge.

Her companion? Not so much.

There wasn't a single redeeming feature about him. His personality was about as lively as a box of rocks. He obviously didn't have many life skills, and he threw off an overly possessive quality that rubbed Joel the wrong way.

Joel could tell she was uncomfortable, but again, it was none of his business.

The guy also seemed kind of wimpy, but he understood that not every male on the planet had to step up to the plate to run a home and several businesses like he and his brothers had to help his mom when they were younger.

Regardless, Joel would be the best neighbor he could be and not give Autumn another thought except in a normal, neighborly sort of way while grabbing his mail or walking Oscar. And the guy, he'd learn to live with. Joel realized he hadn't even caught the man's name.

Oscar let out a groan as he slowly lumbered into the study to track down his owner. The study had become a favorite place for the two. There was a small corner fireplace and a leather recliner near the window. Joel had a seldom-used desk across the room on the far wall and floor-to-ceiling shelves around the room filled with all the books he'd collected over the years. There really wasn't a book he came across that he didn't like or didn't feel the need to keep. It was a good thing the home had lots of square footage.

"What do you say, Oscar? Should we go for another walk?" Joel glanced out the window and caught himself holding in a sigh.

There wasn't a reason in the world to be eyeing the B&B.

Oscar sat by the recliner and propped his chin

on the leather armrest. He had no intention of going anywhere.

"Fine."

Joel grabbed the book he'd started before his shift this morning and sat in the recliner as Oscar resettled his chin. He'd been volunteering as a medic for so many years he'd lost count, but it was a good outlet so he didn't get restless.

Being at the resort his family owned got tiresome, and when he was out helping people, it made him feel good. Instead of having to worry about entertaining VIP clients and maintaining occupancy rates, he could assist people in their time of need.

He glanced out the window again and rolled his eyes. This was ridiculous. Working at his family's ski resort introduced him to lots of beautiful women. Seeing an attractive female wasn't an anomaly in his life, so why was he all of a sudden so interested in a good-looking neighbor?

As he cracked open the book, he heard a car come down the road. He forced his eyes to stay on the page. Oscar stretched and stood up, wandering over to the window to stare, but Joel kept his focus on the blurred words while Oscar sat down and waited.

The car engine turned off, and seconds later, a car door shut. Joel waited for the sound of the second door to close, and when it didn't, he caught himself looking out the window.

Autumn was walking around the car, making her way to the back of the moving van. She checked it to make sure it was locked, but Joel didn't see any sign of the guy. He craned his neck slightly, refusing to leave the recliner, while he searched the sidewalk, still seeing no hint.

She was just as beautiful as he remembered. She'd swept her hair into a loose ponytail, and it looked like she'd changed from her jeans into a sundress, but she was too far away to see much else.

Not that he was looking.

Oscar's tail slapped down on the wood floor, and Joel jumped in his chair, startled from being caught spying by his dog.

"Ready for that walk?" Joel asked, standing up.

Why did he always become enamored with the ones who were unavailable?

Oscar reluctantly walked over to the basket by the door and picked up his leash with his teeth, bringing it over to Joel.

Probably because he knew he'd never have to commit. It kept things simple.

A nervous excitement drilled through him, which told him he needed to head in the opposite direction once they got outside.

He clipped the leash onto Oscar's collar, grabbed his jacket, and walked out the front door.

Spotting Autumn staring at the house, arms crossed and head tilted, he was drawn to wonder what she was imagining . . . or was she wondering what had she gotten herself into? He doubted the latter. Her exuberance earlier made it seem like she was fully ready to take on the challenges ahead with the B&B. And there would be plenty of challenges.

By his calculations, the interior was in as rough shape as the exterior, and that was only based on when he last saw the inside about a year ago. He could only imagine how much more that year of neglect had done to the bones of the house, not to mention all the work she'd have just to make the place look good once everything else was repaired. It certainly wouldn't be the first Tucker residence that needed to be saved from demolition in this town.

Oscar pulled in the woman's direction, and against his better judgment, he followed his dog's lead and wound up only feet away from her.

She turned, briefly smiling at them both, but her gaze immediately fell to Oscar. He was always a charmer.

"Oh, my gosh. Who's the cute boy? Are you the cute boy?" Autumn squatted in front of Oscar, scratching his ears and chin as his tongue hung out, eating up every second.

"I thought I was the cute boy." Joel scratched his jaw and laughed. "But whatever."

She looked up at Joel and winked, and he couldn't help but wish the guy from earlier had suddenly taken a hike.

"You're the most handsome man on the block," she told Oscar as her attention fell back to him with more pats. "Yes, you are."

"I already knew I didn't have much of a shot, but this just sealed the deal." Joel's smile made Autumn feel completely at ease and her laughter filled the air.

She stood and patted Joel's shoulder. "You're a close second."

"Don't let your fiancé hear that." He grinned and glanced toward the overgrown property, wondering when he'd reappear.

"Oh, he's definitely not my fiancé."

"Boyfriend then?"

Her gaze connected with Joel's and a mischievous look threaded through her eyes. "It's complicated."

"Isn't it always?" Joel chuckled.

"It does appear that way." She nodded and smoothed her hands over the skirt of her dress. "Thanks for that tip earlier. We'd probably still be locked out if I hadn't pushed my way to the door and followed your directions. When I got up there, I saw what you were talking about." What bothered her more was why in the world Ronald couldn't figure out how to open the door. Even without Joel's help, she would have gotten them inside.

"No problem at all. That's what neighbors are for." He glanced at Oscar, who appeared to roll his eyes.

"Well, I hope I'm not much trouble as a neighbor."

"I can't imagine you ever could be." Joel's voice softened, which took him by surprise.

"So, no cowboy hat?" she asked, shifting from one foot to the other.

Joel was surprised she remembered he was wearing one earlier. He'd almost forgotten himself. It wasn't his usual look, but he'd been out with hotel guests on a horseback ride. One of the summer perks of owning a resort.

"Nah. I save that for trail rides."

She glanced at his cowboy boots before bringing her gaze back to his. "Well, it's a good look."

"Don't see it much in California?"

"Not in LA, no." She looked back at the house and shook her head. "How long has the place looked like this?"

"Several years. About ten years ago, little things started turning into big things, and then he just got too sick."

She hugged herself and rocked back on her heels. "You knew him well?"

"I did. After your aunt died, he was never the same."

He couldn't place the source of embarrassment that flickered through her gaze. She cleared her throat. "Tomorrow's going to be a long day. I should get going."

"Is there anything I can help with?" Joel looked up at the old mansion, expecting to see the man peering from one of the dirty windows.

"I don't think so. I've got a couple of guys coming out to unload tomorrow."

Joel's brows shot up. "You didn't need to do that. I have brothers. We can come over and knock this out for you in a couple of hours. Tops. If your *it's complicated* wouldn't mind."

She laughed and shook her head. "He's leaving on a flight tomorrow morning."

"He didn't want to be around to help?" Joel looked extremely surprised.

Autumn's forehead creased slightly and she nodded. "It was more me who didn't want Ronald to be around."

"Oh." Joel bit his bottom lip. "It really *is* complicated."

And now he could call the man Ronald. He

supposed it was good to have a name with the face.

"Indeed." She laughed and nodded, but a curious expression crossed her face. "He's at the Thistleberry Inn and is heading back to California tomorrow."

"I didn't mean to pry." But the truth was that he wanted to pry, and to find out the guy wasn't even sleeping here made his curiosity soar. There was a part of him that wanted to know every little detail. "There's probably a lot going on, and it's none of my business."

"There is so little to say about him or us that I'm not sure you could pry even if you tried." Realizing what tumbled out, she reversed course. "I mean, he's a nice guy, and I'm sure he's very capable at many things, but I'm not sure he's—" She stopped herself. "I'm sorry. I shouldn't have said anything bad about him. He drove all the way up here for no reason. I feel awful talking bad about him."

"I doubt it was for no reason. Men are pretty easy to read, and he definitely had a motive to drive all this way." Joel drew a breath and glanced at the mansion, holding in his sigh. She had a long way to go to get it up and running. "Anyway, I'm just a guy out walking his dog." Joel laughed, holding up the dog leash. "Your secret is safe with Oscar and me. In fact, I'm not even sure what you were trying to say, so you're even safer."

She bent down to pet Oscar one last time but looked up at Joel through her thick lashes. "I promise you won't have to become my therapist. I think I'm just exhausted from the long drive, and then I tend to ramble and life goes downhill. It's a cycle." Her small talk made his night a whole lot better, and he knew he'd happily play therapist for her. He was equally pleased to find out the man he'd barely met was already heading out of state.

"I'm just in that house right over there." He pointed behind him, and Oscar stood up and shook his head, ears flapping. "If you need anything, day or night, let me know. I'm only a knock away."

Joel cringed at how much he sounded like an Allstate commercial. He usually had moves and smooth one-liners.

A car came up behind them, and Joel spun around to see who was behind the wheel. The street was usually quiet at this time of night. Every once in a while, one of his brothers might stop by out of the blue, but generally, this street was pretty dull. He was surprised to see Charlie, one of only six cab drivers for the small resort town of Silver Ridge, pulling up to the curb in front of the convertible.

Joel's eyes drilled to the back seat where Ronald sat, looking extremely irate. He swore he heard a disgruntled exhale from Autumn as she walked slowly toward the cab. Ronald was already jumping out of the small car and bounding in her direction as Oscar sat up and whined.

Ronald glanced at Joel and Oscar, his eyes narrowing at the taller one.

"So you're already making your move, and I'm not even out of town, huh, buddy?" Ronald barely glanced at Autumn as he charged toward Joel.

"Just walking my dog, man." Joel shook his head, but his lips curled in a smirk, which only infuriated Ronald even more.

A low hum from Oscar stopped Ronald in his tracks, and Joel knew he'd have to give him extra biscuits when they got home.

"I know what you're up to. I saw it the moment you sauntered over here playing cowboy earlier this evening." Ronald puffed out his chest, but it did little in comparison to Joel's.

"The cowboy gotcha inside the house, though, so . . ." Joel's brow curled and Autumn stifled a chuckle. "Might not have been too much of an act."

"Listen here." Ronald pointed his finger in Joel's face, and he just shook his head instead of talking.

"Shoot. I'm listening." Joel tipped his head and waited for Ronald to say something.

Anything.

He needed a good laugh.

After several seconds of silence, Ronald spun around, walked past Autumn, and marched up the stairs to the front door.

"He's a real charmer," Joel muttered under his breath before making a clicking noise for Oscar to follow him down the sidewalk. "If you need any help tomorrow, you know where to find me."

Autumn gave a quick nod and followed after Ronald, which was the best thing for everyone involved, really. Complication was something that Joel never excelled at and did his very best to avoid at all costs.

Exactly. It wasn't his place to get involved or make the guy look as incompetent as he was, and if Autumn liked him, then—

Piercing screams from behind echoed through the air, and everything Joel had figured out only

seconds before came crashing down.
She needed help.

**Available on Amazon!**

# BOOKS BY KARICE BOLTON

## SUNSHINE BREAKFAST CLUB

DASH OF LOVE

## MR. MISTAKE SERIES

MR. MISTAKE
MR. ACCIDENT
MR. WRONG
MR. RIGHT

## ISLAND COUNTY SERIES

FINDING LOVE IN FORGOTTEN COVE
LOVE REDONE IN HIDDEN HARBOR
TANGLED LOVE ON PELICAN POINT
FOREVER LOVE ON FIREWEED ISLAND
TEMPTING LOVE ON HOLLY LANE
CHANCE AT LOVE ON MYSTIC BAY
IRRESISTIBLE LOVE AT SILVER FALLS
LUCKY IN LOVE ON HOUND ISLAND
MISTLETOE MISCHIEF
ACCIDENTAL LOVE ON MEADOW COVE LANE
DISCOVERING LOVE ON CRANBERRY LANE
CHRISTMAS ON FIREWEED
IMAGINING LOVE ON WILLOW ROAD
CHRISTMAS CRUSH ON FIREWEED

## BEYOND LOVE SERIES

BEYOND CONTROL
BEYOND DOUBT

BEYOND REASON
BEYOND INTENT
BEYOND CHANCE
BEYOND PROMISE
BEYOND the MISTLETOE

## CLOUDBERRY INN SERIES
IMAGINING YOU
REMEMBERING YOU
LEAVING YOU
LOVING YOU

## SILVER RIDGE SERIES
A HAPPY TRUTH ABOUT LOVE
A LITTLE SECRET ABOUT LOVE
A FUNNY THING ABOUT LOVE
A SURPRISING FACT ABOUT LOVE
A SIMPLE WISH ABOUT LOVE

## LUKE FLETCHER SERIES
HIDDEN SINS
BURIED SINS
REDEMPTION
MIA

## BLOOD TORN DUET
BLOOD TORN
BLOOD CURSED

## V MAFIA SERIES
BLAKE

DEVIN
JAXSON

## THE WITCH AVENUE SERIES
LONELY SOULS
ALTERED SOULS
RELEASED SOULS
SHATTERED SOULS

## THE WATCHERS TRILOGY
AWAKENING
LEGIONS
CATACLYSM
TAKEN NOVELLA (A Watchers Prequel)

## AFTERWORLD SERIES
RecruitZ
AlibiZ
UprisingZ

# Contact Karice

Don't forget to join Karice's newsletter by visiting

her website at karicebolton.com and don't miss out

on all the updates and sneak peeks by joining her

Facebook Group (Karice Bolton Book Buzz).

To contact the author, please visit her online at

www.karicebolton.com or via

Twitter/Facebook/Pinterest @KariceBolton.

www.ingramcontent.com/pod-product-compliance
Lightning Source LLC
Chambersburg PA
CBHW030638260626
47157CB00007B/2387

* 9 7 9 8 9 8 5 1 9 4 7 4 6 *